# THE CRONE OF MIDNIGHT EMBERS

# EMBERS

IRIS BEAGLEHOLE

# I

## DELIA

Delia groaned, rolling over and squinting at the morning light as if it was deliberately trying to cause her personal offence. At first it was only exhaustion, but as she turned her head, the hangover quaked inside her skull with a searing pain. She covered her head and rolled over onto her front, tangling the sheets.

That's when the worst part hit her. "What have I done?"

The entire West End would be talking about her. Her ears were burning; actually, her entire head was burning, due to the physical consequences of drinking one too many smoky whiskey sours after 'the event', which may have included an act or two of righteous revenge.

The familiar sound of the Darth Vader music blared out. Gilly had changed Delia's ring tone to the Imperial March as a joke after their theatre company had put on that one-woman Star Wars show.

Delia felt a pang in her chest. She hadn't seen her daughter or her two adorable grandkids for a while. So not only was her head throbbing with pain, her chest heavy with embarrassment, but Delia was emotionally low already, longing for time with her grandchildren and her grown-up child with the silly sense of humour. She pushed the pain away because it was too much to bear.

Delia wasn't going to answer the phone, not at all. But she did glance at it, just to make sure she wasn't not-answering something important.

Kitty's name flashed up on the screen.

Delia sighed and pressed the green button. "Is it as bad as I think it is?" Delia asked her best friend in the world, Kitty Hatton.

"Oh, Deals! You were a star," Kitty crooned.

"Don't lie."

"I'm serious. The whole town will be talking about you. I bet it'll even make it into the London papers."

Delia groaned again; it was becoming her theme song.

"Don't worry, love," Kitty said reassuringly. "It won't be long until you've processed your emotional hangover."

"And the regular hangover that I seem to have as well."

"Oh yes. It was rather nice whiskey, wasn't it?" said Kitty.

"Thank you for helping me drown my sorrows," Delia said.

"Anytime, darling. You know it will all be worth it. When you think about that awful prick."

"A worthless, pathetic little man," Delia muttered.

"Exactly," said Kitty, "and the look on his face. When you emptied his possessions onto the floor, including his mistress's undergarments, poured his special vanilla vodka all over the pile, and set it on fire! It was genius."

Delia sighed. "It wasn't the affairs that made me do it."

"Of course not, love," said Kitty. "It was far worse than that."

"Actually, the affairs were a welcome distraction," Delia admitted. "When you're married to someone like that for so long you begin to pray he'll leave you alone."

Kitty chortled. "Still, it was embarrassing for him. He likes to think he's an upstanding member of society."

"An upstanding little prick," Delia grumbled. "How dare he force me out of my own business?"

"It was very wrong of him," Kitty said, consoling her. "But what are you going to do now?"

"Hide under the biggest rock I can find," said Delia. "I'm sixty-three years old and far too old for hangovers and shame. What am I supposed to do?"

"Go back into acting," said Kitty. "You were brilliant in theatre."

Delia pushed a painful memory out of her mind before it had time to surface. "I don't have the energy for it."

"Start another business then?"

"Even the thought makes me tired. If I never have to look at another costing spreadsheet again, it'll be too soon."

"Well, take early retirement and sue that bastard for all he's worth."

"I suppose I'll have to," said Delia. "He's taken everything else from me."

"Oh, now, now," said Kitty. "That's not true, you still have your brilliant wits and your brilliant daughter and all your wonderful experience. Maybe Jerry did you a favour. This divorce sets you free. Think of it as a fresh start."

Delia couldn't suppress the wave of bitter anger, bursting forth from her chest. A beam of sunlight caught her eye, bringing more hang-over pain with it. She glared across the room at the curtain that never closed properly in her small temporary rented flat.

All of a sudden flames burst forth, engulfing the drapes.

"Blimey biscuits!" she cried out, dropping the phone. She leapt up from the bed, bracing herself against the crashing boulders that insisted on tormenting her skull. She tore the curtain down and stomped on it, coughing as she waved her hand through the smoke to clear it and opened the window to stop the alarm being set off.

"Delia, Delia!" a small voice cried out.

Delia picked up the phone again. "Sorry," she said to Kitty. "Minor disaster. I think my curtain just spontaneously combusted. What do you think that's about?"

"Faulty wiring," said Kitty matter-of-factly.

"I don't think there's any wiring in the curtain," Delia muttered. "Maybe it was the sunlight. It's quite bright, you know."

"It's winter," said Kitty. "I don't know. Perhaps you have a pyromaniacal ghost. Call in a professional. See what they say."

Delia couldn't help feeling that Kitty was deflecting. "Did you do something? Were you trying to distract me from my woes by setting booby traps around the apartment?"

"Of course not, darling," said Kitty. "Anyway, I'd better go. I have brunch with Roger later."

Delia made a cooing noise. "How is Roger?"

"Just as romantic as always, dear. So typical, he's probably going to bring me some plastic flowers again. And a bottle of cheap bubbly."

Delia couldn't help but chuckle; her best friend had been dating quite an odd character indeed. It was almost as if he didn't understand normal human customs.

"I'll call you later," Kitty said briskly, and hung up the phone.

Delia rolled onto her back, staring at the ceiling.

"This is my life now, is it?" she muttered, before glancing around the room at the only-partially-curtained window of the small cramped-but-modern flat.

It had been the first property that was tolerable that she'd found in a tight rental market, after Jerry's betrayal. At the time, anything would do. Delia had just needed somewhere to stay until the divorce settlement came through.

But now, Delia couldn't stand it for one moment longer.

She pulled on the first items of clothing she could find in her wardrobe, which happened to be the same plain black turtleneck and grey knitted cape with black jeans that she almost always wore. She quickly washed her face, applied her scarlet lipstick, and attacked her mostly grey hair with a brush.

"Strange," she muttered.

Amid the grey and silver and sparse strands of her natural black

4

hair, a distinctive red streak stood out, curling from her roots down past her left shoulder.

"I don't remember getting that drunk that I'd let Kitty dye my hair."

She squinted at herself in the mirror. Despite the hangover which seemed to now be fading fast, she didn't actually look too bad. While her face had just as many wrinkles as it had the day before, there was a new clarity in her complexion, and the dark circles she'd anticipated were hardly there at all.

"One hot crone," she muttered to herself, "ready to kick some arse." And that was absolutely true, and the arse in question was Jerry.

# 2
## MARJIE

"Flaming teapots!" Marjie muttered, waving a tea towel over the pot. She glared at the flame, which seemed to shrivel and pop out of existence under her gaze before fizzling out. She risked a glance around the shop, but it was a quiet morning. The early customers had cleared out, which probably meant the fire was spontaneous – not a prank played on her by a mischievous teen like little Felix, who would surely have hung around to crow with glee if he'd bothered to set up such a thing.

Marjie's tea shop always radiated comfort. Today it smelled of cinnamon and vanilla. Her custom brews and baking filled the shop with a tapestry of spices and herbs. Her latest concoction, a new experimental syrup, was bubbling on the stove, a perplexing blend of rosemary, sage, and dried juniper berries.

She'd been stirring it idly moments before and had then checked the clock, surprised she'd missed her own morning teatime. Marjie had drifted around the kitchen, half daydreaming, only to be shocked to her senses by a flame, erupting red and lively, dancing atop her new teapot.

It startled her because the flame hadn't the decency to be caused by something practical. It had appeared with a whimsical spontaneity. Something magical was stirring, something fiery.

"But why?" she muttered to herself.

Marjie had never been particularly good with fire, herself. Her magical specialty was...well, tea and cake, mostly, and party decorations. She had never considered herself to be a particularly powerful witch, though recently she'd felt more of a boost in her own energy.

She narrowed her eyes at the red teapot. She'd only put it on the bench moments ago, ready to brew herself a fresh pot of English breakfast tea. Now, she wondered whether the innocent looking object was cursed.

No, that wasn't it.

She let her mind relax and tuned into her own intuition, which was definitely her other magical speciality.

*This feels...ancient and powerful...*

*It can't be...*

Marjie opened her eyes, but the feeling of an ancient awakening lingered, and Marjie couldn't help but shiver.

She looked around again, wishing there was someone to talk to about all this, but Rosemary and Athena were busy preparing for a dangerous winter solstice mission and her dear friend Papa Jack was looking after Rosemary's chocolate shop as he often did. She made a note to call in later and bring him his favourite thyme and parmesan scones. But right now, she needed to talk to an expert.

Marjie reached for the phone, her hands still smelling of sage and juniper.

There was only one person knowledgeable enough to indulge her worries: Agatha Twigg, historian and curmudgeon extraordinaire.

"Agatha, it's Marjie," she said into the receiver. "You remember that dream I told you about, the one with the fire?"

A pause, followed by a gruff affirmation on the other end. Marjie knew that Agatha did remember. She had the memory of an owl. She remembered everything, a fact that made her particularly handy in their shared concern of tracking the ebb and flow of mystical events.

Finally, Agatha grumbled, "What's a crone got to do to enjoy a quiet morning?"

"Agatha, this is serious. I believe something's afoot," Marjie confessed. "My teapot just set itself on fire."

Another pause. An exhaled a puff that Marjie could practically hear rolling its eyes. "Tea's supposed to be hot, Marjie."

"Not flaming, Agatha!" retorted Marjie, though she couldn't help but chuckle. Agatha's brand of dry wit was a comforting constant.

Marjie was thankful for the unusually quiet morning. No one would overhear as they speculated, in hushed tones, on the meaning of this sign.

Marjie described the flame, the unexpected thrill of its appearance, the echo of the dream she'd had. Could it be that her intuition was right? The ancient powers that were often dismissed as merely legend could be real. Something big was stirring.

"I told you I've felt different lately," said Marjie.

"Of course you do," Agatha said dismissively. "Your whole life was upturned at Samhain."

"Not just that. It's my magic. Don't tell me you aren't feeling something too."

Agatha grunted noncommittally, an affirmation in disguise. "So what?" she said. "Don't tell me you're suggesting we pay *her* a visit?"

Marjie took a sharp inhale of breath. Of course, there was one person who knew far more than Agatha about ancient magic such as this. But the one they often referred to, often without naming her, always brought a tingle of fear to Marjie's spine.

The forest witch did not like company.

That only made Marjie want to befriend her even more, though all her attempts so far had failed.

"It's worth a try," said Marjie. "What kind of biscuits should I try to offer her this time?"

Agatha's eyeroll was almost audible as she scoffed.

"What?" said Marjie. "Surely there's some kind of treat that might help to win her over, if only we can figure out what it is."

Agatha chuckled. "Pack the ginger snaps." With a final snort, she hung up.

Marjie stared at the phone, a bitter and tangy taste of anticipation on her tongue. The fire was a sign, a stir in the fabric of their tranquil lives. Something was coming and Marjie was about due for an adventure.

# 3
## DELIA

The day ahead stretched out before Delia like an arduous quest,
not that she had anything particular to do.

Delia wanted to see Gilly and the grandkids more than anything.
She longed to see the little ones. Merryn was seven years old and
wonderfully cynical. She always had interesting questions for Delia,
and was brutally honest in the most delightful way. Keyne was only five
and had a sweet, otherworldly presence, as though he was away with
the fairies, or perhaps psychic. He wasn't dense, rather he had a lightness about him that could easily be mistaken for naivety.

Delia sighed. She missed them so much but had been attempting to
give Gilly space. After all, the last time she had tried to visit, she'd been
told in no uncertain terms that her presence wasn't welcome.

The thought caused her pain; ever since Gillian was little, they had
been close. Now, Gilly, a mother herself, seemed to be pulling away,
right when Delia needed her most.

"How depressing to have to rely on your children for emotional
support," Delia muttered to herself as she sat at her usual table in the
local café, waiting for her cappuccino.

The waitstaff seemed too busy flirting with each other to notice her, and though the barista had made the aforementioned coffee, it sat on the counter, seemingly forgotten.

Delia considered retrieving it herself, fearing that by the time the waiter brought it over, it would be stone cold.

Finally, he approached.

Delia squinted at him over her horned-rimmed sunglasses.

"Sorry for the wait," the waiter said, grinning at her.

Delia frowned, unimpressed. "It better not be cold, or I'm getting another one on the house."

"Of course, madam," he replied, not unpatronisingly, then turned on his heel and pranced off.

The ceramic cup was barely lukewarm.

Delia breathed a deep sigh as she picked it up, feeling her rage boil over.

As she looked down at her coffee, it began to bubble, the milk frothing over the sides.

She yelped at the burning heat, plonking the cup back onto the saucer. Her mind scrambled for some kind of logic that didn't seem to make sense, so instead, it improvised.

Delia stared suspiciously at the ceramic vessel holding her favourite beverage.

"Blimey, coffee cups these days have really changed," she mumbled. "New technology, I suppose."

The woman next to her gave her a strange look.

"Don't mind me," Delia said. "I'm just talking to my imaginary friends." She gestured around the table.

The woman dropped her smug expression, blushed, and glanced down at her plate of Sally Lunn.

After a few moments, Delia braved a sip of her coffee. It didn't make sense. The cup hadn't even been warm when she first picked it up and now she could barely hold it. At least the beverage, now piping hot, warmed her against the chill of the late morning winter air.

"I've been through worse," she muttered to herself, taking a second sip. "Things will get better," she said reassuringly, ignoring another baffled glance from the Sally Lunn woman and feeling quietly amused.

The dramatic music from her phone interrupted her reverie.

It was probably Kitty, and Delia had just about enough of her for one morning. However, she glanced at her phone, just in case, and immediately answered it.

"Gilly?"

"Mum, I'm so sorry," Gillian's voice came through the phone.

"What's going on, love?" Delia asked.

There was a pause on the other end of the line. "I can't really explain..." said Gilly. "I mean..." There was another pause before Gillian found her voice again. "I've just been offered an excellent promotion, and I'm moving with the kids."

"Moving out of London?" Delia asked, mortified.

"Yes, that's right," Gillian confirmed. "It's an unexpected job offer. I think I was headhunted."

She said this in quite an uncomfortable tone.

"That sounds nice, dear, but do you really have to move? I mean, what legal partnership worth their salt isn't in London?"

"It's rather an old establishment," Gilly replied. "Well-regarded. And I'm moving to a small place called Burkenswood."

Delia wrinkled her nose. "Over towards Cornwall?" she asked, trying to keep judgment from her voice. Cornwall was beautiful, sure, but it was no London, and Gilly was a city woman, not a country bumpkin.

"It was just too good to refuse," Gilly said.

"And you're taking the kids, but not Neville?"

Neville, Gilly's husband of seven years, was not Delia's favourite person. Perhaps there was a silver lining in all of this.

"Neville and I are taking a break," Gilly explained.

"Oh, love," Delia replied sympathetically. "How are Merryn and Keyne coping with all this change?"

"Surprisingly well," said Gilly, her voice warming.

Delia smiled, thinking of the children. It had been weeks since she'd seen them. "Why don't you come over, and I'll make you a cup of tea?"

"In your tiny flat?" Gilly asked with a hint of humour. "Do you even have room for me in there, let alone the kids?"

"I'm sorry about my inadequate accommodations," said Delia, only slightly sarcastically. "How about I come over to your place instead?"

"Oh no, that would be impossible. I...I've already started packing, and it's chaos here."

Delia sighed. "What's really going on, love?"

"I just need some time alone," Gilly replied. "I'll call you later, Mum."

The phone beeped as the call cut off.

Delia slumped forward, quickly drinking back the remainder of her still-hot beverage.

She couldn't help feeling a pang of resentment. Not towards Gilly, but towards the men – Jerry and Neville.

Surely Neville was the reason her daughter was acting so strange and distant. Or was it that Gillian was taking her father's side in the divorce? It didn't make sense. Gillian had always been closer to Delia than Jerry...unless Jerry had bribed her with a hefty portion of their marital savings, but that didn't seem right either.

The snarky waiter glared at her from across the café as he gossiped with a colleague. He smirked as she glared back. A small twinge of rage pricked at Delia, and a moment later, the waiter's tea towel inexplicably burst into flames.

He dropped it and stomped on it in surprise.

Delia's lips quirked. "A strange coincidence," she muttered. "Almost as if my anger has some sort of combustion properties."

She giggled at that, drawing a few curious glances from the other customers, but she ignored them.

Picking up her phone again, she began to look up Burkenswood.

"Dreary little place," she murmured, skimming through images of the city. "But what's this?"

Something caught her eye. One of the top ten things to do locally, aside from walking up a hill or visiting the small square garden with a weather vane, was to drive an hour or so to the seaside.

The images showed an adorable little township that seemed vaguely familiar.

In fact, Delia thought she must have been there at some point on a childhood holiday with her grandmother, Etty.

*Myrtlewood.*

The name popped into her head. But it didn't show up on the map.

"I'm sure that's what it's called." She tried several different spellings, well-aware that English was a strange and unpredictable language, especially in England, where place names were rarely spelt phonetically at all.

"I'm sure it's there," Delia said, zooming in to her phone screen, on a small section of the coast.

Then, partly because she was at a loose end and didn't have anything else to do, and partly due to the strange sense of excitement that she hadn't experienced in quite some time, Delia wondered if she might enjoy taking a little drive.

For some reason, London was giving her a cloying anxious sensation, and she had no idea why, but surely the sea air would do her some good.

# 4

## THE CLERIC

The Cleric flinched as he heard the sound of loud footsteps echoing down the hall towards him.

The door to the sanctum burst open, the sound echoing off the stone walls.

In strode a figure radiating an austere authority.

"Cleric." The word was uttered curtly. This was Father Benedict, the Crimson Shepherd, a name and title that stirred whispers among the order.

He had only returned to the order headquarters recently after many years in the field on secret reconnaissance. The Cleric had not enjoyed the new atmosphere of seriousness and fear that he'd brought with him like a chilling wind.

"Father Benedict," the Cleric said, bowing his head slightly, a mixture of reverence and anxiety in his voice.

A moment passed in which the silence between them was dense, humming with tension that wrapped around the Cleric like a fog.

From behind a set of heavy, reinforced doors came a low, unsettling growl. The Cleric paled but Father Benedict didn't flinch, his focus instead on the vast array of scrolls and maps spread out on the stone table.

"The fire witch?" Father Benedict asked, cutting to the chase.

"She's awoken, Father," the Cleric said. "It is as foretold. Signs of her power have begun to surface."

The Cleric could have sworn that Father Benedict blushed. Was the mere mention of this awful woman's power affecting him? Women were rarely mentioned within the cloistered walls of the Order.

The Shepherd quickly recovered. "Good. The wheel turns as it must," he said, his gaze on the flickering flame in the heart of the room. "And the hunter?"

"Hunter? Oh you mean our tracker?"

"Of course," said the Shepherd sternly.

"Ready to move," the Cleric responded swiftly. "The fire witch will be under constant surveillance."

"Ensure it remains that way," Father Benedict commanded. "The Elemental Crones must not join forces before we are ready."

The Cleric swallowed audibly. "And if they do?"

"Then we take necessary action," Father Benedict's voice rang out in the chamber. He then gestured vaguely towards the ominous doors, behind which the unsettling growls were growing louder. "We have... contingency plans."

His words hanging in the air, Father Benedict swept out of the sanctum, leaving the Cleric alone with his trepidation. It was finally happening. The Order of Crimson had been preparing for the rising evil for many years, ready to harness the wayward power and turn it toward the good. The Cleric only wished he had been let in on the secrets, but he was too lowly. Father Benedict may be imposing and terrifying, but perhaps that was because he knew so much more.

The doors rattled again and a low growl rolled out around the room.

"Contingency plans, indeed," the Cleric muttered, a smile springing to his face before his well-conditioned humility rose up to suppress it back into a neutral expression. There was no place for frivolity in the Order. There was only The Mission, and the time for action was fast approaching.

# 5

## DELIA

Years of Pilates and theatre training hadn't prepared Delia for the prospect of being attacked in broad daylight on a London street by a man in a red hooded cloak, however, it did put her in a more advantageous position than most sixty-three-year-olds.

Okay, so it had been a couple of years since she'd attended a single Pilates class, but in that moment, she was grateful for muscle memory. Despite slightly creaky hips and the warning of arthritis in her knuckles, her instincts took over as the heavily moustached stranger with an unnecessarily long goatee lunged towards her, malice in his eyes. He drew a dagger from his belt and raised it above her.

Delia had expected many things from life. But being the target of a seemingly crazed attacker was not one. Her heart pounded. A bead of cold sweat trickled down her temple, a chill contrasted sharply with the hot rush of adrenaline in her veins. Her knuckles clenched and unclenched involuntarily.

As the attacker lunged, time seemed to dilate, each second stretching out into an eternity. Despite her creaky left hip and other mysterious gnawing pain in her joints, the ingrained instincts of a lifetime of disciplined routine took over.

She pivoted, her dancer's grace still miraculously intact. Her foot swung in a sharp arc towards his ankle. There was a grunt, a moment of satisfaction as she realised her aim had been true.

Ignoring the protesting pain from her foot, Delia took advantage of the man's temporary imbalance, her knee propelling upwards towards his groin.

A shout echoed from behind Delia.

The man's surprised gasp was cut short as he crumpled, his dagger clattering uselessly onto the pavement.

She watched as he collapsed onto the ground, the shock of what she had done mingling with a distant sense of satisfaction. The scene appeared surreal to her. But the sharp pain in her knee and the swift rise and fall of her chest reminded her it was all too real.

Just then, something crashed into her from behind – a man – rugged, with a leather brimmed hat and black oilskin jacket like some kind of cowboy. He was staring directly at her, his dark, steely eyes wide with shock. She remembered him from the café. He'd been sitting right behind her. Did he see the attack? Was he trying to help?

His gaze shifted, moving past her to the man lying at her feet. His eyes narrowed as he took in the sight of the brooch pinned on the attacker's cloak. It was round and made of dark, oxidized metal depicting a triangle, pointing downwards with a deep crimson marking inside that looked like a rune.

The man from the café reached for the brim of his hat as he looked at the brooch. A strange look passed over his face — part recognition, part grim determination.

And then, as quickly as he'd appeared, he was gone, swallowed up by the bustling London crowd.

Delia was left standing there, the fallen man at her feet, the echoes of a stranger's shout still ringing in her ears, her chest heaving, the rush of victory ebbing away to leave a cold knot of fear.

*What just happened?*

She had just taken down a man who'd meant her harm. She'd been sure of it a moment ago, though it was an absurd thought.

The poor sod lay sprawled and groaning on the pavement in front of her.

As quickly as the surreal bubble of the fight had wrapped around her, it popped, the sounds of London rushing back in a wave. She scanned her surroundings, realising that the rest of the street remained oblivious to the drama that had just unfolded.

As Delia's pulse started to normalise, she pieced together the bizarreness of the scenario. The attacker, the man from the café, the familiar brooch – none of it made sense.

Did she accidentally get caught up in someone's live action role-playing game? Was this some kind of public improv theatre?

She leaned over the man to check if he was alright. Aside from a slight whimper, she was sure he was fine and just being overly dramatic.

Still, assault was not going to look good on her record, especially after committing very minor arson the night before.

As her rational brain returned to her, Delia was sure she'd just injured some kind of Renaissance cosplay enthusiast. She quickly scanned her surroundings, noting that no one seemed to be paying her any attention, and sprinted off as fast as her dance-trained muscles could carry her.

It took a while for her brain, pulse, and breathing to return to normal. Something didn't quite make sense about the scenario. In the moment of the attack, Delia had been absolutely sure that the man was targeting her, evident in the murderous look in his eyes. But how likely was that, really?

Then it hit her—

Jerry.

Of course, her bitter and vindictive ex must be messing with her, sending one of his B-grade actors to try and shake her confidence or worse. If she was incapacitated or bedridden by a theatrical hitman, she wouldn't have the energy to sue him for all he was worth.

Rolling her eyes at the absurdity, Delia headed to her car, more determined than ever to escape London and Jerry's antics. The seaside getaway suddenly seemed very appealing after the morning she'd had.

# 6

## THE ROGUE

O ne hour earlier, in a hidden corner of the West End, the tracker
found his perch on an unassuming street corner.

He was a man of a thousand names, but his code name was usually
the Rogue. This time he had been contracted by powers that lurked in
the shadows, whispering their commands through encoded messages.
His eyes, aged and wise, tracked the movements of the witch as she left
her flat for her usual morning ritual at the café.

He gripped the leather brim of his hat, pulling it slightly lower. It
was important not to be recognised, especially on reconnaissance.

The bounty hunter wasn't afraid of the people who passed him by,
busily walking to work or coffee dates. No. But there were others who
might always be watching.

He only looked out of place from close up. From a distance his
leather hat could be mistaken for a fedora, his clothing non-descript
enough to pass in casual settings. Facial hair was no-longer frowned
upon. Occasionally, he was called a hipster, but only by people who
apologised moments later under the steely glare of his gaze. It wasn't
his first glimpse of the witch, but something was different this time.

After a safe enough distance had elapsed, he followed her as he had done three mornings in a row.

He crossed through Covent Garden without a second glance. The paved suburb was no longer recognisable as any kind of garden. He couldn't remember when it last was. Memories tended to blur together after a while.

As the witch made her way along the street, he followed, a shadow adrift in the sea of people.

It was a simple job and tedious work, but his employers for this job were a stoic and powerful crowd, they paid well, and besides, he needed something to occupy the long, dreary, passages of existence. For the last century he'd taken any contract that came up, a temporary panacea for the ache of boredom. Some of them had been bloody and brutal, but death was no threat, and morality was for mortals concerned with their place in the afterlife. Ethical fashions changed every few decades or so, and the bounty hunter had never had much interest in what was popular. He had seen his fair share of sunrises, each one less impressive than the last, and it took quite a lot to pique his interest.

Today, something was different.

The witch, last he'd seen her, had walked with a weight on her shoulders, an exhaustion that blighted her energetic field. But today, the subtly perceptible light that radiated from her was clear, almost bright. He could barely look at her without squinting, but it wasn't ordinary light, it was some other power. Her hair seemed different too.

He'd been keeping a distance – always wise when tracking someone over a period of days. But now he needed to report on the development. And to do that, he had to get closer.

Taking a seat in the back of the café, the bounty hunter watched as Delia ordered her coffee, her casual demeanour belying the powerful aura that seemed to shimmer around her. Despite his extensive experience with various magical beings over the centuries in his line of work, he couldn't figure it out.

A spark of rage ignited within him – he didn't like puzzles he didn't ask for. He loved and hated them, but he didn't like them. They interrupted the tedium, but also shook his sense of self, which had already worn down to the very bone.

But there she was, a riddle that beckoned him.

As if sensing his gaze, Delia looked over her shoulder, her eyes catching his before he shifted focus. It was a close call.

The rogue hunter was not used to being the one at a loss.

The enchantress had deceived him. He knew he had to tread carefully; he may not owe anyone any loyalties, but his reputation as a mercenary was all he had.

His tired heart was pounding in an unrecognisable rhythm.

*The job is simple,* he reassured himself. *Observe, report, and don't get involved.*

Yet, there was this gnawing curiosity, growing louder with each passing minute.

He kept his head down, not daring to look again. Not yet.

His thoughts were abruptly broken as Delia stood to leave the café.

He waited a moment and then stood, abandoning his cold black coffee.

He should wait longer, he knew that, but instinct took over. If something had changed, he needed to know what it was and report back immediately.

As he left the warmth of the café and returned to the bustle of the street, he caught a glimpse of her up ahead just as a figure cloaked in crimson stepped into her path.

The bounty hunter's seasoned eyes narrowed as he watched the man lay a hand on Delia's arm. His instinct flared brighter, the inertia of observation shattered as every nerve in his ancient body prepared for action.

# 7

## DELIA

"These ridiculous map apps," Delia grumbled under her breath, punctuating her statement with a colourful array of choice words that would have undoubtedly offended her former husband's rather dainty ears.

She stopped the car and grimaced. Her eyes darted between the tiny glowing screen of her phone and the unending tangle of country roads sprawling out before her. She was sure she'd just driven down this way, only she definitely hadn't doubled back. Could the road have looped around without her realising it?

An exasperated huff left her lips as she drove on. "Why in the blazes do they make all these blasted roads that lead to nowhere?" Her query hung unanswered in the air, as she fruitlessly tried to figure out the puzzle that would lead her to the elusive village.

She was absolutely sure it was out this way, though it was only a faded memory from the recesses of her childhood, along with other special recollections of Etty.

Her grandmother, fondly known only as 'Etty', was an enigma of a woman. Shunning motherly monikers and colours, her wardrobe consisted of black, which only became more striking as she aged.

When Delia came to the shocking realisation that Etty lived no longer than sixty-five, her world momentarily faltered. The chain-smoking, fierce matriarch had eventually fallen prey to emphysema – or so Delia had been informed at the distressingly closed-casket funeral.

But young Delia cherished memories of escapades and adventures with her grandmother, and now, teetering closer to sixty-five herself, she felt an undeniable urge to reconnect somehow – if not to her roots, then to fragments of a bygone era, filled with the remnants of vivid happiness that she hadn't experienced since childhood.

The road ahead turned into a dead end.

"By all the freaking gods!" Delia pulled over and cursed at the sea of endless paddocks, stretching out like a green quilt patchworked with hedgerows and the odd stunted tree. "How do I get to Myrtlewood?"

Letting out a hefty sigh, she closed her eyes for a moment.

"Now's not the time to lose it, Delia," she reminded herself, placing a gentle hand on her chest.

She was actually doing fairly well, considering the ludicrous shenanigans of the previous night, the thumping hangover earlier that morning, the shock of her curtain spontaneously combusting, and the bizarre attack by a rogue cosplayer possibly in league with her ex!

That was a lot to deal with in one day and she realised she'd been coping superbly.

Allowing herself a moment of satisfaction, a grin began to tug at the corners of her lips, followed by a laugh.

Slowly, she opened her eyes and found herself captivated by the picturesque sight of sunlight, bathing winter fields around her.

Lifting her horn-rimmed sunglasses onto her head, she squinted down the road. It wasn't precisely a dead-end, as she'd first assumed. Now that she looked again, a continuation of road nudged its way into view before twisting out of sight around a bend.

Firing up the car again, she pressed down on the accelerator, heading towards the mysteriously unfolding road.

It unfurled before her, a ribbon of gravel amidst the sea of green.

"An optical illusion," she mused to herself, the words whispered on the wind. "Either that, or I really have lost my marbles." With that, she eased into the bend, the village of Myrtlewood drawing ever closer.

# 8

## THE SHEPHERD

The dawn was bleeding into the sky as Father Benedict began his strict regimen of morning exercises.

That wretched woman had been in his dreams again, but, as usual, the hard pounding of his own discipline restored things to their proper order inside his mind.

The cold stone under his bare feet, the rhythmic echoes of his movements reverberating against the austere walls of his quarters, the taste of the cold morning air on his tongue, all grounding him in his obligations.

Hardship, he had learned, wasn't only a teacher; it was humbling and path-paving. And his path, as he'd always known it, was to restore the Order to its former dignity and rightful place in the world.

His eyes caught sight of his reflection in the small mirror hanging on the wall. The face of a man tested by time and circumstance, marked by the purity of his dedication to the Order and the burden he had willingly carried looked back at him. Each wrinkle, each crease, was a badge of honour earned over decades of clandestine work in the field, each assignment more secretive than the last. He would never speak of this work, except if expressly asked by his superiors.

He turned from his reflection, settling in the austere simplicity of his quarters. A suitably firm cot, a small desk, a plain wooden chair.

He completed his exercises and took a seat at the desk to attend to the breakfast one of the underlings had brought in. The sunlight streaming in from the small window created dancing patterns on the wooden surface. The warmth on his skin was a simple indulgence, but he tried to ignore it. Any indulgence could lead him down a dangerous path and he had to hold himself together to be a force forged tougher than steel.

A simple bowl of gruel awaited him, steaming gently, and a hardy chunk of brown bread sat beside it, accompanied by a modicum of cheese. He disregarded the cheddar, shaking his head. There would be no lavish feasts for him, no pleasure, only humble sustenance.

The Order preached and lived by austerity, and Father Benedict would be its embodiment.

Every mouthful was savoured, not for its culinary merit, but for the sense of ritual it brought with it. The act of eating, of fuelling his body for the day's tasks, was a part of his commitment to the Order and The Mission. The food would strengthen him, preparing him for what lay ahead.

Father Benedict finished his meal in silence, his gaze straying towards the window. The courtyard was coming alive, the Order's members setting about their day. It was a stark reminder of his responsibility and the task that lay before him.

This was as it should be: an existence stripped down to its core, shorn of frills and distractions, in service to a mission so monumental that it had swallowed his identity whole.

A knock interrupted his introspection, and the Cleric entered. "Father Benedict," he began, bowing slightly. "The fire witch, she is on the move."

Benedict exhaled slowly, closing his eyes for a brief moment.

The world was careening violently out of balance – just as it had been for centuries, but now there was an opportunity to right things for good.

The Order had to act, and swiftly, putting their centuries of strategising into action. But there was also the neglected flock to tend to.

Memories of his harsh masters and the brutal routines they'd inflicted upon him during his early years of training flickered in his mind. A childhood spent in the austere embrace of the Order had done him good, and in return, he would achieve the recognition and authority to return things to their rightful place. Determination ignited within him.

The Cleric cleared his throat. "Erm, you wanted to begin the new training regime today..."

Father Benedict regarded the Cleric carefully. A simpering weakling, but not without his uses. He had been quick to follow orders and now plans were in place to restore the inner order of the Order, but first, the world needed to be set right, the ancient forces rebalanced.

Father Benedict's gaze swept back to the bustling courtyard, Order members scurrying about like confused ants, indulging, no doubt, in all kinds of sinful pleasures as they pretended to play out their roles. None of them had borne the sacrifices he had, but all could be whipped into shape given the proper discipline. Unfortunately, that would have to wait.

"The time has come," he murmured, more to himself than to the Cleric. "The Mission takes precedence."

# 9

## DELIA

A captivating tingle ran down Delia's arms as she neared the township. The cottages looked different here – they were old-fashioned, but that wasn't quite it; lots of cottages were old around this part of the country, but the ones in Myrtlewood were different. They were more charming somehow.

She drove along the country road, admiring the peaceful farmland that gradually morphed into the village. She admired a particularly notable old manor house stood on a hill, overlooking the village and the sea.

The sight of the ocean was breathtaking.

Delia couldn't help but sigh as the horizon opened up before her.

Taking a detour, she found herself by the beach. The crashing waves were not exactly inviting – swimming was out of the question, especially at this time of year when a thin layer of ice still covered the ground until afternoon and snow seemed a distinct possibility.

Still, there was something incredibly peaceful about the sea. She had loved the ocean as a child, but it had been years since she'd truly enjoyed spending any length of time at the seaside due to the rigorous routines of rehearsals and ever-looming shows.

Because of the chill in the air, Delia decided to stay in her car, though she did open the window to breathe in the fresh salty sea air.

The afternoon was already beginning to draw to a close; the sky was starting to darken. It wouldn't be long before sunset.

She had come all the way here with nowhere to stay, but it would be a long drive back to London. Instead, she promptly drove back towards the village, parking in front of a delightfully quaint tea shop that was thankfully still open.

As Delia got out of the car, she noticed a woman with rather curly red hair eyeing her cautiously, although based on what the woman was wearing Delia rather thought that she might be the one to be cautious. The bright floral dress clashed distinctly with a yellow and purple striped apron.

However, Delia wasn't one to be the fashion police. Besides, the outfit blended in nicely with the excessively colourful and floral decor of the tea shop itself. She returned the woman's gaze with a tight-lipped smile and proceeded to enter the shop.

"Hello, dear," said the tea shop woman, clearing plates onto a tray. "You're right on time."

"Oh?" Delia was slightly puzzled before her brain made a quick leap in logic, and she added, "Oh yes, I am glad I caught you before you closed."

"My name is Marjie," said the woman, who promptly strode over and pulled Delia into a hug. It was an odd gesture for someone she'd just met.

"People certainly are friendly in these parts," Delia said, though she had to admit the hug felt good. It had been a while since she'd hugged anyone other than Kitty or Gillian and even those had been rather brisk and fleeting recently.

Marjie's hug, on the other hand, was warm and nurturing in a way that put Delia right at ease.

Marjie gestured to a table by the window. "You'll be having tea?"

"Coffee, please," Delia replied, taking a seat.

Marjie wrinkled her nose. "I should have known," she muttered, shaking her head as she disappeared into the kitchen. Barely a minute passed before she returned with a little coffee pot and a matching teacup in an elegant midnight blue and silver pattern that reminded Delia of the 1920s. There was a little matching jug of cream, and a rather decadent-looking chocolate tart.

"I didn't order..." Delia began.

"No, but I could tell what you needed," Marjie interjected. "Now eat up, we haven't got all day."

Delia looked at her, puzzled, and then quickly reasoned that Marjie must be keen to close the shop soon. Indeed, she quickly bustled back off to the kitchen, leaving Delia alone with her thoughts – and the rather moreish-looking tart.

The coffee wasn't as strong as she was used to, but it left an invigorating zing even after a single sip.

Delia eyed the tart. It was full of sugar and other carbohydrates, exactly the kind of thing Jerry would have disapproved of, especially on his keto diet kick. That only made Delia more delighted to try it. However, she was thoroughly unprepared for the intense flavour which elicited such a sensation of pleasure that words were inadequate to describe it.

"How's that then?" Marjie asked from behind the counter.

Delia looked around but found no one else in the shop. She grinned. "This tart is heavenly. You've pleased me like no other woman!" she replied, shocking herself with the kind of humour she usually reserved for her best friend.

Marjie laughed heartily.

Delia joined in the laughter. She had the strange feeling she was making a new friend, something that hadn't happened in a long time, at least not with someone around her own age.

In the theatre, she tended to fall into a mentor role, especially with the younger actors. Of course, she had Kitty, but that left her with a rather small social circle of people she genuinely liked and would consider proper friends.

"How long have you lived here, Marjie?" Delia asked.

"All my life, I'd say," Marjie replied. "With a few trips here and there...I wouldn't want you to think I'm not worldly!"

"Heaven forbid," said Delia. "The thought never crossed my mind."

"You're from London, then?" said Marjie. "I can tell from your accent."

"Born and raised," said Delia.

"But you're a witch."

Delia squinted, unsure whether this was some kind of insult. The way Marjie said it, it sounded more like a compliment. She shrugged in response.

"I think you might just be the one we've been waiting for," Marjie mumbled.

Delia looked at her, slightly perplexed.

Her brain failed to come up with an adequate explanation, so she took another bite of the chocolate tart instead. She didn't much care for explanations when her entire sensory capacity was focused on savouring the deliciousness.

As she sat there, she heard a small squeak. Delia turned to the window to see a puppy, golden brown and white, with its black nose pressed right up against the window. She grinned at the little beagle whose tail wagged expectantly. "I'm afraid these are all mine," she said, returning to her savouring.

It was a few moments again before she considered Marjie's comment and wondered what kind of village she'd got herself into. Marjie had given her a rather friendly hug. Was she part of a cult? Delia decided to change the subject. "Where can I find the best accommodations around here?"

"There's the local pub," said Marjie. "Or you could come up to the house and stay with me if Rosemary doesn't mind. There's plenty of room."

"Err, thank you," said Delia, uncomfortable with the invitation to stay with someone she'd only just met. "The pub sounds perfect." She smiled politely and rolled back her shoulders, reaffirming her healthy boundaries. She wouldn't be taken in by any kind of hippy commune, no matter how good their baking was.

# IO

## AGATHA

Agatha Twigg sat amidst the dusty tomes and parchment scrolls that filled her secluded library. The room smelled of ancient ink, vellum, and leather bindings, the scent of time captured in many decades of accumulated knowledge. A single desk lamp cast a warm glow over her work, throwing long shadows among the stacks of books.

The phone on the desk interrupted the stillness, its shrill ring echoing through the hushed chamber. Agatha looked at the device with a frown, cursing before answering.

"Agatha, it's Marjie," said the voice on the other end, brimming with excitement. "I think I've found the fourth Crone."

Agatha's eyebrows shot up. The fourth Crone? This was another one of Marjie's fanciful ideas. Marjie was like a child, easily excited, and quick to see signs where there were none. Agatha took it upon herself to be the voice of reason, though on days like this, she'd much prefer to be having a sherry with Covvey at the pub than taming the wild imaginings of her meddlesome friend.

"Marjie, you know how I feel about speculation. We've been over this," Agatha replied, her voice heavy with exhaustion. "Not everything's a sign."

"She's here, Agatha, in Myrtlewood. Staying at the pub," Marjie blurted out.

Agatha pause, considering this new information. "Why didn't ye say so?"

Marjie wasn't going to shut up until Agatha had met the woman, so it might as well be over a sherry or two, if only to put Marjie's mind at ease.

Agatha hung up the phone, still doubtful. Her rational mind told her there was nothing more to this, though she had been sensing something recently, some sort of power growing stronger.

And then there were the books. Randomly levitating books were not an everyday occurrence, even for a witch. They were, in fact, rather a nuisance, but the books themselves were only a minor inconvenience compared to the shadows of darkness she occasionally sensed at the edges of her mind.

Agatha grumbled as she pushed herself back in her chair. She rubbed her temples, feeling the weight of all the years of lore and duty pressing in on her. Even with her years of experience and wisdom, the thought of a rising ancient power was intimidating.

Yet, the world had a habit of producing unexpected occurrences lately.

Maybe, just maybe, Marjie was onto something with all her speculation about fabled crones. Not that Agatha would admit that to her. She allowed herself a quiet chuckle before rising from her chair. Nothing was confirmed amid the pile of ancient rumours Agatha had unearthed in her own private collection. They'd spent more than a few evenings at the pub gossiping about who the Crones of Myrtlewood would be, if they were to rise again, and they had a few likely candidates, themselves included of course. The ancient power the Crones wielded was said to be immense enough to defeat the evil that rose every hundred or so years, and so it apparently had been, over and over again, that four would be chosen to bear the mantle, the responsibility, and the powers that came with it.

Whether Marjie's claims were fanciful or not, it would not hurt to meet this woman. If nothing else, it would provide a break from the dusty solitude of her library and a few sherries. And who knew? The world was an unpredictable place, and the future was never set in stone. Maybe this would be a new chapter in their story. And Agatha would be damned if she let it unfold without her.

# II

## DELIA

By the time Delia arrived at the Witch's Wort pub, it was late afternoon, but the overcast sky made it look more like evening. She shivered as she stepped out of her car.

It was a typical English establishment, a bit shabby on the inside but cosy, with wooden tables and low-hanging ceilings and rather quiet for this time of the afternoon.

It didn't smell like beer, which gave Delia some hope that the accommodations upstairs wouldn't be too grubby.

The woman behind the counter eyed her suspiciously. "Can I help you ma'am?" Her dark blonde hair was arranged in pigtail plaits despite the fact she was at least forty.

Delia raised an eyebrow. "You're not really used to strangers around these parts, are you? It's no wonder. I couldn't find you on the map."

The woman put down the tankard she'd been polishing and gave Delia a more considered look and then smiled warmly. "Not on a regular map, no. But you found us, so you must be meant to be here."

Delia shrugged, hoping this wasn't some other cult reference. There was quite enough cultish behaviour in the wider theatre world, what with method acting and improv groups, something she'd rather steer clear of.

"I was wondering if I could rent a room for the night."

"Of course, love," said the woman.

She took down Delia's details in a book, accepted payment, and then handed over a key with a rather adorable acorn keychain. "Upstairs to the left, room number three. My name's Sherry, by the way. Let me know if you have any questions. Hope you enjoy your stay."

Delia smiled at her; the sentiment seemed genuine enough. "I hope so too," she said, taking the key and a small overnight bag.

She headed through the empty pub and upstairs to room number three. It wasn't lavish, but it was nicely made up; slightly shabby, as she'd expected, but clean and cosy.

There was an old wooden sofa by the window and a queen-size bed with white sheets and a plummy purple duvet.

Delia sprawled on the bed, mulling over what a mess she'd got herself into and what she was doing with her life, and then pulled herself together promptly. After all, she was a grown woman having a little unplanned adventure, and there was nothing wrong with that.

Removing herself from the indecorous bed-sprawling, she moved across to the sofa instead and stared out the window across the gorgeous little township.

Lights were beginning to come on, and she could see right across the village from the elevated position of the room.

The glimpse of the sea in the distance was lovely, and really, it was the perfect setting to have a little break and take her mind off things. Sure, it might have been nicer to be holidaying in luxury at a swanky resort by the seaside, but for now, this would do nicely.

Curling up on the sofa, Delia found herself drifting into a doze.

THE SWING FLEW HIGHER *and higher. She giggled as Etty pushed her.* *"Bigger! Bigger! Up! Up! Wheee!" young Delia cried in delight.*

*The sky darkened and a crow swooped across it.*

*Black clouds of smoke appeared.*

*"Delia!" Etty screamed as a great monster — a beast — emerged from the smoke.*

DELIA TRIED to scream but instead woke with a strangled cry, only to find herself in the perfect safety of the sofa, and a good few decades older than she had been in her dream with the backache to prove it.

Delia sighed. The nightmares had been happening more and more recently.

It was strange because she'd barely thought about her grand-mother, Etty, in decades, and now all of a sudden, she had started dreaming about her almost nightly.

Delia's psychiatrist — because of course she needed one working in theatre — had told her it was probably a reflection of her own fear of mortality, of getting older, which might well be true.

It wasn't a particularly pleasant revelation for Delia, who thought mortality was for atheists and Christians — those overly concerned with life ending or the fate of their soul — not actors, and certainly not direc-tors who preferred to live in their own little worlds and forge immortal legacies.

The sky was growing darker now, and although the room was particularly quiet and she could hear nothing from the pub below, Delia thought it might be time to head downstairs and see what the Witch's Wort had to offer for dinner.

# 12

## DELIA

Despite how quiet and peaceful her room had been, Delia quickly realised as she made her way downstairs, that the pub, which had been sedate earlier, was now bustling with the dinner rush.

Stepping into the quaintly lit dining area, she glanced around, her gaze lingering on the chalkboard specials. Delia found herself suddenly starving; the events of the day had left her with little time for food.

She decided to treat herself. After all, what was the point of a break if she couldn't indulge a little?

She found herself a quiet spot in the corner and, nudging her anxieties aside, she slid into a booth and scanned the room. It was a different sort of stage, one filled with a cast of locals who had their parts down pat. If anyone noticed her at all, she would be the new face, the surprise character who had walked into their ongoing play.

Sherry brought her a menu, smiling and greeting her warmly before leaving Delia alone to peruse.

There was nothing here that Jerry would have approved of. In fact, during the early '60s health kick, he would have ordered the steak and chips – hold the chips – with an extra salad. Delia, however, was having none of it. Or rather, everything looked rather delicious to her.

She contemplated the pattern her life had taken, the roles she had played, both on and off stage. She mused over the ghost of her grandmother, her estranged husband, her psychiatrist's words, and the abruptness of her departure from her old life. And as she waited for her meal, she found herself slowly releasing the tension of the day, sinking into the musical chatter and clink of the pub.

Sherry returned and Delia ordered the beef and Guinness stew and a glass of red wine.

It came only moments later, accompanied by a big piece of crusty bread slathered in fresh golden butter. She quickly devoured the entire bowl.

The pub's ambiance, its lively rhythm, and the comfort of hot food on a cold night began to work their magic. She was a long way from the spotlights and applause, the drama and the intrigue. Here, in this shabby but cosy pub, she felt a glimmer of something she hadn't felt in a while – the freedom to be Delia, not the actor, not the director, but just Delia. And with that, she felt a cautious flicker of hope that she might actually enjoy this unexpected intermission of a holiday.

As she sipped her wine, she checked her emails on her phone. There was a slightly concerning message from her solicitor implying that Jerry might somehow have tricked her out of the vast majority of their accumulated wealth.

Delia felt a stab of annoyance. The lawyer was supposed to be hers, not Jerry's. Her ex-husband had already spitefully said that he'd hired more expensive representation, leaving their usual solicitor for Delia. She hadn't bothered to find anyone new because the thought was daunting, but now, well, either her solicitor was useless or Jerry had gotten to him somehow.

It was actually more than annoyance that plagued her now, but she didn't want to launch into a tirade of swearing while sitting alone in a pub in a strange town, in case it drew the wrong kind of attention.

She swallowed her burning rage, called Gilly, and left a message: "Your father's trying to rip me off. I might need you to represent me after all. By the way, I've taken myself on a holiday to Myrtlewood. Do you know of it? It's a little village not too far from where you are. Just letting you know, in case you decide you want to spend some time with your mother after all."

Delia hung up the phone, smirking at the slightly passive-aggressive message. Gilly could handle it. She could handle a lot more than that. For a moment, Delia was lost in sorrow, missing Gilly and the grandkids, then she pushed the emotion away. It did her no good to wallow in self-pity.

Delia set aside her phone and took a big sip of her wine. That was when she noticed a stern old woman staring at her from a table nearby.

"Can I help you?" Delia asked.

"I don't suppose you can," the old woman said, peering over her round spectacles.

It struck her then that despite the woman's scraggly white hair, cane, and hunched petite frame, she was probably not much older than Delia herself.

However, Delia didn't feel old. She didn't need a cane, like the woman who was now glaring at her, and thanks to laser eye surgery Delia's vision was mostly passable except for small print and other ridiculously impractical things that should have been made illegal by now.

She watched as the woman, who was now clearly glaring at her, propped herself up with her cane and shuffled over to Delia's table.

"Are you a witch?" The woman jabbed a finger at Delia.

"Excuse me?" Delia bristled. "That's the second time I've been called a witch today. What is it? The outfit?" She looked down at the predominantly black clothing she was wearing. "Maybe it is the outfit," she mused.

"Perhaps not, then," said the woman with an eyeroll. "What are you doing here?"

"Enough, Agatha," said a gruff voice. A man approached. He must have been in his sixties, but could have starred as an older version of

Henry Cavill, with long grey-white hair, a scarred face, and muscular build. He placed a hand on the obviously slightly deranged woman's shoulder.

Delia sighed. "Is this what I've got to look forward to in my old age? Losing my marbles?" she asked the man before realising that if this was indeed the case she was being rather rude about it.

"How dare you!" said Agatha. She turned back to the man, shaking his hand off her shoulder. "Covvey, leave us alone," she growled at him, then leaned down towards Delia with breath smelling of overly sweet sherry. "You're not from around here."

"London," Delia said, "if you must know." She felt sorry for the woman. After all, she obviously didn't possess all of her faculties. Delia wasn't afraid, at least not physically. She was sure she could take Agatha. However, there was a sternness to the old woman that was quite unsettling.

In fact, if Delia hadn't spent the best part of the last three decades staring down arrogant actors, she might have withered under Agatha's steely gaze.

"What's going on here?" Another man approached with sandy hair and blue-green eyes. He looked to be in his forties, tall, well-built, and handsome, but far too young for Delia – not that she was looking for any kind of romantic company at the moment.

"Nothing, Liam," Covvey grumbled. "None of your business, stay out of it."

The younger man who Covvey called Liam raised his hands in innocence and looked to Delia. "Are you alright, miss?"

It has been a long time since Delia had been called miss, and by the way Liam was smiling at her, she was sure he was a terrible flirt.

She laughed and shook her head as the men proceeded to glare at each other while Agatha continued to stare daggers at her.

Delia tried not to pay attention to the old woman who seemed to see right through her, sizing her up in every aspect. Then Agatha simply turned away and stomped back to her table.

"Strange place," Delia said, wondering if it had been a mistake to come here at all.

"Sorry about that," said Sherry, approaching the table. "Look, Agatha is one of our regulars. She can be a bit troubling at times. Here, I brought you some mulled mead, on the house."

"Mulled mead?" Delia asked. "The last time I had that was at a medieval interactive performance ball."

Sherry blushed slightly.

Delia looked around, noting the slightly odd way the people of Myrtlewood were dressed. Were they all involved in old-timey fairs? At least they weren't all trying to look the same, or even attempting pretentious uniqueness like most of Delia's theatre troupe.

She took a sip of the mead, having promptly finished her wine, and felt it warming her delightfully. Maybe this place wasn't so bad after all.

Her phone buzzed again.

*Gilly calling.*

"Hello, love," Delia answered immediately.

"Mum, what are you doing?"

"I just took myself on a little holiday, that's all."

"To Myrtlewood?" Gilly asked, incredulous. "Seriously? Do you even know what that place is?"

"It is eccentric, I'll give you that," Delia conceded, looking around at the rather odd collection of locals.

"Get out of there, get back to London. It's not safe...I mean, for a woman your age to be travelling alone. You're vulnerable."

"It's a damn sight safer than London," Delia retorted, not enjoying being told what to do by her own progeny. "Your father sent some ridiculous actor in a cape to attack me on the street, in broad daylight, today. In the West End, no less."

"Really? Is that what he told you?"

"No, but who else would be responsible than an out-of-work actor paid by my disgruntled ex? I can't think of any other possible explanation. He went right for me. I'm sure Jerry is just trying to rattle me. He's trying to take everything."

"I saw the email," Gilly said. "Thanks for forwarding it."

Delia sighed. "Will you represent me? I know you'll do a better job than that ridiculous man Smithers. I'm sure he's an old friend of your father's."

"I can't. You know that, Mum. It would be a conflict of interest, representing one of my parents against the other one. But someone at my firm will be able to pick it up. Besides, I'm a barrister, not a solicitor."

"Of course," Delia said, feeling slightly disappointed. "Oh well, send the files to someone. Make sure they're good."

"Are you staying in Myrtlewood long, then?" Gilly asked in a rather sulky tone.

Delia looked around. "You know, I just might. I've been feeling slightly depressed in London in that terrible little flat...And besides, I feel like being close to the sea will do me a world of good."

"You know it's a—" Gilly started and then stopped.

"A what dear?"

"Oh, never mind, Mum. Just take care of yourself and let me know if you see anything strange."

"Everything's strange around here, I'm sure," Delia said. "That's why I quite like it. It's inspiring. Maybe I'll write another play."

"It's nice to hear you say that," Gilly said. "It's been such a long time since you've written anything."

Delia smiled into the phone. "And when will I get to see my daughter and my grandchildren?"

"I'm terribly busy," Gilly replied.

Delia tried to hold back the crushing weight of disappointment. She hated being pushed away like a discarded old rag.

"Although..." Gilly continued. "Maybe the kids could come and stay with you for a bit if you had somewhere to keep them."

"Really?" Delia said, hopeful. "Now that could be nice, it'd keep me occupied."

"You're a worry, Mum," said Gilly. "I'm sorry I haven't been able to help you through...whatever it is you're going through lately. Things have been a little bit hectic. But I'll see you at some point soon."

"Good luck with the move," Delia said as they ended the call.

Was it just her, or was everyone acting slightly strangely? Perhaps she was losing some of her faculties.

Why was Gilly so resistant to the idea of Delia being in Myrtle-wood? Perhaps there had been some kind of controversy over the town.

She looked around the pub again. There were an awful number of people dressed in cloaks and robes of different hues, and there might be some sort of local hippie commune or cult, but Delia wasn't going to be drawn into anything like that. Certainly not. After all, the 1970s were long past.

She sighed and took another sip of the mulled mead, allowing it to soothe her nerves.

It really was quite a delightful drop, and despite Gilly's hesitations, this town wasn't so bad. Delia's mind began turning excitedly. Maybe she could even rent a cottage here for a little while, somewhere with enough room for the grandchildren to run around the yard. That would help Gilly out too, and hopefully get their mother-daughter relation-ship back on track.

Delia looked up to see the woman from the tea shop standing at the bar. Marjie caught her eye and gave her a wave.

A moment later, Marjie bustled over with two more cups of mulled mead, one of which she pushed over to Delia.

"Hello, dear," she said. "I'm sorry if we got off on the wrong foot earlier."

"Did we?" Delia asked, to which Marjie gave her a cautious look.

"You see, dear, we're not really used to strangers in this part of the world. The consequence of that is that we're not very good at talking to people we don't know."

"Understandable," Delia replied with a shrug. She considered herself an introvert and had been thinking about taking herself back upstairs for a nice quiet night of solitude.

However, Marjie was warm and smiling. And Delia had the strange sensation again, that they might just become friends. She supposed she could stay for one more drink as long as no one called her a witch or tried to convert her to anything.

"I hope this doesn't give me a terrible hangover," Delia said, after a big gulp of mead.

"Of course not," Marjie replied with a grin. "It's enchanted against that."

Delia gave her a quizzical look. Marjie put her hand over her mouth. "You really don't know, do you?"

"Know what?" Delia asked.

Marjie shook her head. "Never mind, I still think..." Her voice trailed off. "Tell me about yourself," Marjie said, changing tack.

At first, Delia felt guarded. Why would she tell a near stranger about her life? But, by and by, she found her entire story pouring out as Marjie *oohed* and *aahed* and said reassuring things, contributing a rather abridged story of her own life – growing up in Myrtlewood, her husband's unfortunate death, the cause of which she didn't seem to want to reveal, and she talked a lot about a woman named Rosemary and her daughter Athena, who Delia assumed must be close family of Marjie's.

"I'm living with them now," Marjie informed her. "In Thorn Manor, up on the hill. It's a lovely old house. It's very special. They like having me around." She smiled to herself.

Delia felt a stab of jealousy. If only Gilly was like that.

There had been a change recently. Six months ago, Delia's daughter was calling on her all the time and then suddenly it was like she didn't want anything to do with her. Something had happened. Delia wondered if it was a new lover, somebody she wouldn't approve of.

"Oh dear," said Marjie, glancing towards the doorway.

"What is it?"

"Something strange, a disturbance," Marjie muttered as she looked from the main entrance to another curtained door hear the counter.

Delia could see nothing strange, however there must have been some sign she missed because suddenly there was a kerfuffle.

A man in a red hooded cape lurched in through the front door, bearing a sword, only to be tackled to the ground by several customers near the bar including both Liam and Covvey. The old blighter growled.

It must have been the mead, but Delia could have sworn she saw a furry paw slash at the hooded assailant's face, clawing at him.

"Is there a dog?" Delia asked, standing up to make sense of the tussled limbs as more people joined the fight.

"I'm sure there isn't," said Marjie blandly.

Delia narrowed her eyes. "Strange," she murmured as she and Marjie watched as the commotion subsided; the red-cloaked man was pinned to the floor.

"What's strange, dear?" Marjie asked.

"Somebody a lot like that tried to attack me earlier."

Marjie raised an eyebrow. "Really? In Myrtlewood?"

"No, no, in London," Delia corrected.

"Ah," said Marjie gave her a knowing look. "I just knew it! I don't suppose you've been setting anything on fire lately?"

Delia's eyes widened in shock. She put down her cup of mead and dashed away upstairs, closed the door to her room, and locked it, then she sank down with her back to it.

"It must just be the mead," she muttered to herself. "I'm definitely not losing my marbles. Not yet. Not yet."

# 13
## COVVEY

The day had already worn thin for Covvey when he planted himself at the bar, battle-ready for a pint of the darkest ale Myrtlewood had to offer. He was focused, as always, on his next move – seeking solace at the bottom of a pint glass, or at least at the bottom of the fifth, but something wasn't right. An anticipatory prickle on the back of his neck meant something. Danger.

The blood coursing through his veins prickled with the excitement of the hunt.

He let out a huff of irritation and glanced longingly at the pint Sherry was pulling, but before he could even mourn his interrupted evening, the pub door swung open and Covvey's instincts made him turn instantly towards it. A man, shrouded in a red cloak – the sort of robe that screams 'look at me, I'm about to make an unfortunate life decision'.

Covvey felt the rumble of a low growl issue from his throat as the man's hand crept towards the hilt of a poorly concealed sword.

A gasp rang around the pub and several patrons stepped aside.

Covvey's growl merely deepened.

The sword was cheaply forged, and brandished with a flourish that reminded Covvey of a play-fighting toddler.

Before the man could so much as croak a battle cry, Covvey had sized him up. He noted the distance he'd have to lunge to do any damage, the stranger's stance, the blinking confusion warring with overconfidence.

Covvey hung back as the man barrelled forward, sword flailing like a willow branch in a gale. Covvey stepped forward, and with a snap, his fist paid a brisk visit to the man's kidneys. The result was a pained gasp as the man doubled over.

Just then, Liam, resembling an over-excited puppy, rushed headlong into the fray, swinging a punch that might've been impressive had it landed anywhere but the open air.

The red-cloaked menace had recovered his composure. In an unexpected display of agility, he bobbed under Liam's wild advance and connected a solid jab to his jaw. Liam didn't flinch, he simply growled.

Covvey rolled his eyes as Liam brushed his light hair out of his face, his eyes wide as a deer's in a headlamp. He was there to 'help'. In Covvey's understanding, the man was a massive impediment, stumbling around like a baby in his first fight.

Only moments ago, he'd been in the process of holding Agatha back from attacking a rather endearing and mysterious newcomer when Liam had barged in, uninvited. Now here he was again, his scent heavy, as ever, with the curse that had haunted the magical world for centuries.

"Haven't you learned yet?" Covvey growled at Liam. "Stay out of my way."

The attacker lunged again, his sword arching in a clumsy swoop. Ducking, Covvey felt the cold whoosh of the blade over his scalp, a far closer shave than he usually preferred. With a well-placed punch to the wrist, the sword was dislodged, clattering away like a dropped butterknife.

In the ensuing chaos, Covvey let loose. His fists found their targets like homing pigeons, while the cloaked man's attempts at retaliation swung wide, connecting with nothing more than embarrassment. Covvey's punch sent the red-cloaked attacker sprawling onto the floor.

The room sighed collectively, the tension deflating like an old balloon.

Over the fallen fool, Covvey stood tall and unwavering while Liam advanced again.

"We should tie him up," Liam said. "Figure out why he's here."

Covvey's gut twisted with an instinctual dislike, an ancestral hatred for Liam's kind, which had only been enhanced by his interruption, his charming baby face, and his idiocy.

"Let him be." Covvey's growl echoed off the wooden beams, rumbling in the quiet that had descended. "He's got no place here."

The red-hooded man scrambled to his feet, shedding his dignity like a dog in summer.

"Don't come back," Covvey added as the man dashed away.

Everyone in the pub seemed to return to their drinks and conversations.

"What did you do that for?" Liam grumbled. "Now we've lost our chance to find out why that lunatic showed up here and attacked."

Covvey shook his head as he reached for his pint. "Lunatic?" he snorted. "That's a bit rich coming from you."

Liam's eyes blazed, furious. "You just let him go because I had a better idea and you wanted to override it."

Covvey took a refreshing swig of ale. "And what would you have us do? Tie him up and torture him? Hold him hostage? What kind of town would we be if we allowed that here?"

Liam shook his head. "We could have questioned him and turned him over to the authorities."

Covvey chuckled. "That would only double the number of idiots down at the police station. Perkins has his hands full just trying to get in everyone's way. How do you think he'd handle a hooded bandit?"

Liam glared as he took a sip of his own pint, which only made

Covvey chuckle more. It was shaping up to be a fine evening, already one fight and he'd managed to brass off a young upstart. Covvey didn't hate the lad by any stretch. Liam meant well, but his actions always reeked of showmanship and ego. It was tiring.

Covvey turned away. His gaze fell on the newcomer, Delia, a new face in the crowd, her eyes wide as she watched him. Something about her pricked at his senses, an odd scent, or a spark in her eyes. Something was different about her. Perhaps Liam had been right after all. There was a new mystery in the air and the red-cloaked sap might have had some useful intel, but anyone with such poor battle skills was bound to be a lost cause on intelligence of both sorts.

His instincts told him the new woman might well be attracting danger, but by the time Covvey ordered his second pint, she had disappeared, so all that would have to be a mystery for another time. For now, Covvey sighed and turned back to the bar. The night had just begun and he still hadn't finished his first pint.

# 14

## DELIA

With a warm, shimmery feeling, Delia snuggled under the covers, gradually remembering where she was and everything that had happened the day before.

Opening her eyes, she braced herself for a headache, but there was nothing. "Marjie was right about that mead," she muttered as she stretched, pulling back the covers.

She looked towards the window.

In her slightly befuddled state, she'd forgotten to close the curtains and sunlight spilled into the room.

"Lovely," Delia said, taking a breath of the crisp morning air.

She slid out of bed, feeling better than she had in a long time.

Then, the embarrassment hit her. She'd bolted from the pub without so much as a mumbled excuse, fearing for her own sanity. Had Marjie really said something so strange? Or did Delia just take her out of context and run away? So much for making new friends.

Still, the weather outside was gorgeous and her spirits lifted despite her lingering shame. In good form, she decided not to let something so silly ruin her day.

It was definitely time to go back to the seaside and enjoy the winter sunlight. It wasn't especially far, and Delia felt she could do with a good walk.

So, after a quick shower and coffee downstairs at the pub, which was thankfully open early and completely empty, Delia began wandering across the village.

She made sure to give Marjie's teashop a wide berth to avoid further embarrassment.

She crossed the town square, which was decorated with a large circle of grass in the middle and surrounded by trees. On her way, she spotted a delightful-looking chocolate shop which was not yet open, a second-hand bookshop, and several other establishments she decided she would peruse later.

As she carried on walking, the village gave way to farmland. Delia wasn't exactly sure how to get to the ocean, but she had driven from there the day before. It couldn't be that hard – surely heading west would take her to the ocean.

# 15

## FERG

Ferg smoothed his purple velvet cape over the back of his office chair, the regal fabric a stark contrast to the well-organised stacks of paperwork he'd previously lined up on his desk.

"Ready for another day of fabulous bureaucracy," he said to himself with a satisfied grin.

He cast his gaze across his dark walnut panelled office, the municipal nerve centre of Myrtlewood.

Since his most fortuitous election to the honourable role of mayor, he had spent rather a lot of time arranging things to suit his adulation for both order and ceremony.

Every parchment, tome, and magical gadget had its specific place, an orchestra of peculiarity composed under the baton of Ferg's meticulous hand.

His eyes came to rest on the large shelves housing a collection of mayoral paraphernalia, a mix of mundane and magical. Among these stood the Stargazer Spectrometer, a delicate assembly of rotating lenses and intricate cogs that deciphered the magic latent in celestial bodies. The Hourglass Oracle, a dual-ended sand timer encased in an ornate frame, whispered silent but profound truths of time. And the grandest of all, the Public Service Papyrus, a gift to the town from the Arch Magistrate, herself. It stood proudly to attention, a self-inking quill on a sheet of enchanted paper that penned down important town events and kept excellent notes – a practical and timesaving tool for a busy and magnificent mayor such as himself.

All these were meticulously arranged for maximum practicality and aesthetic appeal among the chalices, athames, and other ceremonial items.

But just because things had been arranged well, it did not mean they could not be arranged again!

This morning, as Ferg meticulously polished the spectrometer, the star-wheel suddenly shuddered, lenses spinning into a frenzied whirl. He frowned. He had already recalibrated it several times after some mysterious winter magic had interrupted the town, and referred each instance to the authorities, however, this time, the dial spun in the opposite direction.

It was an unmistakable alert – a different magical disturbance was afoot. His hand paused, staring at the chaotic dance of the golden cogs.

Ferg raised an eyebrow. "Hmm, a storm's brewing, and not in the meteorological sense."

He eyed the weather vane, its miniaturised thunderclouds swirling in a frantic dance. The disturbance in the magical realm suggested the arrival of a powerful entity. Or perhaps – his mind darted frantically to his wildest hopes – it could be a different kind of message altogether, a good omen, for example, of a well-received theatre production. He sighed dramatically. If only the Myrtlewood Players could get their act together in time for Yule.

Either way, Ferg felt an insistent pull, an inkling that he should be somewhere else.

As he contemplated exactly where, a loud rumbling sound issued forth. It took Ferg a split second to realise it was not any of the magical implements alerting him to danger, it was, in fact, his stomach protesting.

He was late for his second breakfast.

This gave him more of a clue as to where he needed to be. Generally, it had to have food, and more specifically, it had to be Marjoram Reeve's teashop.

"Never ignore a hunch," he muttered, adjusting his mayoral sash, the plush fabric vibrant against his tweed jacket. He threw on his velvet cape with a dramatic flourish and, with one last look around his marvellous office, Ferg set out for the teashop, a skip in his step and anticipation humming in his veins.

Marjoram Reeves, more commonly known as Marjie, was pouring a pot of her finest Earl Grey when Ferg burst into the shop, his grand entrance only slightly undermined by the tinkling of the humble door chime. The familiar scent of cinnamon and vanilla enveloped him, an olfactory comfort that met his approval every time.

He gave a modest bow. "Merry meet and good day to you."

"Ah, Ferg dear," said Marjie, her red curls bouncing in rather an uncouth manner as a warm smile spread across her face. "You're just in time. I suppose you fancy a cheese scone?"

Ferg gave a curt nod. "Indeed, I'm late for my scone and I'm anticipating enjoying it, so I hope you haven't put anything stranger in the batch than half-a-teaspoon of thyme."

Marjie tutted. "I'll bring it right over."

Ferg hesitated for a moment.

"Yes?" said Marjie. "Anything else, dear? I've given up on asking if you'd like to change your order, so you don't have to worry about that, although the new elderflower tarts are a fabulous treat."

"I'll take that under consideration," said Ferg, and he meant it, being rather partial to elderflower as he was. "However, I also came here to inquire whether anything unusual has happened recently. My spectrometer went off this morning. Is there anything I should know about as the official leader of this fine township?"

His sharp gaze took in the slightly pinched look on Marjie's face.

Ferg sat down at his favourite table, allowing Marjoram an appropriate amount of time to consider his important question and formulate a response.

"Well, Ferg," she began, bringing him his cheese scone. It was steaming pleasantly, clearly still warm from the oven. "There's a new witch in town, by the name of Delia. She's been in here and we've had a few chats. Seems like a good sort, but perhaps rather new to magic despite the fact that she's about my age. She says she's just here on holiday, from London."

Ferg took a bite of the scone, mulling over the information. "A new witch, you say? And from London? Now that's interesting! Tell me, what's her background?"

Marjie paused, a teasing glint in her eye. "Theatre."

"Theatre?" Ferg almost choked on his scone. "Well, isn't that a spot of luck? Might be a fine addition to our troupe."

"I get the impression she's a rather well-known director," said Marjie. "Meaning she probably doesn't like being told what to do."

Ferg shook his head in disapproval. Still, it was his responsibility to get to the bottom of the disturbance revealed to him by his spectrometer, and also to fish out any new talent in town and put it to good use.

Ferg cut his scone into quarters and ate it in the proper way, with precisely the right amount of butter, washed down with English Breakfast tea.

As soon as he had finished his morning ritual, he retrieved a small portable altar from his pocket and performed a quick locator spell, his fingers moving in intricate patterns over the table. The flicker of magic revealed the location of this 'Delia'.

It seemed she'd recently been at the pub, where she'd no doubt enjoyed the local accommodations, and if his predictions were correct, her current trajectory aimed towards a nearby beach.

"Well, Marjoram, I must bid you farewell and head off to welcome the new witch. It's my mayoral duty after all," Ferg declared, leaving a few coins on the table as he stood.

A less effective mayor would be content to simply let people come and go, without bothering to go to any effort. However, Ferg was no slacker. He may have shed many of his previous roles in order to have the time for his new title. He was no longer a gardener, taxi driver, or receptionist, but he did still have a role in leading the local theatre group and the seasonal festivals, of course. If this new witch stayed on in Myrtlewood she must surely have some potential to tap into, and even if she didn't, it was worth inspecting her.

"The spectrometer never lies," he muttered as he left the cosy warmth of the teashop and headed out into the cold winter morning. "And if I'm not mistaken, something dangerous is coming."

Whether Delia was the danger or not, was yet to be determined.

# 16

## DELIA

"I say there," called a man as he approached. He was wrapped in a long, purple velvet cape, with short hair and rather gangly limbs.

At first, Delia worried he might attack, as certain cape-wearing individuals had been known to do recently. Yet, the man seemed friendly enough.

"Hello, you're not from around here, are you?" he asked. "Allow me to introduce myself." He bowed elegantly. "My name is Ferg, but my title is Lord Mayor of Myrtlewood. You may call me His Majestic Highness...."

"Okay," responded Delia, giving him a suspicious look and wondering if all the people in this town were batty.

"I am the elected mayor of Myrtlewood," Ferg continued.

"Really? People voted for you?" Delia asked, incredulous.

"Of course they did." Ferg examined his fingernails as if they were rather interesting. "Some people did, and the other contender was disqualified."

"I see," Delia replied with a smile.

"And how may I be of service?" Ferg asked, with a theatrical flourish.

"I'm fine, thank you," said Delia. However, after a moment's hesitation, her desire for self-determination clashed with her practical eagerness to reach the ocean as soon as possible and rest her legs. Her hip was playing up again and it was beginning to wear on her good mood. "Actually, could you point me in the direction of the beach?"

"Certainly," replied Ferg. "Just take the road next on your left and continue along to the end. You'll find a quiet cul-de-sac and a narrow path leading down towards the ocean. There'll be a little sign in purple."

"Of course," Delia said. "Thank you."

Ferg gave her a polite nod, then continued on his way. From a distance, it sounded as if he was reciting some kind of chant, possibly some form of municipal rite.

Delia shook her head as if to dislodge her confusion and continued on her walk, following the directions of his Majestic-whatever-he-was. As it turned out, they were rather good directions.

It wasn't long before she found herself on a narrow winding path which led from the cul-de-sac and looked out over the ocean as it sloped down towards the sandy shores.

The sea breeze picked up, bringing with it a fresh saltiness that invigorated Delia's senses and calmed her mind. "I'm exactly where I need to be," she told herself.

Of course, she didn't know what was coming, nor what she would do next. But she was determined that whatever it was, it would be fabulous.

# 17

## THE ROGUE

Acrisp wind blew across the Myrtlewood shoreline, and the briny scent of the sea stirred something in Declan's blood. His senses, honed by the ancient nature of his being, were on high alert. From his vantage point at the edge of the beach, the Rogue observed Delia. This woman was different from his usual marks. The Rogue was just doing his job, of course, observing, keeping the brim of his hat low to obscure his face. To the casual observer, she was a woman alone, standing on a beach lost in her thoughts. Only, he knew she was dangerous.

He had done his job, tracked her to Myrtlewood. Bad news for his employers. This town was protected far better than most parts of the country, though the Rogue really had no idea what the Order of Crimson was plotting. She'd spent the night in the local pub and another attack had failed miserably – too miserably. Either the Order was more daft than anyone realised, or their incompetence was deliberate.

The Rogue suspected the latter, though their motives remained unclear. This morning, Delia Spark had risen early, startling him out of his rest across the road amid a small cluster of trees. He didn't mind sleeping outside, in fact he preferred it. The cold air biting his skin was a welcome sensation, and buildings weren't to be trusted. He'd seen too many of them crumble, burn, or trap unsuspecting victims.

The beach was fairly empty, despite the sunny winter day, but he was far enough away to observe her without being noticed. People rarely noticed what was around them, in his experience, and Delia seemed transfixed by the incoming tide, her silvery hair with its bright red streak blowing in the wind as if casting a spell of its own – a flame dancing amidst a sea of tranquillity.

They'd labelled her 'fire witch' in the dossier, an entity of potent abilities, capable of wielding fire at will. He'd thought it nothing more than colourful exaggeration – until he'd seen the evidence. The fire in the London café has appeared spontaneous, but what kind of witch sets alight the tea towel of a dallying waiter with a simple angry glance?

As he observed her, she turned and their eyes met. Panic speared through him, an unfamiliar response from his usually steady nerves. He tipped his hat in a nonchalant greeting and turned to walk away. The last thing he needed was to be recognised.

Yet, before he could make his retreat, he heard quick footsteps and her voice rang out, catching him off guard. "Hey! Aren't you the man from London?"

He shook his head, denying the accusations, and watched as confusion flickered in her amber eyes.

"From the café?" She demanded a response.

He shook his head. Words were unnecessary; his denial was in his silence. He saw the confusion ripple across her face but made no move to ease it. He needed to keep his distance. This woman, this witch, had far too much power for anyone's good. It set his instincts alight with caution. It was an enigma, a challenge, and a threat all at once.

Delia stood her ground. "I'm sure I saw you – it was just yesterday."

Rage rushed over him then, an unbidden reaction to his internal struggle. Rage was a familiar sensation, an emotion he'd worn like a second skin through his long life. But this rage was different.

Even as he dismissed her, an invisible force pulled against his survival instincts, which beaconed at him to keep a safe distance. His steps faltered.

What was this witch's true power?

"I'm sure we've met before," Delia said, her eyes searching his face with a disconcerting curiosity. "I'm sorry if I've forgotten your name."

"You haven't," the Rogue assured, and attempted to sidestep her. She followed his movement with a tenacity that made his stomach knot.

"And you are?" Delia asked, narrowing her eyes at him.

He hesitated, but against his better judgement, the word slipped from his lips. "Declan."

Her eyes widened for a moment, as if she hadn't expected him to answer. "Be honest with me, Declan. Were you in London recently, at a café?"

"No," Declan replied too quickly.

"Liar," she retorted, her words sharp. "Are you following me?"

He held up his hands. "I assure you, I'm not. Perhaps I have a doppelganger?"

"A doppelganger?" she echoed, not buying it for a second.

"Or it's a coincidence?"

"A coincidence?" She snorted, rolling her eyes. "Is Jerry behind this?"

Declan blinked. "Who's Jerry?"

"The ex," she clarified, eyes narrowing further.

"No, I don't know Jerry." That much was true. "I'm just passing through town, that's all."

"You have a lookalike, then?" she asked, her tone scathing.

He shrugged. "It's a big world, lots of faces."

She shook her head, looking frustrated and, somehow, resilient. "I absolutely refuse to lose my marbles," she muttered to herself.

Declan's shoulders relaxed as she walked away, but his supernatural hearing picked up her muttering, "I'm sure it was him. But he's not one of *them*. He didn't attack me...He shouted at that man on the street...So was he trying to protect me? Rubbish. I don't need protecting. Idiot."

A cold prickle ran down Declan's spine. There was an immense power in Delia, that much was obvious. It thrummed in the air around her, an energy that stirred the ancient instincts in him. A power that felt like it could burn the world or save it. And Declan, the watcher in the shadows, wondered how much of that power she herself even realised she had.

As he left her standing on the beach, a sense of foreboding washed over him. She was his mission, nothing more. Yet, as the waves lapped at his feet, he couldn't help but feel he was walking towards an inferno, like a moth hyper-focused on the source of its own doom.

This woman was no damsel in distress. She was a force to be reckoned with. She was the Fire Crone.

# 18

## MARJIE

The pub was a bustling hub of activity, its rafters echoing with the chatter of locals as they chatted and joked with goblets and pints of the Myrtlewood's finest beverages between them. Amidst this jovial chaos, in a cosy corner, Marjie and Agatha sat discussing the town's latest arrival.

"She's new," Marjie admitted. "Brand new. New to magic, to us, to this entire world, I gather."

Agatha scoffed. "Well, it can't be her."

Marjie shook her head. "I have an intuition about this."

"Oh, bother you and your intuitions!" Agatha blustered.

"Well, at least my intuition doesn't need two glasses of sherry to function," Marjie quipped. "And it never leads me astray. Well, except perhaps with Herb."

The past month or so since Marjie had lost her husband had been such a blur, helped along by many soothing potions, cups of tea, and the year-long spa pass Rosemary had given her, opening the floodgates to as many massages and magical healing sessions as her broken heart could crave.

Some days, the waves of grief were heavier, always tinged with conflicting feelings because of everything Herb had done.

But it was getting easier, and helping Rosemary and Athena was a welcome distraction, as was Delia's arrival in Myrtlewood, which whispered to Marjie of ancient prophecies, and had her keeping a closer eye on her teapots lest they burst into flames again.

"Intuition is just indecision masquerading as wisdom," Agatha continued on. "I've seen more reliable guidance in a broken compass."

Marjie sighed. "You would say that; your intuition is so rusty, you'd need a tetanus shot to use it."

Agatha shook her head, a few stray strands of silver bobbing around her face as she took a gulp of her sherry. "I can't go on mere intuition. You know that. I need logic, reason, and several large, preferably old, books to help me make sense of a situation."

Marjie's eyes glinted with the spark of determination. "But we need to find *the fourth*. I'm telling you, we already have."

"The threat is growing..." Agatha's eyes narrowed, an internal battle of trust and scepticism playing out within their depths. "We need all the Crones."

"We don't even know if we are among them, do we?" said Marjie.

Agatha rolled her eyes. "What does your intuition tell you about that?"

Marjie sighed, the corners of her lips tugging upwards in a resigned smile. "You are incorrigible." She paused, drumming her fingers against the wooden table. "Right, well, if you're not convinced, how about we test her? We'll send her on a little mission to someone who will size her up. Nothing dangerous."

Agatha grinned, a slightly terrifying sight. "Just send her to Ingrid."

"I said nothing dangerous," Marjie interjected.

"If anyone's a Crone of Myrtlewood, it's Ingrid," Agatha said flatly.

Marjie hummed in agreement. "You're right. But how do we convince the poor woman to go into that blasted forest?"

"It's simple," said Agatha. "Just give Delia instructions. She's your friend."

Marjie let out a chuckle, shaking her head slightly. "I'm afraid not. I'd rather put my foot in it. I asked her if she's been setting things on fire lately."

Agatha squinted at her. "What makes you so sure she's fire and not earth?"

"My teapot burst into flames the very day she arrived in town."

"Surely she knows what she is?" said Agatha. "What did she do when you asked her?"

"She just ran away."

"Maybe she is fire, then," said Agatha. "Earth would hold her ground. Though I'd expect fire to fight back..."

Marjie shrugged. "It's not like I attacked her. Maybe she's scared of her power. Or maybe she just thinks I'm a kooky old bat."

Agatha smirked, her blue eyes sparkling with mirth. "Well, you are that," she responded, a teasing lilt to her voice. Despite the jab, there was a warmth to her words.

Marjie smiled. "I'd return the compliment, but I don't want to be so rude."

They grinned at each other for a moment.

"Alright then," said Marjie. "Let's do it."

# 19
## DELIA

As Delia approached the table, she had the distinct impression that Marjie and Agatha were embroiled in some sort of secret discussion. She thought about backing away quietly, however, catching wind of her name, curiosity got the best of her.

Embarrassment for how she'd behaved the night before, running off to her room – which was certainly worthy of gossip – made her want to run and hide again, but she was made of stronger stuff than that. Instead, she took another step closer. She couldn't leave things hanging with Marjie, who'd shown her so much generosity, and besides, Delia was starting to admit to herself that very strange things were happening all around her that her rational brain could not explain away. Either she was mad or the world was, and perhaps Marjie could help her figure out which.

"Excuse me," Delia said, causing Marjie to jump in her seat.

Agatha, on the other hand, merely raised her head slowly and smiled a lizard-like grin. "Hello, Delia," she said. "Take a seat."

"I don't want to disturb you," Delia said. "I just...wanted to apologise for last night."

"Oh, no need to apologise, love," Marjie responded. "Myrtlewood is a strange place. I'm sorry if I upset you. I was simply wondering—"

"Sit, sit," Agatha insisted, pointing to the seat across from her.

Delia sighed, pulled out the chair, and sat down. "I don't like being told what to do."

"Good," Agatha replied. "That's an important quality to have."

Delia nodded. "Alright, then. What is it you wanted to tell me?" She turned back to Marjie.

"I...err...the fire thing was a metaphor," Marjie spluttered.

"Really?" Delia raised an eyebrow. "It just so happens there have been a handful of fires popping up around me. Mostly small ones. Are you some sort of psychic, is that it?"

"Not exactly," said Marjie. "Although, I do have a strong sense of intuition."

Agatha coughed profusely on her sherry.

"I've had a very strange time," Delia admitted. "And I want to know why."

"Well, it just so happens that we know somebody who might be able to help you," said Agatha, leaning over the table and peering over her small round spectacles.

"Oh yes?" Delia asked. "Tell me more." She reclined casually in her chair, refusing to be staunched out by the slightly barmy older woman.

"Well, there's a woman who lives in the woods who's very wise," Marjie chimed in. "You might want to pay her a visit."

"In the woods?" Delia asked. "How mythic."

"Indeed," said Agatha sternly.

"We can provide directions," Marjie added. "They won't be particularly precise, but I have utmost confidence that you will find her."

"You might," said Agatha.

"Okay, then," Delia replied, too curious to pass up a mystery such as this.

Marjie scribbled some notes on a napkin and handed them over to Delia. There was a small, not particularly precise-looking map.

"Do you think this will be enough?" Delia asked.

"I'm sure you'll find her, dear," Marjie assured her, and perhaps she would have patted Delia on the shoulder or given Delia another nurturing hug, but thought better of it.

"Alright, then," said Delia, getting up from the table and pushing the chair back in.

"Oh, and Delia," said Agatha.

"What?" Delia asked, looking back towards Agatha's stern gaze.

"I like your hair."

"Thank you," said Delia, running her hand through her mane, which had mostly dislodged from its clip, likely due to the sea breeze. The red strands tumbled out. "I can't remember how this happened," she muttered. "I think it was my friend Kitty's doing when we were drunk."

Marjie and Agatha both gave her a knowing look and a nod. She backed away cautiously and then made her way briskly upstairs, sure that there was a bigger mystery at play that she was somehow missing.

# 20

## THE CLERIC

In the recesses of the dim, damp sanctum of the Order, several monks sat, their quills scratching against parchment as they copied out sacred scrolls that could never see the light of day. The Cleric frowned at them. If it wasn't for that library refurbishment he could get some peace.

He glanced again at his own table, cluttered with research documents, scrolls, and old books that might prove useful to the Order's most sacrosanct quest.

These young scribes were only performing a rote task, whereas the Cleric had much more important work to attend to. He scowled before remembering his humility.

It was always a challenge for those committed to the most important of tasks to ensure they did not become too self-important. The Mission was the priority, and besides, he did not want to turn out as arrogant as Father Benedict, who looked upon his brethren with such disdain, as though they were impure lambs, not even worthy of slaughter.

The scribes were so entranced in their work that the Cleric was the first to near the hushed echo of familiar footsteps. The footfall carried a certain heaviness, a tangible authority that everyone in the vicinity could feel.

It announced the approach of none other than the man that the Cleric wished he could avoid, Father Benedict, now also known as the Crimson Shepherd: a man whose presence was much like a winter frost in the midst of summer, though, as it was already winter, his entry only chilled the room further.

The Cleric, having learned the fine art of footstep identification during his years in the Order, braced himself for the inevitable. The heavy wooden doors groaned in reluctant surrender as Father Benedict entered.

"Cleric," came the Shepherd's voice, a razor wrapped in velvet. It never ceased to astound the Cleric how a single word could carry such chilling formality.

"Father Benedict," the Cleric replied, managing a bow of his head, a gesture meant to convey both respect and a healthy dose of fear, though, in truth, it was only fear he felt. Respect has to be earned and the Shepherd had done nothing but disapprove of how things were being run around here since his return.

While the silence danced and twisted between them, an unsettling growl issued from behind the reinforced doors.

The beast was awake again.

Could it be that he responded to Father Benedict as his master? The Cleric's pallor might have given away his terror at the thought if he hadn't had so many years of practice hiding it. Father Benedict, on the other hand, remained unfazed, his gaze locked onto the plethora of scrolls and maps covering the stone table.

"Updates on the fire witch?" he inquired, cutting through the dread-filled silence like a hot knife through rancid butter.

"The tracker has reported that she remains in Myrtlewood, Father."

Father Benedict contemplated the news. His gaze softened, but only for the briefest of moments.

"How did she respond to the message we sent?"

The Cleric lowered his gaze. "I don't believe it reached her."

Father Benedict scowled.

"We knew the town had certain protections," the Cleric reminded him. "Frank came back rather flustered. Thinks he was attacked by a wolf man. He won't leave his chambers."

Father Benedict chuckled. The Cleric's neck prickled at the rare sound, waiting for danger, for the Shepherd to lash out, or at least say something scathing.

His eyes merely carried over the scribes, busily scrawling and pretending not to listen.

Father Benedict nodded in approval of their efforts, not that they saw the rare gesture which amounted to lavish praise.

The Cleric felt a stab of jealousy, his mind racing to think of something that would win him some form of compliment, but before he could think of anything the Shepherd spoke again.

"What other developments?"

"Err, there have been no further fires," the Cleric responded, the words tumbling out in relief. "It seems she's laying low."

"Interesting," said the Shepherd, his eyes gleaming in the dim light. "Time for Operation Delta, then."

The Cleric's heart dropped like a stone in a well.

*The ominous Operation Delta.*

Nobody but the Shepherd knew exactly what it entailed, except that several dozen of the order's finest had been assembled for training and stern talkings-to. The Shepherd had hand-picked them, not even bothering to ask the Cleric's opinion or filling him in on the tactics.

The Cleric had found himself spinning into vengeful thoughts several times over his exclusion, seeking penance in extra prayers for his desires to sabotage his superior. But it was clear as day that whatever it was, it would be set in motion. The wheels were turning, and there was no stopping it now.

"Very good, Father," said the Cleric, bowing his head to stop the rage in his eyes from betraying him.

"As you were." With that, the Shepherd strode out, leaving the Cleric alone with his growing dread.

"All in a day's work, then," the Cleric muttered to himself, his voice ricocheting off the walls of the cavernous sanctum.

The scribes turned to him, curious expressions on their faces, but he dismissed them with a wave of his hand. The less they knew, the better. Apparently that was true for everyone around here.

The Cleric stared at the spot where Father Benedict had stood, and wondered, not for the first time, what cosmic dice had been rolled for him to end up here, in this mysterious world of witches, trackers, and stupidly named initiatives like Operation Delta.

# 21

## DELIA

It wasn't much of a map. Delia studied the squiggly lines that Marjie had drawn on the napkin, now even more creased from having been crumpled in a pocket.

She'd made her way to the correct street as best she could decipher and parked her car near the forest, but it had taken longer than expected to find the path that Marjie had indicated.

In fact, Delia would have been surprised if there was a path at all through these woods. It struck her that while all the trees around town had lost their leaves for the winter, this forest was still rather green. She was no expert on vegetation, but she was sure some of these trees weren't evergreens. She squinted into the shadows, trying to find a way in.

Dense clusters of trees with brambles down below made it difficult terrain to navigate.

She was about to turn around and head back when movement across the road caught her eye. It was him: the cowboy! The man from the beach who she was sure was also at the café in London, with his ridiculous cowboy hat and his striking scarred face, and now he was walking in her direction.

It wasn't clear if he had spotted her yet.

Hastily, Delia lunged behind the nearest tree, waiting for him to pass by. He walked on without looking in her direction and Delia breathed a sigh of relief.

She glanced around and found to her surprise that a path had appeared behind her into the forest. She was sure that hadn't been there a moment ago.

"What's with this town and optical illusions?" she muttered to herself. "Maybe I need to get my eyes checked."

She removed her sunglasses, which were getting in the way in the dim light of the forest. She pocketed them remembering how Gilly always said they made her look like a celebrity, or a hipster – it didn't bother Delia either way.

She peered around, surveying the forest and the path. Thankfully, there was no sign of the cowboy, as she decided to label him in her mind.

She wondered if he was following her.

Was this another one of Jerry's tricks? Did he know where she was? Was he sending more ambiguous characters after her, just to spook her or push her towards early dementia?

"I'm not having any of that," Delia said sternly as she started picking her way down the path. She could have sworn she heard a quiet voice ask, "Any of what?" but brushed it off, attributing it to her overactive imagination. The alternative didn't bear thinking about.

The forest track was initially fairly flat, but as it continued, it wound up and around, becoming narrower and steeper with gnarled tree roots and jagged rocks in the way.

She briefly considered turning back and retreating to her car, but then thought better of it. What if the cowboy was there, waiting for her?

The thought that he might have followed her into the woods was even more alarming. If he was indeed there, turning back towards him would do her no good.

Despite her husband's dalliances, or perhaps because of them, Delia had long ago vowed to stay away from emotionally unavailable men of dubious moral character, regardless of their popularity in certain romance novels. One look at the cowboy was enough for her to see he was as morally grey and aloof as they come. Men like that were dangerous and bad for the complexion.

She continued on through the forest, her thoughts spinning with all sorts of frightening possibilities.

Wild animals could be lurking in the woods or she could get lost and no one would be able to find her in here.

Was this all part of some cult's initiation? Was it some kind of hazing that Marjie and Agatha had sent her on? Did she need to spend a night on a spirit quest in the woods? Was she going to be attacked by a rabid animal?

Briefly, she reassured herself that at least all the bears and wolves had been driven out of England. As tragic as that was, it was currently a consoling thought.

*Sure, there could be rabid squirrels,* she mused with a laugh, but the thought grew increasingly terrifying as Delia continued on. *Or perhaps even rabid weasels, or giant deer with massive antlers that could ram me at any moment...*

"If I were in a play right now," Delia mused aloud, "I'd either be about to encounter a gingerbread house, a masked attacker, or confront the emptiness of my own soul."

None of those options were particularly appealing.

"Ahh!" she cried out as she tripped on a tree root, flailing towards the ground, her thigh colliding with a jagged rock. She cried out expletives, though there was no one to hear her, or at least, that was what she fervently hoped.

Brushing herself off, she found no serious damage done. She rubbed her swelling thigh, feeling the bruise blooming tenderly. She didn't bother to inspect it further.

Delia looked around and sighed. "Where on earth is this cottage?"

"I think you'll find it's up ahead, about a mile to the north," stated a small drawling voice. Delia nearly jumped out of her skin. She looked around but saw no one in sight.

"Am I really going mad?" she murmured.

There was a slight shuffling sound and two black paws appeared over the boulder Delia had fallen against, followed by a furry black head with pointy ears. The kitten stared at her as if making an assessment.

"Cute," said Delia. "What are you doing out here in the forest all alone? Are you lost like me?"

"Take that back," said the cat, glaring.

Delia squealed and gasped, bringing her hand to her mouth.

"And as for whether you're mad, I'd say not quite yet. But you're not far off."

In panic, Delia screamed.

Pushing herself up, she began to run as fast as her slightly injured body could take her, deeper into the woods, off the path. It occurred to her in the utter franticness of her flight that she couldn't run from her own mind.

"Just think, think," she told herself. "Think clearly. No rabid weasels, no talking cats. No spontaneous fires. Just pure, clear reality. Normal brain, *normal*." She scolded her mind as she hid behind a tree, keeping an eye out for signs of more bizarre occurrences.

"I don't see how that's going to help you," the drawling voice said as the cat leapt after her.

"You're not *real*," Delia said as the feline positioned itself on a rock and began to lick its paw.

"That's a tad insulting," it replied. "How would you like to be told that you're not real?"

"No! Go away!" Delia shrieked, scampering further into the forest.

Deeper and deeper she scrambled, brushing past brambles and stumbling over tree roots. The sky above darkened, and she kept going, not knowing where her feet were leading her.

It felt as though she might have lost all sense. "Maybe I have to lose it all to get it all back," she reasoned, somewhat unreasonably, but not knowing what else to do, she carried on, ambling through the forest until, exhausted, she sought refuge in the hollow at the base of a huge, ancient tree.

Its presence was somehow reassuring, all the more so for it not speaking to her.

She reached out for nearby fern fronds, pulling them over herself in hopes of hiding.

"I just need to rest," she muttered to herself. "Just for a moment. Maybe for a year. My brain is tired from everything that's happened. It's too much change. And perhaps, no, probably...definitely, I must have inhaled some spores from a psychedelic mushroom."

She hoped that said spores were not fatally poisonous because, if so, hiding camouflaged in the forest was certainly not the best course of action.

She didn't feel physically ill, just extremely anxious and drained.

She sat there, curled up at the base of the tree, panting frantically, muttering to herself, vaguely aware that this wasn't what a totally sane person would do.

Darkness fell both too quickly and agonisingly slowly.

Delia found herself shivering despite the warmth of her merino wool cape. "Great," she mumbled, "add hypothermia to the list of risky predicaments my brain is cooking up."

She heard a rustling noise as she contemplated the impossibility of her situation. She'd been going around in circles in her mind on whether or not it was better to get up and try to fight her way through the forest now or wait until dawn

The great rustling noise drew closer and Delia hoped it wasn't a dangerous beast.

A light appeared, floating through the forest.

As Delia's eyes adjusted to it, she recognised it as an old-fashioned lantern. Before she could add floating lanterns to her list of hallucinations, she noticed it was attached to a stick, carried by a figure who was hobbling towards her: a cloak and a broad-brimmed hat were just visible, making the figure look unmistakably like a fairy-tale witch.

"What do we have here then?" said the figure in a stern, icy voice.

"Thank God," said Delia.

"God?" said the woman, who was unmistakably some sort of forest witch and possibly an apparition created by Delia's befuddled, psychedelically influenced mind. "Which god are you talking about?"

She peered at Delia through a monocle that gleamed in the lantern light. Her gaze travelled down her narrow nose, crooked in several parts as if it had been broken multiple times. She sized Delia up. "What on earth are you doing here?"

"And you're quite real then?" Delia asked, peering through the fern fronds.

The woman threw back her head and laughed, which came out as a dry and hoarse cackle. "What's that got to do with anything?" she asked. "Come on. I can't leave you out here. That would be bad hospitality."

Bewildered, Delia took the surprisingly strong hand the woman offered her. She pushed back the fern fronds and stood up.

"The name's Ingrid," said the woman, "and don't forget it because I don't particularly like repeating myself."

Delia nodded, relief flooding her. Ingrid was the name Marjie and Agatha had said. Or was it Ethel?

"Now come this way," said Ingrid, gesturing for Delia to follow her. And so she did, because whether or not this woman was a figment of her imagination, Delia felt her options were sorely limited.

It seemed like an age passed as they made their way slowly through the forest. The older woman walked with a cane, which Delia noticed was attached to the lantern by a small, twirly piece of wrought iron.

It would have made a great theatre prop, but Delia had more pressing things to worry about. Such as being in the middle of the forest with an old witch who might be a hallucination, alongside talking cats, rabid squirrels, and spontaneous combustion – all things that her childhood self would have considered likely threats or perhaps even exciting things to encounter in the world, but had not come to pass in Delia's adulthood.

"There's no quicksand around here, is there?" she muttered.

The woman raised an eyebrow, turning toward her. "None that I know of. Why do you ask?"

Delia shrugged. "I always thought quicksand would be more of a threat when I was a child, and if my imagination is making all of this up, I don't see why it should stop at witches and talking cats."

The woman gave her a sober look. "Are you quite finished?" she asked.

Delia shrugged again. "Sure."

"Good," the woman said, "because we've arrived."

"Arrived?" Delia looked around, quite sure that the only thing in sight was more of the forest. But as she continued to follow Ingrid, she noticed the forest path gave way to some stony old steps which led towards a structure with a small flicker of light shining through the windows.

# 22

## MARJIE

M arjie sighed. With a warm sun streaming through the front window of the teashop, the morning was in full swing. The comforting smell of brewing tea mingled with the sweet scent of freshly baked scones. Yet, despite the bustle, Marjie couldn't shake her sense of unease. It hummed under her skin like a discordant note in a symphony.

Despite this, she was confident her jarred nerves didn't show as she smiled at customers, bustling around her shop with practised ease, pouring cups of tea and serving slices of cake.

Lately, her mind couldn't help churning with thoughts of Rosemary and Athena, who were getting themselves into trouble again – deliberately this time – and with their sights set on the Underworld of all places!

"Phew! Busy one today, eh, Marjie?" Papa Jack's booming voice echoed above the clatter of teacups and the excited chatter of Marjie's morning customers. His broad, weathered hands rested comfortably on the counter, and his twinkling eyes sparkled with the same comforting warmth as his usual cup of chamomile.

Marjie smiled at him as she raised a tray laden with cream and jam scones. "I'll be right with you."

Her thoughts returned to her worries as she carried the tray to eagerly waiting customers. Things had really been rather overwhelming, recently. And then there was the whole situation with Herb, his memory a ghost haunting the edges of her mind. Grief, she found, was a strange beast. It would pounce when least expected, leaving her with an aching emptiness or burning rage that echoed through the moments of her life.

On top of all this, Marjie's own powers weren't behaving themselves and she now had the unpredictable Delia to deal with. The poor bewildered woman had only just arrived in town and Marjie – in the heat of argument with that crotchety old bat, Agatha – had agreed to send her off into the forest alone, a decision which now racked her with guilt.

But who was there to comfort the person who usually did all the comforting?

"Marjie, you're daydreaming again," Papa Jack's voice rumbled, pulling her back to reality. He stood at the counter, his eyes twinkling in a broad grin.

"Mmm," Marjie hummed in response, an absent-minded response as she filled the teapot. The blend was perfect, as usual, but her mind was somewhere else entirely.

"Oh, I can see it now." Papa Jack chuckled, pulling a stool up to the counter. "You're miles away. Or at least, as far away as you can be in a shop this size. What's going on, Marjie?"

Marjie gave him a wan smile, pouring him a cup of chamomile tea. "I can't seem to help it, lately. Things have been...different."

Papa Jack nodded, understanding flashing in his eyes. "Change can be like a wild storm, can't it? But remember, even in the midst of the worst gales, we can find shelter."

"I feel terribly guilty," Marjie confessed. "A new witch arrived in town and Agatha and I sent her off into the forest."

"The new woman everyone is talking about? Delia?" said Papa Jack. "From what people are saying, she seems a bit...well, fiery," he said with a chuckle. He blew at the steam rising from the cup. "A little too much paprika in her pasty, if you know what I mean. I'm sure she'll be fine. Why the forest, anyway?"

"I sent her off to find Ingrid." Marjie took a deep breath, the weight of her guilt sitting heavy in her chest. "Alone."

Papa Jack choked on his tea. "Ingrid – the forest witch – the one you're scared of? You said even the woods where she lives are full of hidden dangers."

Marjie frowned. "Well, it was Agatha's idea!"

"And that makes it a good one, does it?" He shook his head, still coughing. "I swear, you and Agatha together is more trouble than a hog in a larder."

Marjie nodded. "Agatha had a point, I'm afraid. Ingrid might be the only one with answers for Delia...but I could have gone with her."

Papa Jack shook his head. "Sometimes people need to go it alone. That forest can be a dangerous place. But I'm sure it's also full of wonders. I trust you made the right choice."

Marjie looked at him, feeling a knot in her chest uncoil slightly. But then the knot tightened again as her thoughts turned inward.

She couldn't risk telling Papa Jack about the ancient magic stirring, or even that her powers were behaving strangely. She was sure she hadn't been the one to set that teapot on fire, and even if she had, it must have been some kind of resonance, an empathic response to Delia's own magic awakening. Agatha hadn't told her much, but she knew that the Crone magic was steeped in secrecy. To speak of it, even to a trusted friend, risked diluting the power before it even had time to form.

"Marjie, my dear." Papa Jack's eyes softened, filled with a compassionate wisdom. "We can't always guarantee things will work out. But what I know is this – you have always done what is needed. You're strong, stronger than you give yourself credit for."

Marjie's lips quirked up into a small, appreciative smile, thankful for his comforting presence, for the shared silence that fell over them as the bustle of the tea shop hummed in the background. His reassurances were like a soothing balm, and for a brief moment, she allowed herself to believe that all would be well.

Delia would be fine.

Perhaps the forest was exactly where she needed to be. Maybe the path they were on, as twisted and dangerous as it seemed, was the right one.

Still, a whisper in her mind echoed with an undeniable truth: Change was brewing, like the strongest of her teas, an understanding which was bitter-sweet.

"I'll give it a few hours," said Marjie. "And if she's not back by then, I'll go after her."

Papa Jack nodded his approval. "I'll even come with you if you like, so long as it's after I finish my shift at the shop. But I'm sure she'll be back well before then."

"Thank you," said Marjie. "That forest is dangerous – and so is Ingrid!"

# 23

## THE SHEPHERD

Father Benedict, the Crimson Shepherd, climbed the many flights of the stone staircase, each step echoing in the hollow tower. He had been summoned to the topmost spire by the Elders, the heavy weight of expectation turning his gut.

At the summit, he entered the square room, because even the towers of The Order of Crimson needed hard angles to keep things in line.

He was met with the austere gazes of the four top-ranking Elders. Their eyes, surrounded by the hollow shadows of the room, were all trained on him as they sat around their stone table.

Elders Mordant, Firth, Quill, and Burrow held titles as archaic as the Order itself, carrying history and wisdom.

"Shepherd," Elder Mordant began, a gaunt figure draped in grey whose eyes were sharp as flint, his voice layered with anticipation and a sprinkle of dread.

"Elders," he returned, bowing his head low, stony-faced but respectful.

"We summoned you here to update us on The Mission," said Elder

Firth, his eyes glinting in his round face like twin flames behind his spectacles. He held his hands clasped in front of him, like a faithful monk in prayer. "We see that you initiated Operation Delta. What news do you have to report?"

Father Benedict let out a measured breath, weighing the right words in silence. He could not keep information from the Elders. To do so would be far too dangerous. He began by detailing the previous occurrences and his rationale for calling his own plan, Operation Delta, into action.

"And since then?" Burrow, the eldest among them, responded. His voice, though frail with age, carried an undeniable authority.

Father Benedict bowed his head again. There was a risk that they already knew, but either way he could incur their wrath. They'd find out soon enough. "The fire witch has disappeared."

His words hung in the air like a leaden weight.

A gasp echoed through the room, the Elders exchanging uneasy glances. Their usual composed demeanour gave way to waves of disbelief and concern.

"Disappeared?!" Elder Quill parroted in outrage, contorting his wiry frame.

"Temporarily, of course," Father Benedict assured them. "The tracker is the best in the country – as I told you. He shadowed her to Myrtlewood and reported on her activities, but then....she vanished into a forest."

"But...our tracing magic?" Elder Mordant asked, his deep voice outraged.

"It has failed us," Father Benedict admitted, feeling the bitterness of defeat tinge his words.

"Unprecedented," Elder Firth murmured, his expression troubled. "We must report this to the higher authority at once."

Father Benedict trembled as he raised his palms. "I have no doubt that—"

"Then she poses a larger threat than you assumed," said Elder Quill, his tone brimming with accusation.

"I think not," Father Benedict responded sharply, his gaze as icy as a midwinter frost. He had dedicated decades of his life to The Mission and he knew every detail intimately. The Elders may have been his superiors in status and title, but given that they could barely keep their own compound in shape, it was hard not to resent them. They lorded it over everyone in their towers with their embroidered robes, while he saw to it that all the work was carried out. He could not merely stand by and let his toiling and strategic efforts be ridiculed or belittled, but to openly speak his mind would be deadly. Instead he opted for tact, his speciality. "Our calculations were accurate. Our plans were meticulous. It's reality that's proven more elusive, as if often does."

Elder Burrow shifted in his chair, the old oak creaking in protest. "This...this could jeopardise the entire mission – disrupt the very Order itself!"

"Life has a way of throwing spanners in the works of even the best laid plans," Father Benedict replied, his voice steady as bedrock.

Elder Mordant shook his head, his disapproval as tangible as the cool stone walls. "This isn't a mere turn, Shepherd. This speaks of our underestimation of her. Perhaps our approach to The Mission needs reassessment."

Father Benedict braced himself as the words stung, an insult to his leadership. Yet, he stood his ground. "I take full responsibility," he said, for with responsibility also came a greater degree of control. "I was born for this Mission, Elders. I know every crevice, every pitfall it holds." His words echoed off the tower's walls. "Rest assured, we will find the fire witch. Operation Delta will resume as efficiently as possible. This isn't the time for fear, but for resolve."

There was a palpable silence before Elder Firth spoke. "Very well, Shepherd. We have no choice but to have faith in the will of the Almighty. Proceed."

Father Benedict took his leave, his heart heavy yet resolute.

The Elders could question his strategies, doubt his decisions, but he knew his course.

They may command respect, but they were not the ones in the thick of the battle, wading through the muck of reality and evil towards the light of purity. His life was but a testament to his work, and he would see it through to its end.

# 24
## DELIA

"Is this where you live? All the way out here?" Delia asked, biting her tongue to stop herself from adding: *And is it made of gingerbread?*

She was momentarily grateful that she wasn't a child to be fattened up. She was sure the sinewy old meat on her bones wasn't worth more than a few pots of stew. Besides, Ingrid, as stern and witchy as she was, didn't seem overly evil.

So, with only a little trepidation and a brief moment of hesitation, Delia followed the mysterious old woman up the remaining steps towards the cottage.

The door sprang open as they approached, though no one stood behind.

Ingrid tromped inside, placing her cane on a stand by the door and blowing out the lantern.

"Make yourself comfortable, I suppose," she said, gesturing towards the armchairs by the fire.

Delia was grateful for the waves of warmth from the fire burning in the hearth. She allowed herself to crumple into one of the seats.

"Not that one," Ingrid said. "That's mine."

Delia shrugged and took the other very similar chair. She let out a long sigh as she warmed her frozen knuckles by the fire. "It's been a long and very strange day," she muttered.

Ingrid didn't respond; she just set about clinking things together in the kitchen. A few moments passed before she approached the hearth.

Using a blackened hook, she extracted a metal kettle that had been hanging just over the fireplace. She carefully poured water into a teapot, which she then set on a small wooden table and produced two earthenware mugs.

"Let it brew for a few minutes," she muttered.

Delia inhaled the herbaceous scent drifting over from the pot. "What is it?"

"My special recipe," replied Ingrid, returning to the kitchen.

She reappeared a moment later with two chipped clay bowls and a ladle. That was when Delia noticed the other scent – savoury and delicious – wafting from a pot hanging above the fire which looked suspiciously like a cauldron.

Before long, Ingrid had ladled generous servings into the bowls and handed one to Delia with a small wooden spoon. "Eat up, you're going to need your strength," she said.

Delia briefly wondered whether it could be poisoned, but decided it wasn't worth asking – if she was in the house of someone evil enough to poison her, the chances of them admitting to it seemed slim.

"It's good and hot," Ingrid said. "Better drink your tea first."

Delia put the bowl down and took a sip of the beverage that Ingrid had poured for her. She thought she could detect traces of peppermint, maybe even chamomile. "What is this?" she asked again.

"Mugwort," said Ingrid. "Among other things. It should give you some strength and clarity."

"That's just what I need," Delia replied.

"Oh, and it aids dreams," Ingrid added, giving her a meaningful look.

"That's not exactly what I'm after. My dreams are already vivid enough," said Delia, but she drank the beverage anyway, grateful for its warmth.

Turning back to the bowl of some kind of stew or soup, she took a spoonful.

It tasted deep and earthy, savoury and salty, even a little bitter. It felt like some kind of medicine that her body immediately recognised as good and healing – fortifying. The brothy soup contained small pieces of vegetables and rather a lot of herbs, even some beans, though Delia wasn't entirely sure, considering the vague textures of food cooked over a long time, but everything seemed to blend into each other in a rather satisfying way.

She consumed the whole meal and then sat back, relaxing into the chair.

"Thank you," she said, turning to Ingrid. "For the food and everything else. I don't know what I would have done if you hadn't come to find me."

"And do you know why you were in the forest in the first place?" Ingrid asked coldly.

"I think I was looking for you, actually," Delia admitted. She rifled through her pocket to find the napkin and handed it over.

"Marjoram Reeves," Ingrid muttered.

"How can you tell?" Delia asked. "Is it her handwriting?"

Ingrid stared down her nose at Delia as if making a formal assessment. "You don't look like much."

Delia puffed herself up. "Excuse me," she said. "I didn't come here to be insulted."

"And do you even know why you did come here?" Ingrid asked.

Delia looked down at her hands. "I've been setting things on fire...or at least, things happen to have been set on fire in the vicinity of where I was, when I happened to be angry. It sounds ridiculous, I know. I tried to rationalise it at first..."

Ingrid chortled. "You don't know the magical world, do you?"

Delia shook her head, not sure of what Ingrid was referring to. "I'm afraid I don't know much of anything at the moment."

Ingrid shook her head. "Well, fires or not, I doubt you're the one we're looking for."

Delia slumped in her chair, feeling rather deflated. She wasn't sure why, but it felt like some kind of cosmic rejection after everything she'd been through to find this woman – risking life and limb and sanity in the dangerous woods – only to be told she wasn't good enough, though for what, she was still unsure.

The anger bubbled up inside her, and the napkin map, still in Ingrid's hands, began to smoke and then burst into flame.

Ingrid cried out, dropping the flaming item and stamping on it on the floor. "Why did you have to go and do that?"

"It wasn't on purpose," Delia spat out. "Now, if you'd kindly tell me how to get out of here, I won't cause you any more trouble."

Ingrid chuckled. "I don't suppose going back out there until daylight would serve you very well. It's a strange forest to navigate at the best of times."

Delia sighed. "Look, I've had the most ridiculous day, and if I have to go out there and face talking cats and rabid weasels, then so be it."

Ingrid stopped laughing and gave her a deadly stare. "What did you say?"

"Rabid weasels...or they might have been squirrels," Delia confessed. "It was what I was afraid of in the woods, though I didn't see them. See, I am nuts. I'm going completely batty."

"What was the other thing you said?"

"Talking cats," Delia said with a dismissive wave. "Now that I was sure I did see at least one of...Though I don't see why that matters in particular. You're hardly impressed that I can set things on fire with my mind."

The cauldron of soup began to smoke, and flames erupted from the top.

Ingrid waved a hand and the flames disappeared; she pierced Delia with a glare. "Settle down, child."

It had been a long time since anyone had called Delia a child. She folded her arms and maybe pouted, just slightly.

Ingrid continued to glare. "Talking cats, you say? Tell me more."

"Are you serious?" Delia asked.

Ingrid gave a firm nod.

"Right then." Delia recounted her strange encounter in the forest.

"Well, I never..." said Ingrid, folding her arms to mirror Delia's and giving her an impressed look.

Delia put one hand on her hip. It was her turn to size Ingrid up. The small woman had an imposing power about her, a sternness perhaps born of living all these years in the wilderness.

"Marjie and that rude old Agatha thought you'd be able to tell me something useful," Delia said sternly. "Would you kindly explain to me why, of all the bizarre things I've said, the talking cat is the one that impresses you? I didn't make that happen..."

"No," admitted Ingrid, "but you understood."

Delia shrugged. "So?"

"So, Delia," said Ingrid with an intensity that brought a chill to the warm room. "Tell me something, what connection does your family have to Myrtlewood?"

Delia shrugged. "I wish I knew. My grandmother, Etty, used to come here. She brought me here as a child."

A knowing look crossed Ingrid's face.

"What?" Delia demanded.

Ingrid merely shook her head. "I'm afraid that Marjoram Reeves was right."

Delia frowned, still feeling rather grumpy. "And what was she right about, exactly?"

Ingrid's glare only intensified. "You are the one we've been looking for."

# 25
## INGRID

Ingrid looked at Delia, now deep in thought, her earlier anger having simmered down to a quiet resentment. Ingrid, despite her outward coldness, felt an odd sense of kinship towards Delia. They were both thrown into the whirlwind of the unknown.

Ingrid drew a deep breath. "It's been a long day, and despite the season, I fear they're only going to get longer from here on in," she said, the stern tone returning to her voice. "But before sleep, there's something I want you to see."

Delia looked at her, brows furrowing. "What is it?" she asked, her voice wary. She had been shown a world she didn't know existed in the span of a day. Her scepticism was understandable.

Ingrid merely gestured for Delia to follow. They made their way to the back of the cottage, where the shadows of the forest loomed large, creating an eerie tapestry of darkness and mystery. Ingrid paused before an ancient-looking tree, its twisted branches reaching out towards the moonlit sky.

"This," Ingrid began, placing her wrinkled hand against the gnarled bark of the tree, "is an Elder tree. It's been here longer than anyone could tell you. It's seen the birth and death of countless generations. Seen the world change, seen the balance of magic shift."

Delia looked at the tree, a flicker of interest in her eyes. "Why are you showing me this?" she asked, her voice softer than before.

"Because"—Ingrid turned towards Delia, her eyes reflecting the soft glow of the moon—"it's important for you to understand that greater forces exist in the world."

Delia shook her head wearily. Great forces like an old tree?

Ingrid simply nodded curtly.

Delia stared at Ingrid, then back at the tree. She reached out, her hand trembling slightly, and touched the bark. The wind seemed to whisper through the leaves as Delia stood there, her hand against the tree.

Delia nodded, not speaking a word. She looked different, Ingrid noted, less defiant, more open.

Ingrid couldn't predict what the morrow would bring, but she felt the stirrings of hope. Trouble had been brewing, that was clear, and it was just possible that some ancient rumours held the key to stopping it.

"Come on now," Ingrid said as Delia shivered against the cold night. "You can kip here for the night. It's not wise to go wandering in the forest at night." She narrowed her eyes.

"Hey, it wasn't night when I started out," Delia protested as Ingrid led her back into the hut.

"No, but it is winter time," said Ingrid. "I'm sure you've learnt your lesson though." She chuckled as she gathered blankets. "Rabid squirrels indeed!"

Ingrid watched Delia settle on the window seat, half-hidden beneath blankets that had seen better decades. For all her initial bluster and fire, the poor woman seemed utterly bewildered.

Ingrid knew she could be intimidating, with her stern demeanour. It was something she'd cultivated like the thyme in her garden. It helped with keeping away bothersome guests. She never suffered fools, and her patience was threadbare. Delia had been a particularly trying fool, and yet, she'd been so wretched, lost and raving and hiding in an old oak hollow, that Ingrid couldn't help but care for her like a bird with a broken wing.

Turning towards her bedroom, Ingrid mumbled a vague sort of goodnight, adding, "Bucket's by the back door, should nature call. But beware the squirrels; they've got a taste for shoelaces."

With that pearl of wisdom delivered, Ingrid hauled her weary bones to her bedroom. The boards creaked under her feet, whispering tales of years gone by.

Her own quarters were an organised chaos of sorts. A counter-clockwise clock – because time was a matter of perspective – hung above a canopy bed of woven reeds. Nearby sat an absurd number of hats perched on a rack, each for an implausible weather condition. Shelves lined one wall, filled with scrolls and books that vibrated with their own brand of magic.

She sniffed the air. It hung heavy, as usual, with the scent of herbs and musky old wood, a testament to years of potions and spells brewed within these walls, but there was something different. The winds had turned course.

"Change is in the air," she muttered to herself. "Oh bother."

Pausing at the window, she took in the view of the forest, illuminated by the waxing gibbous moon. Silver shadows weaved a bewitching tapestry as the night wind played amongst the trees. Somewhere an owl hooted a lonely plea to the night.

Ingrid allowed herself a sigh, a rare expression of fatigue. Things were never as straightforward as they ought to be when it came to Crones. Just when she thought she'd seen all the world had to throw at her, life proved her wrong.

Stripping down to her underclothes, she made herself comfortable in the woven reed bed, its familiar contours moulding around her weather-beaten body. The soft hum of magic from her books was a lullaby she'd grown accustomed to over the years.

As she stared at the cracked ceiling, her thoughts strayed back to

Delia. That girl had more fire in her than she realised. And if Ingrid knew one thing, it was that fire, if not properly managed, could leave nothing but ashes in its wake.

"Best brace myself for a long day come morn," she muttered to herself, before surrendering to the call of sleep.

# 26
## DELIA

Delia pulled the scratchy woollen blanket snugly against her shoulders as she snuggled into the small window seat bed that Ingrid had allowed her to take for the night.

She'd asked so many questions, but Ingrid remained tight-lipped. Nothing was making sense. Yet, as she peered out at the forest, the egg-shaped moon rising on the horizon through the clouds, Delia felt a profound sense of peacefulness such as she'd never really known before.

Perhaps the closest she'd come to this feeling was after a successful theatre premiere, when, clutching a bouquet of roses, she'd allowed herself a few moments of relaxed glory to bask in her triumph. Or maybe it was when she'd first held Gilly, after years of struggling to conceive. Finally she'd achieved motherhood and could tick that off her list. Looking at the peaceful, sleeping face of her new born had given her a sense of satisfaction, but that could have just been the oxytocin.

The tranquillity she felt now, that only deepened as she listened to the hoots of an owl in the forest, wasn't from any particular triumph. She hadn't reached any notable goals, apart from finding a curmudgeonly old woman in a forest, which was hardly a great accomplishment. Yet, something about the forest itself, or perhaps about where she was now in life, seemed to envelop her in a restful way.

There was no job to report to on Monday morning, no actors to corral into doing their jobs properly, or any critics to face. Jerry had taken care of that when he stole the company from under her.

Of course, at the time she'd been seething with anger. Her vengeful act of setting fire to some of his prized possessions, and his mistress's underwear, in front of the entire theatre troupe and their waiting audience on opening night had even made several London headlines, but now it seemed like a distant memory.

Perhaps that act, in itself, was an achievement. Earlier, when she'd checked her phone, surprised to have signal, among the messages were several fan letters praising her daring performance and a disgruntled note from Jerry, who claimed that the entire company was now worthless due to her histrionics.

That only broadened Delia's smile.

If only she could mend things with her daughter and figure out what she was going to do next in life, then everything would presumably be wonderful.

However, the ancient, peaceful wisdom of the forest seemed to whisper to her that she didn't *need* to accomplish anything, not right now.

She could just experience.

She could watch the moonrise and enjoy the sight of clouds drifting into mesmerising patterns. She could revel in the scent of pine and spices, the warmth from the blankets, scratchy as they were, and from the fire that crackled in the grate, and even the pleasant chill wafting in from the window, bringing an invigorating contrast.

Ingrid had used the word 'magic'.

Regardless of how nonsensical Delia found that to be, there was something enchanting about where she found herself, right at this particular moment. And there was something very special about the whole area of Myrtlewood.

"I think I'm going to be staying here for some time," she muttered to herself as she drifted off.

# 27
## THE ROGUE

Night had fallen over the forest, the trees shrouded in the inky blackness of the night. Camped out near Myrtlewood, Declan sent out his magic once again.

Nothing.

He could still feel a peculiar warmth radiating from the place where Delia Spark had vanished. It was an unsettling reminder of the elusive fire witch.

Rage burned through him yet again as he reached down to break off a piece of the fallen log on which he sat before casting it into his campfire.

He stared into the burning light. His eyes traced the edges of the flames, the vibrant red and gold hues dancing and leaping with a life of their own.

Fire, itself, was a kind of magic, one so ancient and useful that even the most mundane beings could not deny it.

Magic was everywhere and yet the majority of sentient beings on this planet were able to screen it out, going about their lives as if it were only make-believe, but fire was hard to deny.

The fire in front of him only fuelled his rage, emanating the powers of the one who he was assigned to track, wild, defiant, and unpredictable.

He spared a glance back towards his camp, which was a rough-hewn refuge, barely more than a temporary shelter in the shadowy wilderness. Hidden amongst the knotted roots of towering trees, he had created a niche, a secret alcove where he could rest, contemplate, and prepare. A low tarpaulin, barely visible under the canopy of leaves, provided a rudimentary roof. The forest floor, carpeted with fallen leaves, served as his bed.

He had been camping this way for centuries, his immortal life etched into the faces of ancient trees and murmuring brooks, in the mountains he'd climbed and the caves he'd sought shelter in. He was a phantom slipping through the wilderness, a ghost in the world of men.

Fire, his constant companion in the cold immortality of his existence, flickered in tune with his inner turmoil. The flames danced and twirled, casting eerie shadows that seemed to echo the spectres of his past.

He looked out into the woods around him.

"Where are you, Delia Spark?" he asked, as if he might receive some kind of reply from the trees themselves. Yet, he was no druid. Never had the trees spoken to him.

The air chilled around him as the night deepened. He rubbed his rough hands together, marked by scars of centuries of hunting, tracking, and fighting.

Yet tonight, they trembled, even as he picked up the crumpled parchment which set out his mission details.

The words inked on it seemed to taunt him, reminding him of his failure. Never before had a target disappeared from his radar.

It was as if Delia Spark had vanished into thin air, her fiery essence still lingering but her physical form gone.

His rage only deepened at the thought of the Order. He'd expected that this failure would at least grant him a dismissal from the contract.

That would be a small mercy. His instincts screamed at him to get as far away as possible from the unnerving fire witch. However, the Order was unyielding. The Cleric had made it clear that he was to continue to track Delia.

After so many centuries, he'd burned through almost everything else – every other shred of humanity except for his rage and the work that kept him going. His vocation kept him focused enough to stave off the madness of endlessness. He wouldn't break a contract. That was why he was trusted in this business.

The soft crackle of burning wood was the only sound breaking the pressing silence of the night. It was a soundtrack to his lengthy life, a refrain in the melody of his existence. Each popping ember, a faded memory; each curl of smoke, a forgotten face.

His equipment was worn and practical, battered by time and use. An old, frayed rucksack, a sturdy knife with a bone handle, a quiver of silver-tipped arrows, each object bore testament to his endless journey, his relentless quest.

The solitude of his forest camp seemed to tighten around him, pressing him down with the weight of his own dread. The usual calm and serenity of nature eluded him, replaced by an oppressive stillness. He wished to be anywhere but there, yet he was ordered to remain in this nightmare.

Sighing deeply, he tucked the parchment back into his rucksack, his eyes returning to the dancing flames. Perhaps, he pondered, the fire before him held a solution. After all, wasn't fire itself a paradox, capable of both creation and destruction?

The magic of fire had spurred the development of humanity, allowing nourishing food to be more readily accessible, leading the nomadic early humanoids to eventually settle down, keeping them warm, warding off predators.

Fire.

It was unpredictable yet followed natural laws. And so, he reasoned, must Delia Spark.

He needed a new approach, a change in his tactics. The fire witch had proven to be as wild as the element she wielded. She was no simple target to track and capture. If he had to stay on this case and fulfil his contract, he'd best match his methods with his quarry.

He grasped a handful of damp leaves from the forest floor and threw it into the blaze.

As the fire crackled and spat, Declan steeled himself for the challenge that lay ahead. If Delia Spark was fire, then he had to be the one who could predict how the flames would burn, an inevitable force meeting an immovable object.

The chill of the night seeped into his bones; the Rogue edged closer to his fire, lost in his thoughts and plotting his next move.

In the cold night, his ancient wounds throbbed with a dull pain, memories of battles past and foes vanquished. Each scar was a trophy, a token of his survival, and a curse. For in his immortal life, each wound healed, every pain faded, but the scars to his soul lingered, invisible and eternal.

He had loved and lost more than he could count, seen friends and foes turn to dust, while he remained behind. It had dulled his emotions and cast him into a solitary existence.

The forest around him should have been a comforting cloak of familiarity, but it seemed alien and hostile. The soft hoots of owls, the rustling leaves, even the scent of wet earth, all seemed a mockery of his turmoil.

A chill had crept into him over the centuries, a hollow emptiness. He had seen empires rise and fall, witnessed the flow of time like a ceaseless river, and all it had left him was a longing for an end. Mortality, with its sweet release, its promise of finality, seemed more alluring with each passing century.

His eyes, hardened by centuries of relentless pursuit, held a new fire within them, mirroring the flames before him. He would find Delia Spark. And perhaps, in doing so, he could find a way to escape the unnerving hold this case had over him.

# 28

## DELIA

**D**elia woke to a clatter of pots and pans.

She yawned and stretched, taking a moment to realise where she was.

Her body felt cramped, having been curled up on the firm window seat, the cold air biting her exposed skin. Her back ached, but not as much as it ought to considering she hadn't been in a real bed.

She rolled over towards the sound, expecting to see Ingrid busy in the kitchen. However, there was nobody in sight; the room appeared completely empty.

Pots and pans continued to clatter.

"How strange," Delia muttered. "Maybe she has some kind of dishwasher."

The thought was absurd. All the way out here, Ingrid didn't even appear to have electricity, let alone modern appliances.

Delia got up and made her way with some trepidation across the room towards the kitchen. Eggs were sizzling in the pan and the teapot was steaming. Ingrid must have been here just moments ago. That was the only explanation, and Delia's addled brain must not have made sense of the timing. There was no way breakfast was cooking itself.

Delia giggled and then jumped as a small earthenware mug slid across the bench towards her, as if somebody had passed it.

The teapot lifted, levitating several inches, and then began to pour itself into said mug.

Delia froze in a rush of terror. Was she being served by a ghost or something even more nefarious?

Her mind raced with the possibilities until it landed on the obvious conclusion.

She threw back her head and laughed.

"Good showing, Ingrid!" she called out. Of course, it had to be rigged. It was the sort of thing they did in the theatre, though she couldn't see any wires.

Whatever this was, it was very clever. She hadn't picked Ingrid for an amateur magician.

The teapot lowered itself to the bench, and the cup moved slowly and gently closer to Delia, as if nudging her to take a sip.

Delia rolled her eyes and slumped forward, retrieving the cup. Just then she noticed movement outside.

It was Ingrid, in her same hat she'd worn the night before, or one very similar to it, stomping through the garden, if the clearing in front of the house with overgrown herb beds could be labelled as such a thing.

"How did she manage to the magic trick from such a distance?" Delia muttered, examining the teapot. It seemed to be quite an ordinary object.

She shook her head, mildly baffled, as the door creaked open and loud footsteps thudded in as Ingrid entered the cottage.

"Your teapot trick is very clever," Delia said.

The corner of Ingrid's mouth quirked up in a half-smile. "Thank you. I'm surprised it didn't send you running for the hills."

"Actually, it almost did," Delia admitted. "But then I figured it must be some kind of clever special effect you've got going on here."

Ingrid raised an eyebrow. "If you like," she said. "Drink your tea."

Delia sat down at the table and took a sip. "I don't suppose you have any coffee?" The herby liquid wasn't exactly what she was used to drinking in the morning.

"Never heard of it." Ingrid chuckled.

Delia narrowed her eyes. "That can't be true."

Ingrid shrugged. "I do my best not to hear about things that are of no consequence to me."

"Fair enough," Delia said. She took another sip of the tea, finding that it relaxed her shoulders. In fact, it seemed to have a relaxing effect on her body while clearing her mind.

Maybe she didn't need coffee after all, although that was almost harder to believe than the existence of floating teapots.

Delia was sure a caffeine withdrawal headache would be coming on any moment. She looked out the window in the vague direction of where she thought the township might lie. "And I suppose I'll be off soon."

Ingrid gave a curt nod. "Breakfast first, I think."

Moments later, the older woman carried over a plate for Delia with a fried egg perched on a piece of coarse bread that looked to be made out of seeds, accompanied by slices of mushrooms, generously seasoned with herbs.

"These aren't going to make me see things again, are they?" Delia asked.

"Can't you see things for yourself?" The question seemed loaded somehow, though Delia didn't quite understand it. "And no, they're quite an edible sort of fungus with no mind-altering benefits, I'm afraid."

Delia nodded, somewhat reassured, although the thought of calling something that she was about to eat fungus was not all that appealing.

Her stomach grumbled, and she dug into the food anyway. It tasted delicious, with complex flavours. It seemed it was exactly what her body needed.

"You're quite self-sufficient, aren't you?" Delia remarked, taking another swig of tea.

Ingrid shrugged. "I don't much like the company of people, which leads me to certain lifestyle choices, you might say."

"How often do you go into town?" Delia asked.

"I must have gone, oh, five years ago."

"You're joking!" Delia's eyes widened in shock.

"Give or take a few years," Ingrid added. "I get what I need from out here. I have some chickens out the back and a good garden. The farm nearby brings me bags of grains and seeds, and meaty bones occasionally in exchange for remedies. It's all I need."

"So...what do you do?" Delia asked. "I mean, aside from all the work it takes to prepare food."

Ingrid chuckled. "What do I do, indeed. I'm a crone, my dear. I simply am. I'm not sure whether I'm a Crone with a capital C. That remains to be determined. But I'm certainly the regular sort."

"Fair enough," Delia said though she felt more confused than ever. She returned her focus to consuming the last of her breakfast. "Alright, I suppose you won't want to come with me back into town, then."

"Not if I can help it," Ingrid replied. "Stick to the main path. You shouldn't get lost. Just keep a clear intention in your mind. That's the important thing."

Delia nodded, feeling that this was sage advice even if her brain made no sense at all.

She wrapped her black cape tightly around her shoulders, thanked Ingrid for her hospitality, and set off through the front door.

She descended the wonky stone steps, passed the overgrown herb garden, and walked along the broad path that led into the forest.

It was peaceful in here in the morning. The birdsong was charming and Delia thoroughly enjoyed the walk, more so due to the nourishing refreshments that Ingrid had provided her. She couldn't even feel the bruises from the night before.

"It can't be so bad...living out here," she muttered to herself. "At least there are no skeezy exes or murderous thespians in sight." She giggled.

# 29

## MATHILDA

T he moon bathed the temple in an ethereal silver glow.

Mathilda stared out, admiring the majestic pillars reaching skyward, their shadows whispering ancient secrets.

She had been here many times before but had never experienced it quite like this.

The Crone Moon was new and fresh in the sky, a thin and tender crescent, and yet somehow its shine was so bright that every detail of engraving in the temple could be seen.

Mathilda's heart drummed in her chest, echoing off the sacred stones.

A caw sounded in the distance. Mathilda turned to the open doorway.

Something was approaching.

With a soft fluttering of wings, a large bird flew into the room, each feather a riot of colours, somehow visible despite the moonlight.

The bird circled the domed room, its grace as serene as a lullaby.

As Mathilda watched, entranced, the creature came to rest in the centre of the dome, peering at her through wise eyes.

Then it ignited.

Bright red flames burst forth, consuming it.

*"No!" Mathilda cried out as the creature burned, but the half-whispered incantation in her mouth was too late to stop the furnace.*

*The flames burned, casting long, dancing shadows against the temple walls.*

*The blaze grew to a brightness so intense that Mathilda shielded her eyes, but then the light died down as the fire burned low.*

*She peered out.*

*From the flames, a shape formed.*

*A new bird – smaller, yet no less beautiful – rose from the ashes. A voice rang out, the sound filling the temple, vibrating through her bones.*

*"The ancient powers of fire have awoken!"*


Mathilda woke with a start, her heart pounding. The dream was still ringing in her mind, vivid and extraordinary: the great temple bathed in silver moonlight, an incandescent bird igniting in brilliant flames, and then, the new-born phoenix rising from the ashes. It was significant.

She shook her head, trying to clear the haze of sleep. Glancing out her window, she realised dawn had long broken. The lush, symmetrically manicured gardens of the Clochar spread out before her, bathed in the bright light of the morning. The ancient commune was already in full-swing while she had slept in; its simple white dwellings and orderly gardens, all built around the sacred temple, were bursting with activity.

With a swift motion, Mathilda threw off her woven linen covers and pulled on her simple, cream robe, then retrieved her cloak from the foot of her bed. It was moss-green like most of the others in the Clochar, but hers was worn and comforting. Her fingers came to rest momentarily on the embroidered hood, adorned with the symbol of the sisterhood: an interwoven emblem of the moon phases, femininity, and nature. She quickly fastened it and hurried out of her modest dwelling, her heart heavy with the weight of her dream.

It had to mean something.

Instead of going to the herb garden she focussed on the temple.

As she hurried through the commune, the air was cool and clean, and the soft sounds of nature filled her ears. Everything in the Clochar was grown or crafted by the hands of the sisters: the lush fruit orchards, the thriving vegetable patches, the meticulously maintained herb gardens. Here, in this serene sanctuary, they lived in harmony with nature, utilising magic as their lifeblood, their power source. It was a tranquil existence, filled with peace and dedicated to the nourishing essence of the divine feminine.

As she reached the temple, she was met by the stern faces of her elders. They were only a decade or two older than Mathilda, but she was still deemed too young to be among them.

Sister Gwyneth, her face lined with the wisdom of countless years and eyes as clear as a summer sky, regarded Mathilda with mild annoyance. Beside her stood Sister Franwen, a somewhat younger woman with fiery red hair and an intensity that could rival the midday sun.

"You're late, Mathilda." Gwyneth's voice as crisp as an autumn morning. "This is not the discipline we expect. Even one as experienced as you must uphold our customs and rhythms."

Mathilda bowed her head. "I'm sorry, Sisters," she apologised.

"And why are you here instead of overseeing the sage harvest as allotted?" Sister Franwen asked.

Mathilda paused for a moment, contemplating her words.

"I believe the reason I was late was out of my control this morning, Sisters," she said. "A potent dream spoke to me..."

She did her best to describe the vision of the fiery phoenix in the heart of the temple, and the elder Sisters exchanged intrigued glances.

"A phoenix, you say?" Gwyneth questioned, her tone cautious but excitement twinkling in her eyes.

"Yes, Sister," Mathilda confirmed. "The bird was consumed by fire and then rose again, new-born. The voice in the dream said the ancient powers of fire had awoken."

"What nonsense," said Franwen.

"This is indeed a fortunate sign." Another voice, deep and wavering, echoed around the temple, as a woman cloaked in a fine woven veil entered from a side door.

"Sister Breag," said Gwyneth, a note of surprise in her voice.

"Do not let our foolish chatter disturb you from your sacred duty," Franwen added.

"Oh shut your face, Fran," said the most respected member of the sisterhood, lifting her veil. Sister Breag smirked slightly at the expression on Franwen's face and then turned to Mathilda, who inclined her head and pressed her palms together in respect. "The ancient powers are indeed awakening," she murmured.

"Then it is true," said Gwyneth, a sense of awe creeping into her voice. "This is a sign, Mathilda. That which was foreseen is coming to pass. We must prepare. We must restore the balance and usher in peace."

Franwen's gaze became steelier. "You must go to the outpost, Mathilda. Keep a watchful eye and report any activity."

Sister Breag and Gwyneth both nodded.

Frustration sparked in Mathilda's chest. "But, Sisters...Am I not old enough? Have I not proven myself? Surely it's time I joined you. I have even forsaken my own kin for the Sisterhood."

"Your dedication is not in question, dear sister," Gwyneth said, her voice filled with understanding but firm. "However, it's not about age or sacrifice. It's about fulfilling your role. The Scrying Bowl of Pendrywn has shown us this."

"Your path lies at the outpost, Mathilda. Trust us," Franwen added, her gaze never leaving Mathilda's.

There was no arguing with that. Mathilda had pledged her life to the Veiled Sisterhood, after all. Her frustration evaporated to be replaced by a sense of duty.

Mathilda nodded, understanding but not entirely agreeing.

"Yes, Sisters. I will head to the outpost."

With a final glance at the elder Sisters, she left the temple. Outside, she lifted her face to the sun, the dream still vivid in her mind. The divine feminine was stirring, and she was a part of it. She would go to the outpost and fulfil her role.

# 30

## DELIA

Delia wandered through the forest, under the bright dappled sunlight and the cooling shade. She found herself feeling lighter than she had in months.

She didn't even care what was going on or whether she was losing her mind, being tricked, or even – the possibility that had begun to dawn on her – that all sorts of strange occurrences normally relegated to the paranormal were actually happening around her. Last night, it seemed totally plausible that she could set fires with her mind, and this morning the crockery was moving all on its own, even if she'd been sure at the time it was an illusion.

At some points she'd come to accept it all as real, and then her rational mind would seek out a logical explanation for it all, though the most obvious one involved a rather gaping absence of marbles.

"Maybe I'm mad or maybe I'm magic," she said to herself, almost skipping down the pathway.

"Why not both?" said a voice.

Delia stopped, suppressing a shudder of fear, and turned her head.

It was the black kitten again.

"You really talk, do you?" she asked.

"Some people perceive it that way." He licked his paw and preened.

Delia took a deep breath. This beast might be disturbing, but he was tiny and hardly a threat.

"Do you have a name?" she asked.

He narrowed his eyes at her. "Mephistos."

Delia chortled. "Mephistos, the cat? That's a rather big name for a small creature."

She could have sworn he growled.

"Okay, Mephistos..."

"And you are?"

"My name's Delia," she said.

"'Course it is, Bedelia."

Delia raised an eyebrow and cleared her throat.

"Excuse me?"

"Bedelia," said the cat again, more clearly this time.

"That's what Etty used to call me," said Delia. "Nobody's called me that in years."

It was odd that Delia was more bewildered by the use of her childhood nickname than she was by the talking cat in that moment.

Delia resumed her walk. The cat followed her along the path, prancing proudly. "And you live out here, do you?" she asked.

"At times," he replied.

"And are you real or a figment of my imagination?" she asked, turning to him.

He glared at her. "What an insulting question." He sounded a lot like an arrogant actor and Delia couldn't help but look around to see whether she was part of a Truman Show-like theatre production with Jerry orchestrating it.

Of course, it would be to her ex-husband's advantage for her to totally lose her marbles, but there was nobody else in sight.

"You're here for an important reason, you know," said Mephistos.

"And what is that?" Delia asked.

"I can tell you no more," he said dramatically, with a wave of his paw. "I bid you good day, Madam."

With that, he turned around and disappeared into the forest.

Delia frowned and bit her lip. That was by far one of the stranger things to have ever happened to her in her life. And yet, some part of her mind registered it as perfectly ordinary.

Perhaps she was absolutely bonkers, or dreaming. Her brain was still intent on rationalising the situation and finding a new normal amongst the chaos.

As she continued on down the path, she reflected over her short visit to Myrtlewood so far. There was some serious secret-keeping going on. Marjie wouldn't tell her, and neither would Agatha.

Ingrid wasn't much help either, despite the lengths Delia had gone to find her.

What was it they hoped or didn't hope for her to be?

And Mephistos, be he real or a figment of her imagination, alluded to something that was possibly all part of the same mystery.

Delia rolled back her shoulders, righting her posture. She wasn't about to be drawn into somebody else's drama. She had had quite enough of that for one lifetime.

She decided she wanted no part of it.

As the forest opened up again to the familiar street, she realised, however, that she did want to stay in Myrtlewood for at least a little while.

# 31
## INGRID

"The uninitiated often dance closest to the abyss." Ingrid stood in the doorway of her hut, the cool winter air brushing against her cheeks, turning them a shade of rose. As she watched Delia walk away, her breath misted in front of her, dissipating quickly in the chill. The ground was hard and frost-kissed, crunching slightly beneath Delia's steps. Gazing at the departing witch as she disappeared into the forest, a cryptic smile played on Ingrid's lips.

Ingrid maintained her position, staring into the forest long after Delia had vanished from sight.

Every so often, a gust of wind would rustle through the trees, causing the few remaining stubborn leaves to shiver and whisper.

Ingrid took in the patterns of nature as they made their music – the distant cawing of crows, the susurration of the wind, and the rhythmic pulse of her own heart.

She thought of the other likely suspects.

Somewhere down the village, Marjoram Reeves was in her usual morning frenzy, no doubt. Ingrid had never visited her teashop, but her imagination gave her a pretty good idea of what it would be like based on the ridiculous baked goods that overly nurturing woman insisted on dropping off to her. Momentarily, Ingrid longed for more gingersnaps before snapping herself out of the craving.

Agatha would probably be sipping sherry by a fire, nose buried in a heavy book, oblivious to the world outside.

Both of them, formidable witches, and yet neither had any idea what was in store for them. Even Ingrid, herself, in all her years, only had clues.

Casting her eyes skyward, she spotted a hawk soaring, its wings outstretched against the cold blue sky, the sun catching its feathers in a brilliant glint. "A sign," she mused. "An omen of challenges to come."

There would be a hunt, a chase. Predators were seeking them out at that very moment, and eventually they'd break through her defences. There was no doubt about that.

Ingrid's thoughts returned to Delia. That spirit, that fire, it was something to behold. But it was also a cause for concern. The magical world was no playground, and she wondered if Delia even had an inkling of the enormity of her true power.

Ingrid felt a need to ground herself. She moved towards her kitchen to brew a cup of calming tea. As she waited for the water to boil, her fingers brushed the edges of her scrying bowl, contemplating the mysteries it might reveal today.

Once her tea was ready, its aroma – a mix of vervain, rosemary, and yarrow – filled her hut, comforting her and awakening her senses. The herbs not only warmed her from the inside but sharpened her intuition.

"Every frost has its thaw, every light its shadow. The question remains: which will prevail?"

Her mind wandered to her winter herb garden. Later, she'd inspect the hardy plants, covered in morning frost, their resilience a testament to nature's wonders – and a reflection of her own journey.

For now, the tea promised solace. It was a moment to reflect and prepare, for the omens hinted at challenges on the horizon.

Ingrid could feel the invigorating properties of the herbs working their magic. Their essence not only warmed her body but calmed her mind and rekindled the clarity of her thoughts. The tea cup, still steaming gently, sat on a wooden table beside her scrying bowl. Even though she had not intended to, her gaze was drawn to its still waters.

Within the water's surface, ripples began to form, unfurling like a slow-moving storm, revealing images both obscure and vivid. At first, she saw the same hawk she had seen earlier, circling overhead, a sentinel in the sky. Then, as the ripples ebbed and flowed, the image shifted, revealing a crimson flame that danced and crackled with a life of its own.

A chill that wasn't from the winter air settled deep within her bones. This flame – so vibrant, so wild – had to be Delia. But surrounding that flame, shadows gathered, growing darker, threatening to extinguish the fiery brightness.

"Some flames, once ignited, consume all in their path. And some shadows are darker than the heart of winter."

Shaking her head to clear it, Ingrid pulled herself away from the scrying bowl. Prophecies and visions had a way of taking root in the mind, and she knew she had to tread carefully. These were dangerous times, and Delia's naivety was a vulnerability, not just for her but for the entire world.

Ingrid had been putting it off, but she knew the time was coming soon where she'd need to seek out Marjie and Agatha, to gather them all together. As much as Marjie's obsession with baking might seem trivial, or Agatha's penchant for books, rationality, and sherry appeared to make her an unlikely candidate for a dangerous adventure, they were both skilled in their own unique ways.

"However, first thing's first," she muttered. Ingrid felt an urge to reconnect with her garden. Bundling up in her thick cloak, she stepped outside.

The frosted herbs glistened in the weak winter sunlight. She walked among them, touching each with a delicate hand. Her protective charms were holding up well against the frosts. The rosemary stood tall, unaffected by the cold, the lavender bushes were in a deep sleep, and the sage was still robust, exuding its earthy scent when touched. Each plant reminded her that life persisted even in the harshest conditions, especially where a little magic was involved.

As she carefully plucked a few leaves, the ominous vision from the scrying bowl replayed in her mind, but the tangible feel of the herbs, the scent of the earth, and the crispness of the air brought her back to the present.

"We must prepare for the worst." Ingrid's voice, though soft, carried a weight, a timbre that hinted at deep truth. "There's a balance in all things, and soon, the scales will tip."

# 32

## DELIA

Having made it quite easily back to her car, Delia drove back to Myrtlewood, determined to sort a few things out.

She entered the teashop, inhaling the scent of vanilla and cinnamon, greeted Marjie with a smile, and ordered a Cornish pasty and a strong coffee.

Marjie beamed as if she was absolutely delighted to see her and brought over the pasty along with a large pot of coffee, accompanied by cream and jam scones that Delia decidedly hadn't ordered.

The carbohydrate content of such a meal would have put Jerry into a stupor. This thought only made Delia want it more.

As she took a bite, she noticed the little beagle puppy was back outside, staring expectantly at her again.

"Whose dog is that?" she asked Marjie.

"What dog, dear?"

Delia turned back to the window to find the puppy must've run off. "Never mind."

Marjie returned and took a seat at the table next to Delia. "So?" she said expectantly, smiling broadly.

"So what?" Delia retorted. She wasn't used to people she hardly knew having the audacity of sitting with her and initiating conversation.

"Did you find her?" Marjie asked, unperturbed by Delia's tone.

"You mean Ingrid?" Delia narrowed her eyes. "Yes, eventually I managed to find her, although I'm not sure whether sending me off into the forest close to nightfall was a good idea. I could have died of hypothermia, and..."

"And what, dear?" Marjie asked.

Delia shook her head, unsure of how much to reveal. Presumably, strangers who rambled about talking cats were at risk of institutionalisation.

"But you found her," Marjie said proudly, returning to the topic at hand.

"She's quite a character, isn't she?"

"You could say that," said Marjie. "I must admit, Agatha and I hardly know Ingrid at all. She keeps to herself."

"So it seems." Delia took a long swig of her coffee, welcoming the caffeine, though, in some ways, she had to admit that she felt better after drinking Ingrid's concoction.

Marjie gasped.

Delia realised she'd muttered her thoughts aloud, though she hadn't said anything particularly strange.

"What?" asked Delia.

"She made you tea!" Marjie sounded outraged.

"Shouldn't she have?"

"She's never offered *me* tea before," Marjie retorted, folding her arms.

"Well, I suppose she's never found you lost, bewildered, and mumbling inconsolably to yourself in the middle of the woods at nightfall. She felt sorry for me, I'm sure."

"That's a fair point," said Marjie, returning to her normal, smiling self. "I'm glad she led you to safety. You got to go inside her cottage, did you?"

Delia nodded.

"What is it like?" Marjie asked excitedly.

"Sort of like a little rustic house, I suppose," Delia responded. "Although she's got some kind of interesting teapot trick that she does —" She clamped her hand over her mouth, not wanting to sound totally insane.

"Tell me what happened," Marjie urged.

"Oh, very well," said Delia. "By the time we got there, it must have been quite late. She fed me some amazing soup—"

"She fed you?!" Marjie sounded very excited indeed.

"I probably needed it."

"Of course you did, dear," said Marjie. "Then what happened?"

"She put me to bed on the window seat. It was quite nice, really."

Marjie's mouth fell open. "I've never known her to show such hospitality."

"It was nice of her...I suppose she didn't know what else to do with me."

"I can't say I'm not a bit jealous," said Marjie. "It's been years...I bring her gifts from time to time, you know – treats from my shop. She hardly even says a word to me, mostly. Occasionally she just mutters about...oh, never mind. I'll tell you later. She's never so much as offered me a cup of tea."

"She's not particularly social, I take it," said Delia.

"You can say that again!" It was Agatha Twigg, who had somehow appeared in the tea shop without Delia noticing.

"Help yourself to food, dear. I'm busy here," said Marjie, waving Agatha in the direction of the cabinet.

"I don't need food. I'm here for gossip," said Agatha, pulling up a chair, though her not needing food did not stop her from helping herself to the scones. "Is that coffee?" she asked, sniffing as she stuffed an entire cream and jam scone into her mouth.

"Help yourself," said Delia. Agatha fetched herself a cup and poured a rather large coffee.

"Right," Agatha said. "Tell us all about your adventure with the infamous Ingrid. Did you actually manage to meet her?"

"Not only that," said Marjie. "Ingrid fed her, gave her tea, and let her stay the night."

"Nonsense! That's not her style at all," Agatha said gruffly.

"Like I was saying before," Delia interjected, "she must have felt sorry for me. Lost in the woods. Like a poor, little lamb."

Agatha took a swig of her coffee and then grinned. It was an unsettling expression on her. "What did she feed you?"

"Soup!" said Marjie. "I bet it had lots of herbs and I bet it was dreadfully nourishing."

"It was," Delia confirmed, feeling a strange swell of pride that she couldn't quite explain. These two women seemed to be jealous of her odd little adventure. Ingrid was obviously a notorious recluse and somebody whom they looked up to, or at least found mysteriously charismatic and intriguing.

Agatha's jaw dropped open, and Marjie gasped again when they heard that Delia had been served breakfast by Ingrid the next day. Delia took care not to mention the floating teapot. In fact, recounting the story to them was more thrilling than the actual experience had been, magic tricks aside. Their excitement was infectious.

"So, what is it about Ingrid, really?" Delia finally asked. "Why are you so fascinated by her?"

Marjie looked down at her fingernails, pretending to be very busy inspecting them.

"It's rather a lot to explain," said Agatha dismissively. "We have a history, you know. This whole town has history..."

"Right, then," Delia muttered, feeling her energy waning. Moments ago, she'd almost felt a bond of friendship with these two. Now, she felt on the outside again.

"You will understand in time," Agatha said.

"Don't tell me that," Delia grumbled. "That's rather patronising."

"Indeed it is," said Agatha. "However, if we were to tell you the whole thing now, you'd leave town before we got through half the story, thinking we were bonkers."

"You're probably right," Delia conceded. "I don't want to join your cult," she continued, somewhat defiantly.

"What cult, dear?" Marjie asked.

"Whatever it is that you sent me into the forest to find out...whether I could be one of you. Well, I'm a bit of a lone wolf myself."

"It's not a cult," said Agatha dryly.

"Oh, no. We don't go in for that kind of thing," said Marjie. "We've had a lot of problems from secret societies, you see."

"Well, then I don't know how else to explain it," Delia said.

Agatha merely shrugged.

"Let's put it this way," Agatha said. "There is a tradition—"

"Yes, yes, tradition," said Marjie, nodding rather vigorously.

"Which involves four older women," Agatha continued. "Getting together and..."

"Causing mischief," said Marjie with a chuckle.

"Now you're talking," Delia responded, unable to suppress a smile. "Where do I sign up?"

Marjie beamed.

"You can't just sign up!" Agatha said, outraged.

"Fine," said Delia flatly, though internally she found the whole situation hilarious. "Oh, by the way, do either of you happen to know of any houses to rent around here? I may want to stick around for a while."

Agatha scowled. "There aren't many houses for rent around here."

"There's only one I can think of off the top of my head," Marjie added. "And it happens to be mine. The only thing is, it might have been the site of a mysterious death."

"Oh," Delia replied. "Sounds morbid."

"More morbid than you can even imagine," Agatha said.

"Don't scare her off," Marjie interjected. "It's been thoroughly cleaned and decontaminated."

Delia wrinkled her nose. "I don't know about that. Do you think it's haunted?"

"Almost certainly," Agatha stated.

"*I* don't think so," Marjie argued. "Herb's not likely to want to come back anytime soon after the grilling I gave him."

"Your husband?" Delia asked. "How exactly did he die?"

"It's rather a long story," Marjie said, seeming reluctant to explain it.

"Best not to talk about it," Agatha quickly added.

"Well, I suppose it wouldn't hurt to view the house," Delia finally said.

"Excellent," Marjie exclaimed. "I close up at three. How about you meet me here, and I'll show you around?"

Delia nodded with a little pang of fear. She poured herself another cup of coffee, wondering what on earth she was getting herself into.

# 33

## THE CLERIC

Every breath that the Cleric drew felt like a small victory as he approached the door of the Crimson Shepherd. His heartbeat pounded in his ears, each pulse, a heavy boom. He ran a damp palm down his robes, as if the simple act of smoothing the fabric could still the whirlpool of trepidation inside him. His fingers trembled, a shivering echo of the anxiety lurching in his belly.

It was good news he brought with him, but his body seemed to respond only with terror where Father Benedict was concerned.

With a deep, steadying breath, the Cleric rapped on the solid and imposing door, each knock echoing his pulsing heartbeat. The muffled "Enter" from within was all the encouragement he needed to push the heavy door open.

Father Benedict's office was as he remembered – a tribute to austerity and order, a testament to precision; every book, every quill, every inkwell was in its rightful place. The very air in the room seemed to have been measured and allocated in a calculated quantity. It was an environment that perfectly mirrored its occupant's personality.

Seated behind his desk, the Crimson Shepherd was an island amid this sea of meticulous order. He was engrossed in a parchment, his quill moving with a methodical rhythm, the scratching against the parchment like a monk's chant in the monastery.

Feeling like a leaf adrift in a storm, the Cleric cleared his throat. It came out as a strangled croak, startling in the near-monastic silence of the room. Father Benedict looked up, grey eyes piercing through him, a silent question in their icy depths.

"Shepherd..." the Cleric started, his voice fluttering like a moth against a lantern. "We have...I mean...there's news..." His words were coming out jumbled, failing to form a coherent sentence.

Father Benedict did not prod, he didn't even blink. The icy gaze held the Cleric transfixed, a rabbit in the beam of a hunter's flashlight.

With a deep inhale, the Cleric fought down the fluttering panic in his belly, willing his voice to steady. "The fire witch...we've located her."

The silence following his proclamation was profound. Father Benedict stared at him, the intensity of his gaze unchanged. But there was a flicker, a tiny flame amidst the ice in his eyes. Was that relief? Or merely satisfaction?

"Where?" Benedict finally spoke; his voice was calm, betraying no emotion.

"Near the outskirts of Myrtlewood...just beyond the forest, sir," the Cleric managed to respond, a sense of accomplishment flooding him. He had delivered the message.

Benedict nodded, his countenance still as unruffled as a mill pond. His gaze returned to the parchment on his desk.

This was not the response the Cleric had anticipated. Surely this news was auspicious for The Mission. Surely it warranted more than a nod. He cleared his throat again. "Operation Delta can...it can proceed."

The Shepherd looked up again. "Very well. Ready the Crimson Guard. We move as planned."

The Cleric saluted, then practically fled the room, the door closing with a solid thunk behind him. He was done. He allowed himself a small indulgence, a celebratory leap, his fist rising to punch the air in victory.

Perhaps Father Benedict had other concerns on his mind, or perhaps he was merely curtailing his own exuberance in some kind of monkly humility, but it was worthy of celebration, nonetheless.

Operation Delta was back in action. The prophecy would unfold as planned. The Shepherd would see to that. Now, he, the Cleric, had his own part to play.

# 34
## DELIA

"I t looks like something out of a fairy tale," said Delia as they pulled up outside a small whitewashed cottage. "Charming."

Marjie smiled at her. "Thank you, dear. Let's go take a closer look."

Delia shrugged. "Why not?"

They both got out of the car and made their way through the overgrown rose garden.

Marjie shuddered. "Oh...Perhaps it was a mistake for me to come back here. I should have just burned the whole place to the ground and sold the land."

Delia, not usually one for physical affection with virtual strangers, put her hand on Marjie's shoulder and patted her. "Are you okay? Would you like to go?"

Marjie took a deep breath. "No, I might as well face it. Just...ignore me if I say anything silly, or if I faint."

"I hope you don't faint," Delia replied. "I'm not sure my upper body strength is up to the task of carrying you."

Marjie pointed to a large garage as they walked past. "That was Herb's shed, you see? It was so awful...horrible business he got himself involved in."

"So I gather," Delia responded, giving the shed a suspicious look. She peered through the windows to see a rather large collection of model trains.

Marjie gave a choked sob.

"Are you sure it's fine for you to be here?"

"Of course it is."

Delia shrugged and glanced back at the trains. "Nasty business indeed. Is there anywhere else you'd like to show me?"

Marjie led her around to the back door of the cottage, which also served as the main entrance.

As she fumbled with her keys, Delia looked over the neglected back vegetable garden. It seemed a shame that nobody was living there to tend to it, though there was something decidedly eerie about the house.

The door swung open and they both hesitated.

"You say it's all been cleaned up," said Delia.

"Oh yes," Marjie replied. "They got all the blood out."

Delia winced. "Erm, and did they do anything else to clear the air, any kind of blessing?"

Marjie gave her a knowing look. "Ah! So, you do believe in—"

"Woo-woo? Sure." Delia shrugged. "Don't be so surprised. I'm sure there's lots of odd things out there that we don't completely understand. Humans are arrogant to presume we know everything when we can't possibly see outside our own experience. Besides, in the theatre, superstition is everything."

"We did have a special clean-up team in here," said Marjie, peering down the hallway. "But I suppose the place could do with another cleansing. Perhaps I will ask Ferg to organise something."

"That mayor chap?" said Delia. "He's a character."

"He's a character and a half," said Marjie. "With an amazing wardrobe. I've hardly ever seen him wearing the same outfit twice."

Delia smiled.

Marjie began to show her around the cottage. It was rather old-fashioned and a little quaint. Not the kind of home Delia ever envisaged for herself. It wasn't all that creepy inside; in fact, it was cosy. She could imagine sprucing the place up a bit, tidying the garden, and even putting in a swing for her grandchildren.

But something made her hesitate.

As they stood in the living room looking around, something caught Delia's eye. Out the window, she caught a flash of red.

Heavy footsteps sounded. A man appeared in the doorway in a dark red cloak. "Surrender, you are surrounded!" he cried.

Delia scowled, glancing from him to the gathering red outside the window. The house was surrounded. "Bloody hell!" Delia cursed. "What is Jerry up to?"

"Jerry, dear?" Marjie said, looking perplexed as she armed herself with a kitchen knife.

"My ex-husband. He's been sending these B-grade actors after me. There's nothing worse than a thespian's corrupted ego."

"Ah," Marjie said sceptically. "Right then."

"Death to the Crones!" cried a voice from outside.

"Surrender..." the man started again.

Marjie brandished her kitchen knife at the man in the doorway. "Now, listen here," she said sternly. "You're trespassing on my property!"

"I doubt he cares about that," said Delia as more red-hooded bearded men entered the room. One of the intruders, a burly man, drew a sword and lunged towards her.

Delia managed to trip him, but he reached for her, dragging her down to the ground, pressing the blade against her throat.

Delia gulped. "I don't know what kind of game Jerry is playing, but it's not going to work," she said weakly.

Marjie somehow seemed to be producing bizarre sparkles, and clouds of purple smoke billowed around the room.

The burly man leaned in close to Delia's ear and whispered, "Tell us the secret of the dragons."

"Dragons? What is this nonsense?" Delia said. With a surge of fiery rage, she pushed her foot between her assailant's legs and managed to flip him so he was no longer pinning her to the ground, dislodging his sword in the process. Delia pushed herself up and kicked away the sword. "This is absurd!" she said, coughing through the purple smoke. Other red-cloaked men lay writhing on the ground around them. Somehow Marjie had taken them out armed with only a kitchen knife and mysterious sparkles. Delia made a note to never get on her new friend's bad side.

"It's not just absurd," Marjie said. A strange, glowing ball of energy emanated from her, enveloping them both in a cocoon of light.

"What is going on?" said Delia, her eyes wide.

"I'm afraid the house is on fire," Marjie said.

Delia could smell the burning and hear the crackling. "Run!"

"Wait, just one moment."

"Wait?" Delia said desperately. "There's no time!"

"I knew I had this installed for a reason. Herb told me I was mad, but..." Marjie pulled a lever next to the kitchen bench. She grabbed hold of Delia abruptly, making her squeak involuntarily.

The ceiling of the cottage, thatched roof and all, burst open.

Delia and Marjie sprang up into the air, the bubble still encasing them, lifting them serenely, while the house burned.

The men outside the cottage did not look up and didn't seem to notice the two women hovering above the house.

"Can't they see us?" Delia asked as the bubble rose further and began drifting away from the scene. A fire engine roared through the streets below, hurtling towards the cottage, sirens blaring, as Marjie and Delia rose higher and higher.

"Just a little cloaking magic," Marjie replied.

Delia looked around again and then stared at Marjie. "Those aren't theatre performers, are they?"

Delia's mind whirred around as they sailed over the village, reassessing everything that had happened over the past few days.

"I'm afraid not," Marjie responded. "And if so, they're terrible actors."

"And you're some kind of magical being, aren't you?"

Marjie shrugged. "Just a witch," she said modestly.

"So witches are real," Delia said flatly as the bubble continue to sail through the air. "It's not just an insult."

"Not an insult at all, dear. Quite a compliment, if you ask me."

Delia realised that the bubble wasn't drifting idly; Marjie was focusing on it, directing it to drift over a forest, drift towards a large manor house near the coast sea.

"The last few days have been strange. I was trying to rationalise all kinds of odd things – I thought I was mad. Maybe I am mad. However, at least I'm in good company."

"I think you'll find, dear, that you are also a witch," Marjie said.

Delia laughed. "Well, that would be fabulous, but I'm afraid you must be mistaken. The most magical thing I've ever done is..."

"Set things on fire?" Marjie offered.

Delia shrugged. "There was that talking cat as well, I suppose."

Marjie beamed at her. "Oh, really? Well, that's news. Come on, tell me all about it over a cup of tea," she suggested as the bubble began to sink down towards the lawn of the rather grand house.

# 35

## THE ROGUE

Twenty-five minutes earlier, Declan had settled in between the thick branches of the tall oak tree he'd climbed to get a better view. His cloak blended in with the rough brown bark.

He had done his job, located the fire witch, and directed the Order to the small cottage belonging to Marjoram Reeves, as his magic had indicated.

At that point, he should have left, gone back to camp and waited for further instructions, but something held him in place. Something about this case scratched at the walls of his tired soul, making him feel raw.

Perched in his hidden spot, he told himself he was supervising, ensuring everything went as planned. The Order didn't want him there to see their secret plan play out, but Declan needed to know what happened. He hardly knew anyone involved, but he couldn't look away.

Through narrowed eyes, he watched as the witches approached the cottage. The red streak in Delia's hair caught the sunlight. A spark of energy seemed to fly through the air between them. She turned her head. He ducked. And by the time he looked up again, the women were entering the cottage. They seemed at ease, unsuspecting. Had he simply imagined that spark, as if the long-dormant part of him now stirring was playing havoc with his imagination.

He waited, wondering what their business was there, his mind drifting, a nagging discomfort in his gut.

Soon enough, the Order's guards and soldiers began to arrive. Ordinary-looking people approached the cottage, only to pull on their red cloaks as they drew near, transforming into some horror cult scene from an '80s movie.

Declan's lips twitched at the thought. He had gone through a phase of obsession with the cinema, which had lasted between the '50s and '80s. There was something about the ease of it, the way it was all curated just for him, the viewer. He hadn't seen a film since 1989, deciding it was all downhill from there. Besides, movies had only been around a short while and would no doubt vanish again soon enough. Such were fads in an immortal life.

As he watched the cottage, his mind wandered to Delia. Did she ever see a crappy movie, or was it all high-brow theatre? Not that it mattered anyway. He had nothing to do with her, and the Order would probably destroy her soon enough. Either way, Delia Spark didn't have long to live.

As if in answer to his thoughts, a great plume of smoke rose up from the house, accompanied by shouts from the red-cloaked Order guards. Declan's heart tightened as the house burned, a sickening realisation settling in.

He returned his attention to his tracking magic, reaching into the small leather rucksack he always carried. Drawing out the knuckle bones, he rubbed them together in his hands, uttering the ancient words that sparked their magic.

More shouts rang out from the fire, but Declan's focus shifted, not to the house itself, but to the air above it. He could see nothing, but the bones spoke to him, hinting that the witches had escaped.

Closing his eyes, he leaned into the magic, his frown of concentration turning into a rare laugh. In his mind's eye, he could see them, floating above the town in a bubble.

In a life as long as his, there were few surprises left, but this...this was delightful.

A pang of regret tightened across his chest. He didn't pick sides. He just did his job and left, yet here he still was. And it seemed he was somehow on the wrong side.

Still, duty was more important than emotional whims. Until the Order released him from the contract, he was bound to them.

Wayward thoughts crept into his mind. He could use the wrong magic, lead the Order astray...but it was none of his business, and once his work here was done, he would skip town and get as far away from the beguiling Delia Spark as possible.

That witch was dangerous, in more ways than one, and he'd do well to remember that.

# 36

## DELIA

Delia shrieked as the bubble hurtled, too fast, towards the ground, bursting in a rather bumpy landing. Both Delia and Marjie landed on their backsides on the lawn.

"Apologies," said Marjie as they scrambled to their feet. "I have some slightly more advanced powers coming in, more than I'm used to, anyway."

Delia eyed her thoughtfully, lost for words. So much had happened, and her brain was still adjusting. "I take it you're not used to bursting through the roof of your own cottage and floating in a bubble through the air?"

Marjie sighed, brushing grass from her floral dress. "Well, we did have that emergency escape hatch set up a long time ago, you know, in case of house fires or other threats. I've never had to use it before, but it pays to be careful...just in case."

"Here I was complaining about the inordinate amount of fire drills in the theatre," Delia muttered.

"What's that, dear?"

"Nothing. Erm, is it normal around these parts to have...*magical* evacuations?" The words sounded foreign and uncomfortable on Delia's tongue, given their new weight and meaning.

"Well, normally, that kind of thing would have just popped us out and left us on the lawn outside. But given the situation, I improvised with the bubble, trying to get a little further afield to avoid whoever those attackers were. I'm fairly sure they're nothing to do with your ex-husband."

Delia felt herself deflate. "It's a shame in a way. At least when I thought it was Jerry sending people after me, it made some kind of convoluted sense. But now I have no idea. You don't have any suspicions about who they are and why they're after us?"

"Well..." Marjie hesitated. "Let's have that tea."

She led Delia towards the house without elaborating further.

"This place is amazing," Delia said, staring at the elaborate old building.

"This is Thorn Manor," said Marjie.

"Ah, you live here?" Delia asked.

"How did you know?" Marjie said, surprised.

"You told me the other day that you were staying here."

"Oh, of course I did," Marjie said, her shoulders relaxing. "Alright. This house belongs to Rosemary. I probably told you that too."

Delia nodded. Marjie pushed the front door open, and the house almost seemed to sigh in welcome. Delia regarded it suspiciously before entering.

"Just me!" Marjie called out, leading Delia towards an open plan kitchen and dining area with a table and window seats at the far side.

The interior of the house was somewhat less grand and more cosy than Delia might have expected from the outside.

It wasn't full of expensive-looking ornaments and didn't have the kind of over-the-top decor Delia had occasionally experienced in houses of rich theatre patrons during fundraiser dinners. That only added to its pleasantness in her eyes. She wouldn't need to worry about damaging an overpriced vase or insulting the taste of the occupants.

The shelves were cluttered with jumbles of crockery and rather a lot of crystals.

A woman stood in the kitchen behind the counter, her long, wavy red hair looking somewhat frazzled. She glanced up as Marjie and Delia entered.

"Are you alright, love?" said Marjie.

The woman who must surely be Rosemary looked from Marjie to Delia with a slightly puzzled expression. "What happened to you?"

"Ohh...err," Marjie mumbled. "Nothing serious. My old cottage burned down, I'm afraid. Just an electrical fire, I'm sure."

Rosemary gave her a questioning look.

"And you, dear?" Marjie asked, changing the subject.

Rosemary frowned, clearly baffled by Marjie's casual response to her house burning down.

"What are you up to?" Marjie prompted again.

Rosemary sighed, clearly deciding to take Marjie's lead and ignore the elephant in the room. "I'm just trying out a new recipe," she mumbled, then glanced at Delia. "Who's this, then?"

"Forgive my manners," said Marjie warmly. "Rosemary. This is my new friend, Delia...err...What's your last name?" Marjie asked.

Delia hesitated, her self-confidence wavering. She would have said 'Venito', as that had been her name for over thirty years. But it struck her that it was no longer appropriate to use Jerry's name. The divorce might not have come through yet, but she no longer wanted to be associated with that awful man or his family.

She sighed deeply, drawing looks of concern from both Marjie and Rosemary. "That's a great question. I'm going through a divorce," she confessed. Marjie and Rosemary both expressed their sympathies.

"So you're in a period of transition then?" said Rosemary.

"In more ways than one, I gather," Marjie added.

Delia nodded and sat down at the table. "To answer your question, my last name was Spark and I suppose that's what it will be again soon."

Marjie raised an eyebrow. "Spark?"

"That's a brilliant name," said Rosemary, grinning. "Delia Spark, like some kind of super-hero."

"That was my mother's name. She took her own mother's name because, I suppose, divorce runs in the family," Delia said.

Rosemary chuckled. "It's a good name," she repeated.

"I daresay it is," Marjie muttered.

"I think you're right," said Delia, taking a sip of the cup of tea that Marjie passed her, which must have been brewed rather quickly considering they'd only just entered the house. Perhaps that was magic as well. After all, if it was possible to escape a housefire in a floating bubble, surely magical tea was likely too.

It was good strong tea, with no sugar and a dash of milk, just the way Delia preferred. Although she would have appreciated a coffee even more.

As if reading her mind, Marjie wandered over to the table with a plate of truffles.

"If I'm not mistaken, these are the espresso ones you've been working on," Marjie said to Rosemary, who nodded.

"Although they don't quite have the kick that I was hoping for," Rosemary added. "But they're not too bad. I've had to do something to keep my mind occupied. Otherwise, all these thoughts of the winter solstice would have driven me mad by now."

"Oh?" Delia said, taking a truffle and popping it into her mouth. The flavour exploded; it was as if she'd guzzled back a quadruple espresso and swallowed a chocolate tart all at the same time. "Oh wow," she added, "that's outrageous, decadent, and invigorating all at once."

Delia took a gulp of tea before helping herself to another truffle.

"I'm glad you like it," said Rosemary. "Coffee has never really been my strong point. I'm more of a tea drinker."

"As is everyone else around here, apparently," Delia muttered.

Rosemary smiled at her.

"You look rather tense, dear," Marjie observed. "Something more calming would be in order." She glanced at Rosemary.

Delia realised that while one hand was on the handle of her teacup, trembling just slightly, the other was firmly gripping the hem of her merino cape.

"I've got some lavender milk drops in the fridge," said Rosemary.

Delia shook her head. "No, I'm fine, thank you. It's just a lot to adjust to, this magic stuff."

Rosemary gave a little laugh. "I'm still adjusting, and I've been here almost a year."

Delia looked from Marjie to Rosemary, confused, then back to Marjie. "Your daughter didn't grow up with magic?" she asked, taken aback.

Marjie's eyes crinkled in a smile as she sipped her tea. "Daughter?"

Delia blushed. "Oh, I just assumed...the way you talk about Rosemary."

"We do feel like family," said Rosemary.

Marjie sighed. "I've never been blessed with children of my own. Which is probably a good thing, considering certain unforeseen issues with my marriage." Rosemary gave her a sympathetic look. "However, just as Rosemary said, she and Athena are family, so you're not far off."

# 37
## MARJIE

W arm sun streamed through the windows of Thorn Manor, bathing the kitchen in its gentle glow. As usual, the space was filled with an air of tranquillity, interrupted only by the soft sounds of Rosemary's movements in the kitchen.

Marjie sat at the table, clutching her tea for emotional comfort. Its soothing aroma seemed to contrast the chaos that had overtaken her life recently. As she took a sip, she found herself watching Delia, who was lost in thought, sitting next to her at the table.

"You know," Delia said suddenly, breaking the silence, "I just had a strange thought, that this house feels...like a living thing. Preposterous, I know. But it's almost like it has a heart full of stories and warmth. Maybe it's just the rather unexpected events of the morning addling my brain..."

Rosemary shot her a grin from the kitchen. "You're not wrong. Thorn Manor is one of my best friends. I'm sure of it!"

Marjie smiled faintly. "Yes, and it has witnessed joy, pain, and changes." The weight of her lost home pressed on her, but she pushed the sorrow away. She had been wanting to move on from that place for a while, but the suddenness of its loss was jarring.

Delia raised an eyebrow, studying Marjie. "You're strong, Marjie. I can tell. I'm sure you're much stronger than you give yourself credit for."

Marjie looked down, fidgeting with her tea cup. "Sometimes, strength is the only choice we have."

Her secrets – what she knew of the legendary Crones and their magic – pressed on her consciousness. The need to share was overwhelming, but now wasn't the time, and she knew its strength lay in secrecy.

Delia leaned forward, her voice soft. "You know, it's okay to lean on others sometimes."

The delightful scent of chocolate and peppermint wafted across the room.

Marjie took a deep breath and another sip of tea. "Thank you, Delia. Just...thank you." She might not be able to share just yet, and she certainly wasn't going to talk about Herb again, or all the memories made in that old cottage that had just gone up in smoke, but in this moment, in the cosy warmth of Thorn Manor and in the company of friends, she felt less alone.

Delia returned the gratitude with a smile that reached her eyes, the sort of smile that said she understood, even if she didn't know all the specifics. The moment lingered, a shared understanding of trust, when the soft clinking of porcelain interrupted their thoughts.

Marjie topped up her tea from the pot and took another sip, feeling the warmth spreading through her. "Sometimes, it's the little moments that matter the most," she whispered, more to herself than anyone else.

Delia looked at her, eyes filled with recognition.

Rosemary sat down, joining in the quiet celebration of resilience. "To new beginnings," she murmured, the three women clinking their cups together.

Marjie sighed contentedly. Yes, her house had burned down and, yes, the uncertainty of the future loomed large. But just as the unknown dangers ahead loomed larger, so too did the excitement stirring within her – for new magic and new friendship – and in that moment she felt fortified. As she nibbled on a truffle, she allowed herself a silent wish, hoping with all her might that her newfound emotional strength would be enough to overcome the enemy – whoever they really were.

# 38
## DELIA

A cloud of green smoke erupted from the kitchen, causing Rosemary to cough and splutter as she apologised profusely.

Marjie quickly opened the windows while Rosemary excused herself and left the room to get cleaning supplies.

Delia took a deep breath, inhaling the strong scent of lavender. "If she's not your daughter, then who exactly is she?"

"That," said Marjie, glancing in the direction Rosemary had just disappeared to, "is one of the most powerful witches of our time."

"Oh, yes?" Delia said, allowing herself to feel amused.

The smoke cleared rather quickly, revealing it wasn't smoke at all, but some kind of magical mist.

Delia and Marjie returned to their tea and some pleasant conversation. Marjie had yet to explain anything properly. Despite this, Delia sensed a stirring of excitement.

In fact, wiggling her fingers and toes, she noticed she felt more invigorated and alive than she had in a very long time.

"You know, I think I could get used to this magic stuff," she said.

Marjie gave her a knowing smile. "Of course you will, dear. You're a natural."

Delia raised an eyebrow. "If I'm such a natural, then why am I only finding out about this now?"

"It happens, sometimes," Marjie replied as Rosemary re-entered the kitchen with a determined look on her face. "Rosemary herself was late to magic, weren't you dear?"

"Yes," said Rosemary. "I only found out about a year ago."

"Sometimes families bury their powers for one reason or another," Marjie explained. "Rosemary's grandmother, a dear friend of mine, was a powerful witch herself. However, she had to hide from a certain secret society which we shall not name."

Delia suspected this society might have something to do with the unfortunate circumstances surrounding Marjie's ex-husband's death. But now did not seem to be the time to ask about that.

"Galdie Thorn decided it was in everyone's best interest to bind the family's magic, even though it made her virtually powerless compared to her former self. She did it to protect Rosemary, Athena, and their entire lineage," Marjie continued.

"Sure she was trying to protect us," Rosemary said, her tone disapproving. "But it did create problems. Do you think that might have happened in your family?"

Delia laughed. "I can't imagine either of my parents being magical. For starters, they're both accountants."

"Nothing wrong with a bit of magical bookkeeping, dear," Marjie quipped.

"But my grandmother...come to think of it, I've been dreaming of her a lot lately. Maybe she was a witch, if witches do exist," Delia replied, still finding the concept a bit hard to believe.

"Which they do," Marjie added encouragingly. She seemed excited by Delia's brief description of Etty as a rather wise and wild old bat. "She sounds like my kind of witch!"

"I think she used to come here, to Myrtlewood."

"Did she now?" said Rosemary.

"I wonder if we even met," Marjie added.

"Oh, you would have been a child," Delia replied. "She passed away a long time ago."

Though sometimes the grief felt much more recent. They had been quite close, after all.

"It can skip generations, you know," said Rosemary. "Granny Thorn had two children; only one of them was magical. My father certainly isn't. He's a professional missionary along with my mother. They can hardly have a single conversation with me without bringing out their bibles and trying to save my soul."

"My condolences," Delia said.

Rosemary threw back her head and laughed. "I like this one. Let's keep her around."

Footsteps echoed through the house. A young woman, the spitting image of Rosemary but with straight hair and more tanned skin, appeared.

"This is my daughter Athena," said Rosemary. "This is Marjie's new friend, Delia. We like her."

"Hi," said Athena, without much enthusiasm.

Delia refrained from making a comment about moody teenagers, which was just as well because in a few moments, Marjie had succinctly described the poor girl's plight. A teenage breakup was one thing, but losing her girlfriend to the underworld and not knowing how to get her back was quite another.

"The winter solstice is our best shot," said Athena, folding her arms. "You don't happen to know anything about that, do you? We've asked everyone in town by now."

Delia shook her head. "I'm afraid I'm a bit lost when it comes to all of this."

"Oh." Athena slumped down in her chair.

"I'll make you a hot chocolate, love," Rosemary said. "Then we can go through some more of Agatha's books."

"Okay," Athena replied with a sigh. "I have to say, Agatha might be grumpy and tense, but her library is amazing. If it wasn't the worst timing, I'd be thrilled to have access to all these books..."

The girl slumped forwards even further. It was clear she was dealing with serious emotional turmoil. Delia could not imagine wanting to go back to being a teenager in a million years, nor even a parent of one. Gillian had had a tough time with all the hormones and exuberance of youth.

Delia tried to convey her empathy by remaining silent; there weren't many words she could come up with that seemed appropriate – that weren't in the form of mildly offensive curse words, anyway.

Glancing at her phone, Delia found another email from Jerry and one from her lawyer.

Her blood boiled as she read it; her now most certainly former-lawyer explained that Jerry had a good case for taking everything that Delia owned and had worked for over several decades in their entire business – due to her actions which Jerry was calling defamation and slander, and the fact that Delia had set fire to his personal items at the theatre.

To top it off, Jerry was proposing to shut down their entire business and declare bankruptcy. At first, Delia was shocked until she realised he would liquidate it and set up a new company, taking all the assets with him. He was trying to weasel everything away – everything Delia had worked so hard to build. He might as well have been the one to set her life on fire.

"That flaming pile of excrement!" she said aloud, and at that, the kitchen sink burst into flames.

"What have you done now, Mum?" Athena asked, looking at Rosemary, who stared wide-eyed at her flaming sink before summoning magical water to douse the flames. The kitchen filled with steam again.

"That wasn't me," said Rosemary, startled. "I didn't even know metal was flammable."

Delia sighed. "I'm sorry. I think it must have been me."

Marjie merely grinned.

"Impressive for someone new to magic," said Rosemary. "I didn't set anything on fire for ages, maybe not until that stupid brat insisted on gate-crashing the school that was being run from this house and I blew up the greenhouse."

"Ah yes," said Delia flatly as Rosemary continued to ramble. "I'm sorry about your sink," she said when she could get a word in. Clearly, it was not in one's best interest to mortally offend or make enemies with one of the most powerful witches in the magical world.

Rosemary waved a hand dismissively. "Never mind that," she said, her tone light-hearted. "However, it's in my nature to be suspicious of strangers. Would you care to explain what you're doing in Myrtlewood? And why you happened to set my sink on fire?"

Delia sighed. "A lot of that comes down to my ex-husband." She gave them a brief summary of her situation, which elicited sympathetic silence, several knowing looks, and nods of understanding.

"If it was me, I might have set the whole house on fire," Athena chimed in.

"Kind of you to say," Delia replied as dryly as she could.

Marjie chortled. "I think you're going to fit in just fine around here."

Delia smiled, feeling a warm and joyful sensation so rare to her that it was a bit of a shock to the system.

She beamed back at Marjie. "You know, I think you might just be right."

# 39
## THE ROGUE

Declan had continued to observe the chaotic scene below him from his vantage point in the oak tree, the cottage consumed by flames, the red-cloaked guards shouting and scrambling. Despite the violence of the situation, the laughter still bubbled in his chest. He couldn't help but admire the ingenuity of the witches.

The way they had escaped, floating above the town in a magical bubble, was both whimsical and clever. It was a tactic he'd never seen before, and in his long life, he had seen much. The notion that there was still magic that could surprise him was both exciting and terrifying.

He should be back at camp, preparing his lunch, but still, he waited in the oak, and he watched.

The guards were now frantically trying to douse the flames, their red cloaks flapping like wings of strange birds. The scene looked surreal, like a frame from one of those old movies he used to enjoy.

He waited until the Order members had cleared off, and the town's fire fighters had come to tend to the blaze. They were too busy to notice him slip silently down from the oak tree and begin walking.

The knuckle bones, still warm in his hand, pulsed with energy. They were an ancient tool, but their magic was as sharp as ever. Through them, he could still sense the witches' presence, their magic trail like a glowing thread weaving through the sky.

A sudden realisation hit him. He could follow that trail if he wanted to. He could keep track of the witches and see where they went.

But why would he? He had no follow up orders yet. He was hired to locate the fire witch, not to follow her and her escapades around like a lost puppy.

Yet something about this case gnawed at him, tugging at his conscience. The fire witch, was not just another target. She was different. Her magic was raw, powerful, and unique. And her eyes, those haunting eyes, seemed to see right through him.

He shook his head, trying to clear the wayward thoughts. He was a professional, a rogue for hire. He had no business getting involved in the affairs of witches and secret orders.

He reached into his rucksack again, his fingers brushing against various magical artefacts and tools he carried. They were all there for a purpose, each one with a specific use. Yet now, he felt a sense of disconnection from them, as if they were relics from a different life.

The Order's intentions were clear as mud, but either they wanted the witches dead or they wanted to use them, manipulate them for their own gain, and then dispose of them. It was a plan as old as time, and one he had seen play out again and again.

Delia was oblivious and he was complicit in her peril. He found himself wishing he could warn her, tell her to be careful, to watch her back. But that was not his place. He was just a hired hand, bound by contract and duty.

As he walked, a sudden gust of wind rustled the leaves around him, and he shivered, despite the warmth of the day. A sense of foreboding settled over him. The game was far from over, and he knew, deep down, that he was not yet done with the fire witch.

He could report back to the Order and wash his hands of the whole affair. But something held him back. A feeling, a nagging thought that he was missing something crucial.

With a sigh, he continued walking, following the strongest strands of magic still trailing through the air, his mind a whirl of conflicting emotions and thoughts.

This was not just another job. It was something more, something that touched a part of him he thought was long buried.

He would continue to watch. For now, he was bound by duty. But the day might come when he would have to choose.

And when that day came, he wondered, would he have the strength to do what was right by his contract, or risk breaking it and unleashing the ancient magic his oath had staved off for centuries? Declan shivered. He had been running for a long time. Was it time to face his shadow, or would he simply continue to drift, without higher purpose? In an eternal life the questions were never-ending.

# 40
## DELIA

elia shifted her gaze from Rosemary to Athena and then back to Marjie. "Now are you finally going to tell me what's going on with all this Crone stuff?" she asked.

"About what, dear?" said Marjie sweetly, stuffing a truffle in her mouth. "Oooh, these are delicious." She glanced at her wrist, which did not have a watch. "Perhaps we should get going."

Delia narrowed her eyes, noticing Marjie's nervous glance towards Athena and Rosemary who were observing them with interest.

"Crone?" Rosemary asked.

"Just an inside joke," Marjie replied quickly. "I'll try to explain it to you later."

Delia planted her hand on her hip, about to protest, when Marjie interrupted her. "Come on, let me show you the garden."

Marjie took Delia's hand and promptly led her through the large living room, out French doors, and onto a pleasant lawn surrounded by forest. "I can't talk about it in front of them," Marjie whispered urgently.

Delia frowned. "Oh, I see. Are you going to explain it to me? Or can you not talk about it in front of me either?"

"Well, that's the problem," said Marjie. "*I* think that I can...but Agatha is not convinced."

"Look," said Delia. "I don't like being mucked around."

"Of course you don't," said Marjie apologetically. "But perhaps you'd be better off if I left the explaining a little longer. I don't know everything myself. Agatha knows more than me, and I dare say, Ingrid probably knows the most."

"Just tell me what you can," said Delia, tugging impatiently at her own sleeve. She needed answers or something else was bound to burst into flames at any moment.

"Well...suffice it to say, there are legends of the four Elemental Crones – powerful older witches of Myrtlewood charged with protecting the town."

Delia felt a tingle down her spine at those words, though she wasn't sure why.

"But legends...that means it's not true?"

Marjie laughed. "Don't be silly, dear. Legends are almost always true. The problem is, there are so many different tellings of them, we never know which ones actually happened."

Delia shrugged. "I suppose that makes some kind of sense...But why aren't you allowed to tell me? Why aren't you allowed to talk about these Crones?"

"Well, Agatha says we mustn't, but I disagree, and she's not here so I'll say this: from what I gather, it's an ancient and secret power that could awaken at any moment, if a particular threat returns," Marjie explained.

"That particular threat..." said Delia. "Would it happen to be related to the ambush we experienced earlier?"

Marjie didn't say a thing.

"Fine, you can't tell me," said Delia. "But perhaps you could just nod if I'm on the right track."

Marjie inclined her head right down towards her chest.

"Subtle," Delia teased.

Marjie wrinkled her nose and smirked.

Delia laughed, feeling suddenly like a child again. "It's all rather exciting, isn't it?"

"Really dear? I thought you'd be bewildered and ready to run miles away by now."

"I don't know," said Delia. "I'm always up for a good performance; it's just never felt so real before."

"Real and dangerous, I'm afraid," said Marjie gravely.

"So, back to the attack earlier..." said Delia. "Did those men come after us because they suspect we might be the legendary Crones?"

Marjie sighed. "I suppose I'd better tell you now. You might say that there have been certain signs of a particular threat stirring for some time now. That's why Agatha and I are determined to find the four Crones of Myrtlewood. We believe that we might be among them."

"And Ingrid and me?" Delia asked.

Marjie nodded. "Ingrid we agree on. Agatha is not sure about you."

Delia shrugged. "That's okay, I'm not offended."

"Good," said Marjie. "But I'm sure. And it sounds like Ingrid thinks so too. I daresay she wouldn't have shown you such hospitality if you were just a random straggler in the forest."

Delia's lip quirked into a half-smile. "I think she quite liked me, actually."

Marjie pouted a little. "You know, most people like me. I'm a feeder and I'm always looking out for people, but that Ingrid is a tough cookie."

"I can tell," said Delia. "Alright...so what happens next?"

Marjie sighed again. "It's been a rough day."

"Your poor house..."

"Well, I can't go back there, can I? And neither can you. Besides, I can't very well rent out a house that's already been destroyed by magical flames. We might want to take precautions."

"Excuse me?" said Delia.

"Well, our escape earlier might have given us an advantage, you know," said Marjie.

"You mean those red-cloaks might think we're dead?"

"They didn't see us escape, did they?" Marjie pointed out.

"But if they're around here it won't be too long until they spot us," said Delia. "I mean, one of them attacked me right in the middle of London."

She looked out into the forest, half-expecting a troop of red-hooded soldiers to appear, but it all seemed perfectly normal.

"Well..." said Marjie. "We might need disguises."

Delia cocked an eyebrow. "I'm listening?"

Delia and Marjie returned to the kitchen, giggling.

"What are you two up to?" Rosemary asked.

"It's a secret," Marjie replied. "I'll tell you when you're sixty."

Delia laughed.

"I just need to do something," said Marjie. "Actually, Delia, you'd better come with me."

"All right," Delia agreed happily, following her new friend. She felt like a twelve-year-old at a sleepover party. "What are we doing?" she asked as they passed through a room filled with small beds, like an old-fashioned nursery, and then continued on down a corridor until they entered a rather grand room.

"This is my bedroom," Marjie explained. "It's one of the guest rooms here, but it's mine for now. There are plenty of rooms here – you can stay the night. It might not be safe to be seen in Myrtlewood yet."

"Depends on how good your disguises are," said Delia.

"I'm going to phone Agatha," Marjie said. "You can look in that trunk over there. That's where most of my costume items are."

Delia, delighted, pored through the quality costumes that had been skilfully handmade while Marjie made a rather cryptic phone call to the notorious Agatha Twigg.

# 41

## THE CLERIC

The Cleric ascended the narrow staircase that led to Father Benedict's chamber in the heart of their stronghold, his heart pounding like a drum in his chest.

Each step added weight to the bad news held in his moist palms. His sweat made the parchment he carried damp; the ink smudged a little, as if trying to escape its duty of bearing the unfortunate tidings.

He couldn't stop his hands from trembling. He felt like a schoolboy called to the headmaster's office, an absurd thought given his position.

With each step, he replayed the failed operation in his mind, seeking some detail, some minor error that could be corrected, some excuse he could present to the Shepherd. But the reality was unchangeable.

The stone walls of the staircase seemed to close in on him as he neared the top, the flickering torchlight throwing monstrous shadows that danced and contorted with his mounting dread.

As he reached the landing, he hesitated before the door. The wooden barrier between him and his superior was etched with their ancient sigils, symbols of the promises they'd made and the duty they carried. Those glyphs seemed to sear into his conscience like a brand.

He inhaled, his hands trembling as if they were doing a juggling act of their own, and he knocked on the door. A moment of heavy silence hung in the air before the Shepherd's deep voice boomed out an invitation to enter.

His breath hitched in his throat. The weight of their heritage bore down on him in that moment, a solemn reminder of the magnitude of his duty.

On the other side of the door, the Cleric realised he wasn't merely about to deliver news. He was about to reveal a twisted puzzle, a riddle that might just throw their whole mission, his whole life's work, into question.

The door swung open revealing Father Benedict, the Crimson Shepherd, tall and imposing.

He eyed the Cleric, unimpressed, then swept his hand through the air to invite him in.

The Cleric stepped into the stark, austere chamber. The room was as severe as its occupant, all stone and dark woods, illuminated by the dim light of guttering candles. Dominating the room was a large, intricate map filled with pins and markers – the visual representation of the Mission – the role he had been born to serve, the very same one that had just suffered a significant setback.

"What news?" Father Benedict asked.

"The—the f—fire witch has...err...well," the Cleric stammered.

"Speak clearly," Father Benedict commanded.

The Cleric bowed his head. "Yes, Shepherd."

"Now, start from the beginning. What happened with Operation Delta?"

"Here is the report," the Cleric said, handing over the wilted scroll.

Father Benedict took it, abruptly tearing the parchment from the Cleric's grasp.

"A fire?" he said gruffly.

The Cleric nodded. "We should have suspected as much...she is a fire witch, after all. However, we never guessed she'd set the whole house alight with her and the other witch inside – the one from the teashop—"

"I can read," Father Benedict interjected.

"Forgive me, Shepherd." The Cleric bowed his head.

He knew the Crimson Shepherd would be displeased at the news, but there was a darkness in his expression, a dangerous ferocity that the Cleric hadn't anticipated.

"We've lost several of our guard – as you can see."

The Shepherd waved his hand dismissively. "To die in the line of duty is an honour."

The Cleric bowed his head, but this time it was simply to hide his own expression. The sentiment might seem noble, but senseless death was inexcusable, and there was no good reason those men had to die. If they'd anticipated the fire witch's behaviour more accurately, planned more carefully, they would have avoided fatalities.

"This scroll has no details on the witch," said Father Benedict slowly. "What happened? Where did she go?"

The Cleric cleared his throat, knowing that the Shepherd would not like the answer. "That remains unclear."

"Unclear?!"

"Yes, Shepherd. It is of course possible that she and the other witch perished in the blaze, however we have no remains..."

"No," said the Shepherd. "That is a contingency we cannot waste time on. She must have escaped."

The Cleric nodded his head gravely.

"The tracker?" Father Benedict asked.

"She has eluded him," the Cleric said, keeping his gaze focused on the Shepherd's angry face. His voice echoed slightly off the cold stone walls.

The Shepherd gave no immediate response. His eyes, cunning and penetrating, held the Cleric's gaze. When he spoke, his voice was as deep and grating as shifting boulders.

"How?"

The Cleric swallowed. "That is inconclusive."

"How?" the Shepherd bellowed. "How is this possible? She was naïve to magic. That much is certain. How does a witch who knows nothing of her power elude the best tracker in the country and barbeque five trained guards?!"

A heavy silence fell. The Shepherd's features remained unmoved, but his eyes bore into the Cleric, making him feel as if he were an ant under a magnifying glass.

"We underestimated her," the Shepherd finally said. "The elders were right. The fire witch is a bigger threat than we thought. Our approach to the mission needs revision. Operation Delta was designed to trap her, corner her, make her a pawn in our chess game, but she refuses to play. It was my plan, but I must take penance."

The silence was deafening. The Cleric didn't know how to reply. It was rare to see his superior humbled like this. He'd never heard of the man ever admitting to a mistake before. The Cleric had expected to be blamed for the failed operation – to be made an example out of, perhaps even to lose his title and position – but the Crimson Shepherd did not stoop to blame. The Cleric couldn't help but feel a welling respect for him.

Finally, Father Benedict spoke again. "Too many years have been spent on The Mission. We cannot afford any more mistakes."

The Cleric made a sound of agreement before adding, "Even the best-laid plans meet with unexpected obstacles. If she lives as you so believe, we will locate the fire witch and The Mission will proceed as intended."

For a moment, Father Benedict held his gaze, and the Cleric felt a ripple of unease. But then the Shepherd nodded.

The Cleric felt the tension in his shoulders ebb away, replaced by a renewed resolve.

He bowed and exited the chamber, closing the heavy door behind him.

The echo of the closing door seemed to reverberate with the enormity of the task at hand – the mission was in jeopardy, and it was his responsibility to set things right. For his part, the Cleric swore to find the Fire Witch and ensure that The Mission was back on track, no matter the cost.

# 42

## AGATHA

Agatha Twigg sat in her lavish library, surrounded by ancient texts, maps, and historical artefacts. The grand fireplace burned steadily, keeping the cold winter's day at bay. The fire's flicker cast a golden glow over her carefully organised desk, where she was immersed in an old tome. A glass of sherry sat beside her, untouched, as her eyes moved over the lines with a scowl. Her mind kept drifting away from the important focus on books to other more irritating developments.

Delia, that newcomer, was causing more trouble than Agatha cared to deal with. The woman's presence had sent ripples through Myrtlewood, and Agatha was none too pleased. She was even more grumpy about Marjie's cheerfulness over the whole affair, and the looming necessity to consult Ingrid, the most cantankerous woman in all of Cornwall, did little to lift her spirits.

And then there was the matter of the Myrtlewood Crones. A fear tugged at Agatha's heart. She'd wanted nothing more than to be one of the fabled Crones, her entire life. Even as a young child, she was always a crone at heart. She didn't mind being teased about wearing cardigans when the other children wore more transient fashions. She'd always preferred books and libraries to parties and dances, tea and toast to soda pop and cookies. Agatha was a natural born crone and she'd studied all her life for this.

What if she wasn't one of them? The idea gnawed at her very soul.

As Agatha's thoughts spiralled, the shrill ring of the telephone jarred her from her contemplation. With a growl, she stalked over to the phone, picked up the receiver, and barked, "Twigg here. Speak!"

"Agatha, it's Marjie," came the voice from the other end. Her voice was cautious, measured. "Fudgesticks."

Agatha's heart skipped a beat at the code word. She glanced over her shoulder as though expecting to find someone eavesdropping. "Fudgesticks?" she repeated, her voice lowering to a whisper.

"Yes, fudgesticks," Marjie confirmed.

"So what now?"

"The recipe needs some adjustment. Perhaps a new ingredient or two."

Agatha's mind whirred as she decoded the message. "I see. And what of the other cook? Has she been informed?"

"Not yet," Marjie said casually. "But the kitchen is getting crowded, Agatha. We do need to consult the head chef."

Agatha's lips thinned at the mention of Ingrid. "Must we? You know how she can be with her recipes."

Marjie's sigh was audible even over the phone. "I'm afraid so, dear. It's a delicate dish, and we can't afford to spoil it."

"I never thought I'd see the day when fudgesticks would cause so much trouble," Agatha muttered, her voice heavy with resignation.

"It's a strange world we live in," Marjie agreed. "But we'll make it through. Just remember to keep stirring, Agatha."

"I will," Agatha said, a determined edge to her voice. "I always do."

With that, she hung up the phone and returned to her chair, her mind abuzz with the coded conversation.

"Fudgesticks!" Agatha cursed.

Delia was more than just a mere annoyance; she was a part of something much bigger, something that threatened to upheave everything Agatha held dear.

She stared into the flames, her thoughts dark and tumultuous. If they were going to navigate this storm, they would need all the help they could get, even if that meant disturbing Ingrid.

With a sigh, Agatha picked up her sherry, finally taking a sip. The warmth spread through her, but it did little to ease the chill in her heart. The game was afoot, and whether she was a legendary Elemental Crone or not, Agatha Twigg would be ready to play her part.

# 43

## DELIA

"What have you got there?" Marjie asked as she hung up the old-fashioned telephone.

"These are brilliant!" Delia said, holding up a ball gown that looked like black spider webs. "But I'm not sure if we'll blend in, unnoticed."

"That's a fair point," Marjie conceded, studying Delia. "That red streak in your hair is very recognisable. Perhaps I could glamour it into being more subtle. In fact, we don't need costumes, we need ordinary clothes."

She opened her wardrobe, revealing a sea of floral prints. "Hmmm," Marjie said, picking out a couple of pinafores. With a wave of her hand, the colours faded to grey. "That'll do," she declared, handing one to Delia. "Put this on and I'll resize it for you."

Delia shrugged and donned the slightly large dress, along with a little jacket that Marjie handed her.

Moments later, with a bit of magical assistance, the outfit fit her perfectly.

"Now I look a little like an accountant," Delia noted.

"You will in a minute," Marjie replied. "Let me see that face."

Delia felt a tingling sensation as Marjie waved her hand around her head.

"Perfect," Marjie said.

Delia looked in the mirror. Her hair, which had recently grown longer and wilder, had now shrunk, transformed into a straight silver bob. All the red was hidden.

"Now you look like an unnoticeable old woman," Marjie observed.

"You know, people complain about being unnoticed," Delia responded, "but I don't mind being invisible...at least ninety percent of the time."

"Well, I tend to stand out wherever I go," Marjie admitted, "though not in this outfit."

She too was looking rather grey, changed into the more mundane attire, her hair transformed to look similar to Delia's.

"Now we're twins." Delia smirked.

"Oh, you're right. It's too similar," Marjie remarked, tweaking her appearance again until she bore a striking resemblance to Queen Elizabeth the second. Delia was about to suggest that Marjie could make a living as a celebrity lookalike. With a bit of white powder she could play the former queen's ghost at parties, but before Delia had time to form the thought into a witty sentence, the door flew open and Agatha Twigg burst into the room.

"You two!" Agatha exclaimed, jaw dropping at the sight of them. "What kind of trouble have you two got yourselves into this time? And what in Hades are you wearing? What's wrong with your hair? You both look old!"

"We are old," Marjie retorted, her tone amused.

Agatha frowned at her. "Is someone going to explain to me what really happened? All I gathered from your phone call was that there was some sort of attack. You did use the code for 'attack,' didn't you?"

"I certainly did," Marjie confirmed, her expression serious. "Fudgesticks."

Agatha nodded grimly and glared at the telephone which promptly exploded.

"What did you do that for?" Marjie grumbled, waving her hand in the air to clear the yellow smoke which the explosion produced.

Delia gaped as she stared at the device. The smoke smelled of lemon and mint, which wasn't all that bad, but she did have to do a quick reality check. Finding herself firmly in a land of nonsense, she returned her attention to the matter at hand.

"Now that we're away from any wires that could be tapped," Agatha said, "would you do me the courtesy of explaining exactly what's going on and why you're both dressed like retired sister wives?"

"We're in disguise, of course," Marjie interrupted, before filling Agatha in on the events that had unfolded at her cottage a couple of hours earlier.

Agatha, for possibly the first time during Delia's short acquaintance with her, looked impressed.

In fact, she was positively beaming and seemed ten years younger as she roared with laughter. "That's brilliant," she said. "That firepower of yours is not to be trifled with."

"Oh no," said Delia, in a wave of guilt. She turned to Marjie. "It wasn't me, was it? Did I set your house on fire?"

"It's for the best, dear," Marjie reassured her. "I couldn't stand to be there. And you probably didn't want to live in that place either, not after what happened with Herb."

"It was a bit morbid, I have to say," said Delia. "I wasn't trying to be an arsonist, but—"

"But nothing," said Marjie. "All's well that ends well. And that house had it coming. Besides, I'm perfectly happy here, and Rosemary and Athena love having me around. It's nice to be wanted, you know?"

Delia tried to smile, but it turned into a grimace. She wished Gillian wanted her around.

"Have you eaten a lemon?" Agatha asked, eyeing Delia's expression.

Delia shrugged. "I don't want to go into the details."

"What do we do now?" Marjie said, directing the question towards Agatha.

"Why do you keep treating me like I'm the leader?" Agatha smirked.

"Because you always insist on being the leader. So it saves time if I ask for your opinion," Marjie shot back.

Agatha snorted. "Alright then." Her beady eyes stared at Delia. "Whether you are or are not one of us—"

"A mythical Crone, you mean?" Delia said.

"Did you tell her!?" Agatha asked Marjie, appalled.

"Nope. She's just figured it out. She's very bright, this one," Marjie responded.

Agatha scowled and looked away, clearly not convinced.

"Besides, we hardly know anything," Marjie continued.

"And I know even less," Delia interjected. "Aside from having deduced, with the brilliant power of my wit and overhearing *your* conversations at the pub, quite frankly, that there are some legendary Crones of Myrtlewood. And nobody actually knows who they are yet. But there's some sort of mysterious, ancient threat, and the Crones are charged with protecting the world from it."

"Ah, yes," Marjie said, sounding satisfied. "That about sums it up."

"Brilliant powers of deduction you have," Agatha grumbled in response.

"Well, at first I thought I was being attacked by my ex-husband's B-grade theatre troupe," said Delia. "But these blokes are going to extremes that far exceed even the most dramatic thespians I know."

Agatha's lips twitched with amusement. "And you're in disguises. This might be brilliant actually, if they think you are dead. Except that they'll come after me."

"And your poor niece," said Marjie.

Agatha laughed. "If they try and attack the farmhouse, they'll have another think coming. That place is booby-trapped up to the nines. Besides, Marla happens to be one of the most dangerous people I've ever met."

It was Marjie's turn to raise an eyebrow. "And they let her teach children..."

"Children are almost as dangerous," Agatha said drily, before turning her attention back to Delia and Marjie, frowning again at their outfits. "In any case, I don't think Delia should be returning home for now. Are you inviting us all to stay here?" She looked around the room appraisingly.

"It's not my place to do that. It's Rosemary's house," Marjie reminded them. "Though I'm sure she won't mind. I suppose I can ask, if that's what's needed."

"And what?" said Delia. "We just sit around and wait for them to figure it out and attack us again?"

"I don't think that's wise," said Agatha. "We need to go to Ingrid."

Marjie turned to her in surprise. "You really think—?"

"Look," said Agatha. "I don't know if Delia is one of us. I don't even know if *we* are 'one of us', so to speak."

"Ingrid seemed to think I am," Delia interjected, feeling rather stroppy. She didn't like being left out.

"Oh yes? Did she now?" Agatha asked, eyebrow raised.

"Yes," said Delia. "For some reason, the fact that I talked to a cat, or rather, that the cat talked to me, was the most convincing thing of all."

"And you didn't think to tell us that?" Agatha asked, sounding mildly annoyed.

"I didn't want you to think I was mad," Delia conceded.

"That Mephistos is trouble," Agatha muttered, "if ever I've seen it. But he insists he can only talk to the Crones."

"Oh yes," said Marjie. "That's why Agatha and I are fairly sure we are among them – though you can never completely trust a cat, as sweet as they can be sometimes."

"Mephistos is no cat," said Agatha. "He's something even more wily. I just haven't figured out what. But he is sure he can't talk to anyone else. That's why he gets so chatty with us whenever we go through that ridiculous forest."

"Well, that explains that," Delia mused. "When I told Ingrid about the cat, she started muttering about me being one of you. I thought she was talking about a cult."

"Oh no, we've had quite enough of that," Agatha assured her.

"That's what I said!" Marjie added.

"Right then." Agatha folded her arms. "What we need is a plan."

# 44

## MATHILDA

Mathilda paced the floor of the old farmhouse. She looked out through the windows as the waxing moon rose over the mountains, longing to be back at her home. Her feet fell heavy on the worn wooden planks. The outpost was a sparse, functional place, occasionally used for retreats by the Veiled Sisterhood, or for training purposes. But today, its silence was maddening.

Frustration gnawed at her as she approached the large, ornate black mirror on the wall. It was her connection to the Clochar, and she used it to report back to the elder sisters. No one had come, and Mathilda was impatient to return.

She recited the charm to activate the mirror.

With a flicker, the mirror's surface clouded and then cleared, revealing the faces of the elder sisters. Gwyneth's wise eyes met Mathilda's, and the sister's voice carried through the air, "No one is coming."

"Patience, Mathilda."

"I have been patient," Mathilda protested, her voice tinged with bitterness. "No one has come, and I am needed elsewhere."

"You must be patient," Sister Breag repeated, her voice calm and composed. "They will come. The Crone Moon is waxing. The hour is drawing near. You'll need not wait much longer, perhaps only a few days until the moon reaches its peak."

Mathilda's eyes narrowed, and she bit back her anger. "Why have I been chosen for this task and not one of the less experienced sisters?"

"You know why," Gwyneth replied, her gaze unwavering. "She is your blood. She will value that kinship bond even if she no longer cares for the Veiled Sisterhood, even though she has shunned our customs, our sacred traditions, our ways. But she'll listen to you. Help her. She and the other Crones can get into that library and get that book, but you must compel her — convince her to bring it to us for safekeeping. We are the only ones who can protect it. The four of them must come to live in our inner sanctum, to awaken their powers, to fortify themselves to face the threat."

Mathilda's heart ached at the mention of her sister. Jealousy flared within her; she didn't want her sister to steal her glory yet again, but she said nothing. She merely agreed with the sisters, saying, "Yes, I understand."

Turning away from the mirror, Mathilda moved towards the kitchen, her thoughts heavy. Her own sister wouldn't listen to the sisterhood anyway, so there would be no point in trying to coerce her. Resentment bubbled within her, as she felt that despite her lifetime in service, she was nothing more than a messenger, chosen for her blood ties to perform a menial task.

Then she shook herself. Humility was one of the values of the order and resentment its foe. She knew that the elder sisters were wise, that they chose her for this task for a reason. It was not about her, but about the greater good.

As she prepared a simple meal of oats and barley, Mathilda's thoughts returned to the dream that had awakened her. The phoenix, the ancient powers, the mission at hand. There was more at stake here than her pride or her place in the order. A battle was coming, and she would play her part.

Mathilda found some comfort in her reflection, in her duty. The weight of her jealousy and frustration lightened, replaced by a determination to do what was necessary.

The Sisterhood had called her, and she would answer, whatever the cost.

# 45

## DELIA

After several additional cups of tea and a couple of espresso truffles pilfered from downstairs, Marjie had decided their best course of action was to visit Ingrid. However, Agatha had decided against the idea, despite being the one to propose it in the first place. She folded her arms stubbornly and sat in one of the chairs next to the small table in Marjie's elegant room and glared at them. "It's too soon," she said for the third time in a row. "And besides, we don't want to bother her."

"How do you know it will be a bother?" asked Marjie.

"Isn't it always the way with Ingrid? Besides, if I were her, I wouldn't want to be bothered. I've been bothered enough as it is today," Agatha retorted, giving Marjie a reproachful look.

Marjie merely smiled merrily back at her.

Delia, ever the pragmatist, decided they weren't getting anywhere.

"Look, you two," she said. "This has been an interesting adventure so far, but I could use a nap. I might just go back to the pub if you don't mind."

"It's not safe," Marjie responded sternly. "We have to stick together."

Agatha waved her hand dismissively. "It'll be fine. They probably think that you're dead and that the Crones are no longer a threat. We can all go home and go back to minding our own business."

"Oh, don't be ridiculous," said Marjie. "I never thought I'd accuse you of wishful thinking, Agatha. But now it seems you're a blind optimist."

Agatha said shook her head.

"Why don't you want to go and see Ingrid?" Delia asked Agatha. "Do you have some better idea of what we should be doing?"

Agatha looked down at the ground. "To be perfectly honest, she scares me."

"That's understandable," said Delia. "But maybe she's turning over a new leaf. After all, she gave me some tea. Maybe she'll offer some to us."

"Now that's wishful thinking," Agatha scoffed. "You think the old hermit crone in the woods is about to throw us a tea party?"

"I've seen stranger things." Marjie chuckled. "Just about every seasonal festival, in fact."

Blaring notes from the Imperial March alerted Delia to her phone ringing. Kitty's name flashed up on the screen.

"Don't answer," said Marjie. "It might me our enemies testing if we're still alive!"

"Don't worry, it's my friend," said Delia. "I better take this or she might mount some kind of search party."

Delia popped out of the room to take the call. "Hello?"

"Darling! What are you up to? I've sent you at least three messages. I even popped round your flat and there was no answer."

Delia sighed. "I'm...out of town."

"You're joking," said Kitty. "When was the last time you did that without telling me? What's really going on, Deals? Have you met a new man?"

Delia had momentary flashes of several encounters with men, none of them of the warm and romantic variety. "Not exactly," she said. "Not the way you're thinking, anyway."

"Oh, really? Where are you exactly?" Kitty asked.

"A little seaside town in Cornwall," Delia responded. "It's a long story. But the short version is that Gilly has a fabulous new job nearby. And..." She searched for the words to try to explain. "I had this nice memory of my grandmother taking me here when I was a little girl and I thought, why am I mucking about in London in this tiny apartment, fretting over Jerry, when some fresh sea air would do me good?"

Kitty cackled a little. "Oh, that's fabulous, darling. Why didn't you tell me? I could have come along."

"I suppose I needed some alone time," Delia replied, trying to mask the nervousness in her tone.

"As if you haven't had enough of that already!"

"I'm an introvert at heart. You know that – despite my theatrical flair."

"So you say," said Kitty, a hint of suspicion in her voice. "I feel like there's more going on that you're not telling me."

"Why would you say something like that?" Delia asked defensively.

"I know you, Deals," Kitty responded. "And I know when you're hiding something from me."

Delia blew out a breath and slumped forward. She wished she could tell Kitty everything, but it was impossible. Just then, she caught her reflection in the hallway mirror. She looked positively haggard, with a strange grey bob and an equally grey Bobbsey Twin outfit. "Oh my gosh, what have I got myself into?" she muttered to herself.

"Just tell me the mafia aren't involved," Kitty chimed in. "I bet the Cornish mafia make a mean poisoned pasty."

"I'm sure that's culturally offensive," said Delia with a chuckle. "And no, there's no mafia to speak of."

Kitty chortled. "I've been reading too many spicy romance books. My imagination's run wild."

Delia couldn't help but giggle at that. If only Kitty knew how much imagination it would take to grasp the reality of the day Delia had actually had.

As much as she wanted to confide in someone from her old life, someone who represented a certain kind of stability, someone who was "normal," so to speak, she couldn't. It occurred to Delia that she barely knew Marjie or Agatha at all, yet here she was, embroiled in some sort of drama that might as well be a magical mafia. Cult or not, the situation was well outside her comfort zone.

"Just trust your gut," said Kitty. "You can tell me all about it later, when you've figured out how to."

Delia's mouth quirked into a smile. "Thank you. You know, I think you're right. I am going to trust my gut."

She hung up the phone and looked at herself in the mirror again. Her gut was telling her she needed time alone and a good nap. Not wanting to brook an argument, she hastily scrawled a note, leaving it in front of the bedroom. Marjie and Agatha were still clearly arguing inside.

As stealthily and quickly as she could, Delia made her way to the front of Thorn Manor. Based on the views she'd caught of the sea nearby, while they were travelling by bubble, Delia had a vague idea of which direction to head.

She was sure she wasn't far from the town. In fact, nowhere in Myrtlewood was very far. She could get into town, pick up her car from where she'd left it outside Marjie's tea shop, and head to the pub for some alone time and a good rest.

She could maintain her ridiculous disguise for now; she was sure nobody would recognise her, probably not even her own daughter.

That should be enough to keep her safe.

And when Marjie and Agatha were quite finished, maybe Delia could fit them into her busy schedule. Or perhaps she would have left town by then. She hadn't decided yet.

With only a moment's hesitation, Delia trusted her urge to take some control back over the situation.

With that thought, she headed off towards the township.

It occurred to Delia, as she began her walk down the quiet country lane, that despite the beautiful sunny winter day, she was incredibly exposed and vulnerable out here. The birds were singing and a gentle breeze drifted through the brambles and bare tree branches nearby, somewhat eerily. She considered turning back to Thorn Manor; it seemed reasonably safe there. But her desire for solitude was overwhelming.

She was suffering from a social hangover, that feeling she often experienced after a big performance. As soon as the curtain closed on the show, she wanted to shut herself away for a week and avoid any interaction. The day had been quite theatrical indeed.

She shook off the hesitation and continued on, ignoring a little tingle of fear.

What would Gilly think if her mother disappeared somewhere in Cornwall, never to be heard of again?

The thought was horrifying, and it was this, above all else, that terrified Delia at that moment, sending her thoughts spinning into dark places.

This inevitably led to her feeling even more bereft.

Had she really abandoned her life's work and her entire career? Did she have nothing else to live for other than being a mother who wasn't needed and a grandmother who hadn't seen anyone in her family for several weeks?

She sighed and continued on. "It's just a low point," she reminded herself. "There's always a low point in any play." Although, as she looked around, she began to wonder if she'd done the thing she always despised in stories – where the main character wandered off, putting themselves in unnecessary danger for some trivial reason.

"At least you can always set them on fire," she mumbled to herself, then laughed, realising she seemed absolutely batty. Regardless, she picked up her pace.

# 46

## THE ROGUE

The dusty gravel road crunched beneath Declan's boots as he tracked Delia towards the old manor house. He squinted at the building's facade, feeling an uncomfortable sense of recognition that he couldn't place. He squinted at the old manor house, a vague memory tugging at his mind.

Over the centuries, he'd trekked across this land many times, but memories faded over time. It was possible he'd been here before, or perhaps it was to a house much like it.

He was caught off guard when he spotted his mark. She strode determinedly away from the manor, clad in a ludicrous grey frock that looked like it belonged to a doll.

Her hair had changed too. Instead of the wild waves he'd stared at on the beach, streaked with red, she now had a silver bob. The disguise may have been a good one. She looked like a totally different person. Nevertheless, he recognised her instantly. His magic saw to that.

*What is she playing at?* Despite the disguise, being out here alone was rash and dangerous. *Does she not realise the Order is after her?*

Recognition flashed in her eyes as she approached him. "You again, cowboy!" she spat, her voice dripping with scorn.

"Cowboy?" His eyes widened in shock. His mind churned, but he kept his silence.

*What's her game? Why is she so brazen?*

"You look like a fool in that stupid hat, skulking around like a scared rat." Delia glared at him. "You're in league with them, aren't you? You worthless, treacherous snake. I'll roast you alive."

Declan's jaw tightened. He wasn't here to exchange pleasantries, but it had been a long time since he'd been so directly and oddly insulted. "Watch your step," he replied, refusing to rise to her bait.

Her eyes narrowed. "You dare threaten me, Declan?"

Her words landed like a stab to his chest. He'd forgotten that he'd told her his real name. Not even the Order knew that.

Delia glared at him. "What do you have to say for yourself? You, who creeps around with those red-hooded cowards? You're one of them, aren't you? You're all the same!"

"I'm no puppet," Declan growled, taking a step closer. "And I'm certainly not afraid of you."

She laughed, a harsh, jarring sound. "Afraid? You should be, you snivelling worm. I'll set you on fire!"

He held her gaze, his heart pounding. Her threats were real; he could see the fear behind her bravado. But he couldn't back down. "Try it," he said coolly.

He took a step closer, a silent challenge, but his mind was screaming at him to escape, to leave this case behind. He didn't know what he was doing here. He wanted out. But he couldn't break a contract. He had to see it through or his magic was at stake. What use was an immortal life without power?

There were always loopholes. He had some leniency on when he made reports, but he'd have to tell them about this encounter sooner or later.

The woman in front of him narrowed her eyes. Her threats were wild, absurd, yet Declan's heart beat faster, his body tense. He took another step, calling her bluff.

"Try it," he repeated quietly, though his thoughts were a chaos of fear, confusion, and a desperate longing to be free of this nightmare.

Her face twisted with rage. "You think I won't?"

He was about to respond when a blaring horn cut through the tension. He turned, just in time to see a cobalt blue Mini Cooper barrelling towards him.

The world seemed to slow as he leapt off the road. He felt the sting of gravel against his skin, the acrid taste of gravel dust in his mouth, the unforgiving embrace of brambles that scraped and tore at him. Panic clawed at his throat as he fell, the ground hard and unyielding beneath him.

He lay there for a moment, disoriented, feeling the echo of Delia's threats and the terror of almost being run over.

*What am I doing here?* he thought desperately, his mind a blur. *I need to escape this case. I don't belong here.*

But as the car's engine faded into the distance and the silent manor house loomed above him, he knew escape was no longer an option. He was trapped, drawn into a confrontation that he neither wanted nor understood. He felt the familiar tingle in his pocket. The summoning stone was activated. He had no choice. He had to meet with the Order again. He could only put it off so long. He was honour bound to tell them of Delia's whereabouts. He could put it off for a little while, but it wouldn't be long before the ties that bound his life together pulled taut and he'd have no choice but to play his part like a pawn on a chessboard.

# 47

## DELIA

Delia was jolted by the blaring horn as the tiny, cobalt blue Mini Cooper pulled up. Marjie and Agatha sat inside, looking incredibly cross.

Delia looked around, but the cowboy had disappeared.

"What were you thinking?" Agatha asked sternly.

Delia shrugged. "I needed fresh air."

"And who was that handsome man?" Marjie asked.

Delia narrowed her eyes. "I suspect he's no one we want to know."

Agatha shook her head. "Ridiculous! You just went wandering off to talk to potential enemies like a naïve child off with the fairies."

Delia took a deep breath and let it out slowly. "Look, you were the one saying we should just go about our lives."

"I didn't mean it," Agatha retorted. "Get in the car."

"You'd better do as she says," Marjie added.

Delia hesitated. "I don't know if I can fit."

"Don't be ridiculous," said Marjie, reaching over the back seat to open the door to reveal a dozen rows of wooden bench seats.

"What on earth?" said Delia. "It looks like a bus, an old-fashioned school bus, in fact."

Agatha frowned. "Marla used to use this car for school trips, back in the day. She's my niece, you know. She's a teacher."

Delia blinked and nodded.

"I just kept the enchantment in there because it's good for storing things, you know," Agatha explained, indicating the rows of seats covered in piles of old books. "I should really get it refitted for my own purposes, shouldn't I?"

"You always say that," Marjie responded, "but it's obviously not high enough priority for you."

"All right, we don't have all day," Agatha said.

Delia looked from one to the other. "Are you kidnapping me then? Do I not have a choice?"

"Well, where were you going?" Marjie asked. "It's not safe to be alone."

"Back to the pub, I suppose. I just need to have a lie down and some time to myself."

"That sounds perfectly sensible, dear," said Marjie as Agatha scowled. "We could have accommodated you at Thorn Manor, of course. But since it's obviously not what you're wanting...Why don't we all go to the pub?"

"Alrighty!" said Agatha so enthusiastically that Delia almost jumped. "Marvellous plan!"

"Okay then." Delia climbed into the spacious school-bus interior of the tiny car. Agatha zoomed off, driving rather like a cartoon race car driver with Delia holding on for dear life and hoping that the old bench seats wouldn't give her splinters.

By the time they reached the pub, Delia was reeling. The journey wasn't far, but it felt like a lifetime with her life flashing before her eyes, holding onto the seat in front of her for dear life. Delia made a vow to herself never to let Agatha drive her anywhere ever again.

"Are you quite alright, dear?" Marjie asked. "I'm sorry about Agatha's driving. You're not going to be sick, are you?"

Delia chuckled. "Lucky for us I don't get motion sickness, or you might have had to remodel the back just to clean up the mess."

Agatha chortled. "We'll be in the bar when you need us."

"Wait a minute. Why are we going to the pub when we're supposed to be hiding out in disguises?" Delia asked.

"We are in disguises!" Marjie enthusiastically gestured between her own grey outfit and Delia's. "Only people who know us well will recognise us now. It's part of the glamour."

"Glamour?" Delia said. "Oh, right...magic."

"And I don't need to be disguised," Agatha said, folding her arms. "I'm no wimp, and I wasn't in that housefire anyway."

Delia sighed. "None of this is making any sense. I'm going to have a *long* nap. And then I'll probably need something to eat, and I want to be alone."

"Of course you do, dear," Marjie said understandingly, as the three of them wandered into the Witch's Wort.

DELIA ENTERED her hotel room feeling famished and exhausted.

She launched herself onto the freshly made bed and groaned into the crisp sheets. Everything from the past day was starting to catch up with her, not to mention the past week.

There was rather a lot to take in and process.

Sure, she'd been called a wicked witch before, and much worse, when she was directing plays with particularly arrogant actors. Occasionally, they even said it to her face.

However, the actual identity of being a witch was another thing entirely.

What did it even really mean? Was there a handbook? She doubted it, given how chaotic the other witches she'd met were. Besides, maybe she didn't want to be a witch. What if she wanted to choose exactly what she was? She hated being told what to do, which was precisely why she became a director – so she could tell other people what to do instead.

There was a knock on the door, and Delia nearly shouted "go away!", but thought better of it. She didn't want to offend any powerful magical beings.

She got up and opened the door just a crack, ready to tell Marjie and Agatha politely to leave her in peace. Instead, it was Sherry standing there with a tray of delicious-smelling food.

"Marjie sent this up for you, love," said Sherry.

It smelled far too good to refuse, so Delia opened the door fully, allowing herself to be treated.

She tucked into the delicious beef pie with a side of chips and salad. She savoured every mouthful.

The sherry accompanying the meal was quite nice too, even though it was a bit sweeter than Delia's usual drink. Sherry (the person) had said it was a gift from Agatha Twigg – her own favourite drop.

After consuming the hearty meal, Delia felt full and sleepy. She deciding to lie down for a minute. A little nap would do her good. She quickly drifted off to sleep.

Delia had only meant to rest for twenty minutes or so, just to gather her bearings, before figuring out what she was going to do next. However, when the Darth Vader theme song blared rudely at her, she jolted awake and realised she'd been out for a couple hours.

"At least the attack of the crones won't be an issue anymore," she muttered to herself and then giggled at her own joke. Surely Marjie and Agatha would have moved on by now, and she could have some peace in the pub.

Reaching for her phone, she saw Gilly's name flashing on the screen and promptly answered. "Hello, my darling."

"Mum, what's going on?" said Gilly's scared-sounding voice. "The police called me. They said there's been a fire."

Delia felt her heart race. "Nothing to be worried about, dear."

"They said you were at the house that burned down – that you possibly hadn't survived. They asked me if I'd heard from you."

Delia's pulse beat, icy, through her veins. "Are you quite sure it was the police?"

"What do you mean?" Gilly asked angrily. "Of course it was. Who else would call me?"

"I think your father's playing tricks on me," Delia lied. The truth was far too strange to explain.

"No, that's ridiculous, Mum. He wouldn't do something like that."

"He's trying to work out where I am," said Delia. "I'm sure of it. And whoever he's employed to do it is nefarious. There was no housefire, just a small accident," she lied again. "He's sent some people after me. They're trying to scare me. That's partly why I came here. I think he's trying to drive me mad so I won't stand a chance in court."

"Sounds a bit far-fetched, Mum. Are you sure you're alright? You might need to see a doctor."

The thought had occurred to Delia, multiple times, that perhaps she'd hallucinated the past seventy-two hours of her life and did indeed need to see a doctor. However, her sharp wit concluded that if she was indeed barking mad, she didn't want to be locked up for it, so she might as well go along for the journey.

"I'm quite sane," Delia assured Gilly. "It's just the only conclusion I can come to. Just...don't talk to any strangers for a while."

"I don't like this, Mum. Something strange is going on. What really has been happening in Myrtlewood? It's a strange place, from what I hear." Gilly's voice was quite tense.

"Oh yes?" said Delia. "What do you know about it?"

There was a silence on the other end of the phone before Gilly sighed. "Never mind. I just...I think you might be better off in London."

"Nonsense," said Delia, although she had been wondering the same thing. "I was actually thinking I might rent a cottage here. The kids could come and stay with me – give you a bit of a break."

Gilly sighed again. "You know. I really could do with a break. The kids aren't adjusting to the...err...move...very well."

Delia had a flash of insight that perhaps she and her daughter were keeping just as many secrets from each other. However, this did not seem like the time to begin confessing, lest she find herself institutionalised. So instead, she made polite and reassuring noises as Gilly gave her a rather concise run-down of what was going on with her new job and the kids.

"Oh, by the way," said Gilly. "I've sent all your paperwork to a lawyer in Myrtlewood. He's very good."

"Is he the best?"

"Yes, I'd say so. He's got rather a lot of experience," said Gilly curtly.

"Oh yes?" said Delia. "Well, I suppose I should meet him."

"I've already made you an appointment," said Gilly. "That's partly why I'm calling. Well, that and to check if you're alive."

"I assure you I'm quite alive," said Delia.

Gilly coughed a little.

"Are you quite alright?"

"I'm fine, Mum," said Gilly. "Well, as fine as I'll ever be."

It didn't sound especially reassuring.

"Your appointment with the lawyer is on Thursday at one p.m. Will that be alright or have you got plans?"

"Not especially," said Delia, wondering what time of day was ideal for visiting an old forest witch and coming up blank.

"Look, I'll text you the details. The solicitor's name is Perseus Burk."

"Funny name," said Delia. "Thursday at one is fine."

"Brilliant," said Gilly. "I better go, Mum. I'm so glad you haven't been burned at the stake or anything."

"Why would you say a thing like that?" said Delia. "Oh...because of the fire."

There was an awkward pause.

"Talk soon, Mum," said Gilly. "Let me know how you get on with the lawyer."

"Yes, and I'll let you know if I find a house to rent too."

"Thanks, Mum," said Gilly. "I love you."

"I love you too," said Delia, feeling rather tender and vulnerable as she hung up the phone.

A new level of fear sank into her bones. Delia was certain whoever was after her knew about her daughter and even had Gilly's number. No ordinary police should have been able to track her down so quickly with so little evidence, given that the only people who knew they were there – other than those in red cloaks – were the handful they'd told about it already. Even if a neighbour had seen them, the chances of Delia being identified were slim.

It all seemed rather a stretch, however there was a thrilling freedom in the possibility that everyone in her old life might find out about the fire and assume that Delia had kicked the bucket. At least they wouldn't expect anything of her. Perhaps it wouldn't be the worst thing to burn down her entire old life – if the Telegraph shared the tragic news of the death of a well-loved director and former actor. It was rather liberating.

Delia continued mentally composing her own obituary – carefully avoiding thinking about the legal complications of accidentally faking her own death.

However, the sense of freedom was short-lived as dread sank in. Delia suddenly wished she hadn't brushed Agatha and Marjie off. She needed their help more than ever, especially now that her daughter might be in danger.

She decided to visit Thorn Manor, which seemed like the safest bet. However, she couldn't bear to stay in her current outfit a moment longer. She threw on some relatively normal black clothes and a red woollen cape. Glancing at herself in the mirror, she was pleased to see she was hardly recognisable with her new bob haircut. The disguise was probably fine.

Hearing cackling laughter downstairs, she found Marjie and Agatha sitting in a corner booth.

"You haven't left yet," said Delia. "It's been hours!"

"This is Agatha's second home," said Marjie. "Besides, I can't exactly go back to my shop. Papa Jack's closing up for me. I see you've changed your dress."

"Yes," said Delia flatly.

Agatha giggled. "Did you enjoy your sherry?"

"Yes, thank you both. The meal was much appreciated." She slumped into a seat at the table. "What now? Have you finished arguing yet?"

"What's wrong, love?" Marjie asked.

Delia grimaced. "Someone called my daughter claiming to be the police, asking if she'd heard from me."

"That's dreadful," said Agatha. "It certainly wasn't the police. Our lot are a bit slow, especially at the moment, with the only competent detective being off on parental leave."

"Besides, how would they know it was me in that house?" said Delia.

"Where does that leave us then?" said Marjie.

"I need more information," said Delia, her knuckles whitening as she gripped the edge of the table. "I need to know if Gilly is at risk. I need to protect her and the children. I need to know what this threat is and how to ensure they're safe."

"Well, we've told you what we know," Marjie responded, her usually cheery demeanour softened.

"You've told me hardly anything," Delia shot back. "You've essentially told me bugger all."

Marjie and Agatha exchanged a glance. Agatha cleared her throat. "We've given you what we have, Delia. But it's clear we need to dig deeper."

# 48

## MARJIE

Marjie folded her arms, glancing between Delia and Agatha. She chuckled. Somehow she'd found herself seated between two of the most argumentative women on the planet.

Agatha had always been a grump, and Delia was fiery and stubborn all at the same time. Marjie found, more and more, that she adored these friends, old and new.

"What are you looking so pleased about?" Agatha asked suspiciously.

"Just the turns of fate," Marjie muttered in response. Just then, she spotted Papa Jack by the bar. His tall frame was nearly swallowed by the shadows, but his eyes caught the light like two flints sparking a fire. He waved her over.

Marjie made her excuses to her companions and got up.

It was an odd sensation she experienced, like stepping into a painting; every move was tinged with a feeling that this was a world slightly off-centre. Perhaps Sherry had been a little too heavy on the charm for the mulled mead.

"Good to see you," Marjie said, beaming at Papa Jack.

"Marjie, my dear," said Papa Jack, his voice so deep it seemed to be dredged from the bottom of the ocean, "I've been looking after the shop as you asked, but..." He hesitated, eyes heavy with concern.

"But?" Marjie asked, tilting her head.

Papa Jack glanced around, as though worried the furniture might eavesdrop. "But I've been worried, is all. I heard about your house."

Marjie smiled warmly. "Oh don't worry yourself over that, my dear. It was faulty wiring – that's all. And besides, you know I'm living with Rosemary at Thorn Manor now."

Papa Jack gave her a questioning look. "There have been strange goings-on around the town."

Marjie chortled. "Stranger than usual?"

She didn't want to drag her good friend into this mess – she couldn't tell him about the Crone magic and the less worried he was the better.

Papa Jack knew her better than that. "You wouldn't be in any kind of danger now, would you?" His gaze was earnest, practically drilling into her soul.

"Oh, no...no, no," Marjie said, brushing off his concerns with a practiced wave of her hand. "You know I can take care of myself."

He reached for her hand and gave it a gentle squeeze, eyes locking onto hers. "I know you can, love, but if you ever need to talk, I'm here for you."

Marjie felt a sudden and inexplicable bafflement. The words were kind, caring even. They were words that had been said before, yet they felt new.

It had only been weeks since her husband, Herb, passed away in such complex circumstances. But Papa Jack had always been a light in the darkness, so kind and caring. His eyes crinkled into a warm smile. A promise. Not just of being here for her now, but in the future as well.

"You've always been here for me," Marjie said softly.

"And I always will be," he replied, his voice warm like a summer's day.

The two of them stood there, in a silence that should have been uncomfortable but wasn't.

When she was ready, when the world had turned a few more times, and the universe had decided to be a bit less peculiar for a change, then perhaps there might be more than just friendship. But that was a thought for another day.

For now, Marjie returned to her seat, leaving Papa Jack by the bar, a solid and dependable presence. A warm smile in a cold world, an anchor when the sea of life got choppy.

# 49

## DELIA

"I think we'd better pay that visit," Marjie suggested as she settled back into her seat with a slight blush fading on her cheeks.

Delia looked across to where the man with the kind eyes whose name she couldn't remember still stood, shooting Marjie one last look before he turned back to the bar.

Oh, alright." Agatha relented.

"Fine," said Delia, "but I'm driving."

"Suit yourself," replied Agatha, and only grumbled slightly as she climbed into the back of Delia's black sedan. "It's a bit cramped in here, and there's hardly any books," she complained.

"I'm sure you'll survive," Marjie quipped sweetly.

Delia couldn't help but be amused. "Right..." she said, starting the engine. "You'll have to tell me everything you know, and please elaborate on the dragons."

"Ugh." Agatha recoiled. "Ghastly beasts!"

"See, the problem is," Marjie said as they drove away from the pub and into the countryside, "if you go back far enough, all you have are legends."

"I thought you said legends are true," Delia interjected.

"Of course they are," Agatha responded, "except nobody knows exactly which version is right."

"Well, tell me all the versions you know," Delia insisted.

"Supposedly, there was a great threat," said Marjie.

"It was the witch burnings, I'm sure of it," Agatha interrupted.

"Maybe the Spanish Inquisition?" Marjie suggested.

"Oh, no, it must have been earlier than that," Agatha argued.

"But wasn't that around the same time as the witch burnings?" Delia asked.

"Look, I'm the historian here," said Agatha, bristling.

"Very well," said Delia wryly. "You tell the story then."

"I'm trying to..." Agatha trailed off. There was a moment of silence before she continued. "Witch burnings weren't concentrated at any one particular time. Witches have been persecuted over the centuries, many, many times, partly because we're powerful, and mostly it's female witches who've been attacked due to the patriarchy."

"Of course," said Delia. "I mean...I already knew all of that. I just didn't know that magic was real."

"Well, what you probably didn't know is that there was magic on both sides," Agatha began. "There's an ancient tale, whispered in the shadows, passed down through generations. Some say it's tied to the Templars, others dismiss it as mere myth. But every legend has a grain of truth."

"What do you believe?" Delia asked, her eyes widening.

Agatha leaned back, her eyes glinting. "Belief is a thin and wispy concept. However there's evidence of an old sect, known as the Order of Crimson."

"Hah!" Agatha scoffed. "More like the Order of Cowardly Buffoons from what I've seen of those musty monks."

"Crimson?" said Marjie. "Well, that explains the red cloaks, I suppose, though some of them are definitely more maroon or burgundy."

Agatha shot her a short glance and Marjie clamped her mouth shut and smiled.

Agatha continued. "They were supposedly created by a figure so enigmatic, ruthless, and terrifying that he was more legend than man. He was a Count known as Von Cassel."

Delia laughed, caught up in the mystique. "Sounds like something out of a B-Grade horror film."

Marjie and Agatha shot her a puzzled look.

"Carry on then," Delia urged, her interest piqued.

"There was once a witch, powerful and wise, a protector of our kind, especially here in Myrtlewood, the haven of magic," Agatha continued. "But even the strongest have their vulnerabilities."

Marjie's voice softened. "She was lonely."

Agatha nodded, her expression grave. "Von Cassel saw that, exploited it, drew her in with false promises, illusions, and charm."

"An act of pure deceit," Marjie murmured, sadness in her eyes.

"The tale goes"—Agatha's voice dropped even lower—"that he seduced her, led her astray, and then, in a place hidden from the world, stripped her of her magic, and destroyed her."

"How tragic," Delia breathed. "But why does this ancient story matter now?"

"That's where the legend becomes a mystery," Agatha said, her eyes distant. "They say our heroine, a figure lost to time, held a secret, a great power that waits in slumber. It's said to awaken with the Crones of Myrtlewood if the dark threat ever stirs again."

Delia's eyes widened. "Has it happened before?"

"Who can say?" Agatha replied, her voice enigmatic. "The cycle of time has been tampered with, twisted. Legends tell of its awakening, but the details are lost, like sodding whispers in the wind!"

"It's all part of the cycle of darkness and light," Marjie added, her voice filled with resolve.

"Indeed," Agatha agreed, her voice softening. "The tale is a warning, a prophecy perhaps, that the destructive magic may someday return."

"And the Crones will rise again?" Delia questioned, her mind spinning with the possibilities.

"It's the stuff of legends," Agatha said, her voice filled with the weight of ancient wisdom. "Not all pleasant, but legends nonetheless."

Delia shivered despite the warmth of the pub. Her mind flashed to the cowboy. Was it possible that he was an ancient evil villain in disguise? She didn't even know what Damian Von Cassel looked like to begin with. Probably nobody did, unless they managed to capture a painting of him.

"I guess we don't know what we're looking for, just like nobody knows what Shakespeare looked like," Delia muttered to herself.

"That's right," Agatha affirmed. "Trust no one."

"Except for us," Marjie added. "You can trust us."

"I suppose," Agatha conceded. "I don't know about *her*, but I tell the truth almost eighty-five percent of the time, according to my records—"

Delia snorted. "How candid of you to admit it."

Agatha glared and continued. "I'll have you know that eighty-five percent is much higher than the average individual who spends all day lying to themselves with a big helping of half-truths and a few jolts of reality here and there."

Delia shook her head, though she had to admit to herself that Agatha might be right. After all, she'd spent the past few days deliberately convincing herself that what she'd experienced couldn't possibly be real, while simultaneously fighting the other most obvious conclusion that she'd lost her marbles. Human minds were indeed strange and shifting worlds unto their own.

She pulled up towards the forest where she'd parked the last time.

"Oh no, not there dear. Further along," Marjie instructed.

"Thanks for the great map you gave me," Delia retorted, her voice laced with sarcasm.

Under Marjie's direction, she drove slightly further along the road.

There was a windy track through forest, rugged and stony, and just wide enough for her car to travel along without being scratched or dented by passing tree branches.

"You can *drive* to Ingrid's house?" Delia asked.

"Not all the way," Marjie corrected her, "but it makes it a bit quicker."

Arriving at a more open, gravelly space, Delia pulled up and parked the car. "Any other surprises that I should be aware of?"

"I think we've had quite enough surprises for one day," Marjie replied. "But we'll see."

"What would you know, Marjie?" said Agatha. "You have about as much foresight as a brick wall."

"Oh really?" said Marjie. "Well, I'd say your aura is off-colour, but it would imply you had one worth noticing."

Delia chuckled.

"And what are you laughing at, you novice?" said Agatha. "I've met familiars with more magical prowess than you."

"Thanks for including me, Agatha," said Delia. "At least I won't feel left out of your little insult-trading club. I'm afraid I'm not up to speed on magic, otherwise I'd say you've got the charm of a rusty cauldron or something."

Marjie chuckled.

They made their way through the forest, taking a very different route from the one Delia had taken the first time.

Being in the woods in the fading afternoon light, accompanied by two rather formidable witches, was a lot more relaxing, despite the imminent threats and her newfound awareness of magic.

Delia found herself grateful for their company, reminding herself not to wander off alone into danger anytime soon lest she become that annoying protagonist again.

It was tricky though. Delia was so used to her independence that the thought of being joined at the hip with Grumpy Crone and Sunshine Crone wasn't particularly appealing with all the bickering.

But thankfully, the arguments largely ceased as they continued their walk through the woods, drawing nearer to Ingrid's house.

# 50

## THE SHEPHERD

Father Benedict paced the cold and uneven stone pavers of the courtyard, his furious steps echoing through the hushed grounds.

Each footfall was a reminder of the fiery anger that was raging within him, as uncontainable as a magical flame.

He shot withering glances at any members of the Order of Crimson who weren't wearing the appropriate stoic expressions or seemed to be slacking off.

His eyes, hard and cold as agates, left no room for compassion or understanding.

The walls of the compound seemed to draw in around him, heightening his frustration. The scent of damp earth mixed with the lingering aroma of burnt herbs from some careless experiment within the Order's hallowed walls, and the taste of bile was rising in his throat.

All these thoughts were just distractions.

Operation Delta had failed. It was a blow. He'd meticulously planned it down to the last detail, but despite the failure, that was not what clawed at his soul. No, it was the missing fire witch, presumed dead. That is what the troop had reported. They'd surrounded the house and it had burst into flames, taking several order members with it. The witches had been inside, and no one was seen to escape, so the report stated that they must have burned up in the blaze, but Father Benedict had read over the passages with scorn and scepticism.

It couldn't be true; it simply couldn't. Such incompetence was unbearable, a stain on the very essence of the Order's honour.

Every rustling leaf and whispering gust of wind seemed to mock him. The other members of the Order, those simpering fools, were to blame. Each one was a symbol of what had gone so horribly wrong, a reminder of the weakness that had permeated the once-proud institution he served.

The very thought of going down to Myrtlewood himself was an itch he couldn't scratch. He couldn't risk being seen in that dreadful town; his mysterious persona was an intricate part of his power, after all. The townsfolk were just the type to mount an attack on him, and he didn't have time for such pesky interruptions.

It took several rounds of the courtyard for the Crimson Shepherd to land on an adequate solution. Let the Cleric go, bumbling as he was. Perhaps disguised, he could head The Mission on the ground. It might even help him develop some leadership skills, something desperately needed around here. Of course the Cleric would be too cowardly to accept the role without question. It would take some convincing.

As he walked, Father Benedict's mind drifted to the austere surroundings. The gnarled old trees seemed to bow to his rage, their branches trembling in the chilling breeze. The air was crisp and clear, yet the scent of impending doom seemed to permeate every molecule.

He stopped suddenly, his eyes fixing on a young initiate who was laughing a bit too loudly with his companion. "Silence!" he barked, his voice echoing like thunder. The laughter died instantly, and the young man's face turned ashen. "Do you find failure amusing? Do you revel in the dishonour it brings upon the Order of Crimson?"

"N-no, Crimson Shepherd," the boy stammered, his voice barely above a whisper.

"You will learn discipline, or you will leave this Order," Father Benedict snapped, his voice dripping with disdain. "We are on the brink of a test, a trial that will determine the very purpose of our existence. Then we will see who is worthy."

With that, he turned sharply and continued his furious march, his mind aflame with thoughts of judgment and wrath. His steps were heavy with the weight of disappointment, his heart a pit of indignation.

Father Benedict's fury was a cold and relentless storm, sweeping through the dark halls of the compound. It was an ancient place, filled with shadowy chambers, hidden passages, and the scent of time itself clinging to the walls like damp cobwebs. The sacred texts that lined the shelves whispered of forbidden magic, the distant echoes of battles won and lost, and of the constant struggle between Order and Chaos.

Operation Delta had been an abject failure, and the missing fire witches were the worst part. The loss was like a gaping wound in Benedict's very soul, a personal affront to his dignity, his honour, his very essence.

As he moved, the compound seemed to echo his fury. The discipline and austerity that had once marked the Order were tainted with inadequacy, and he would stop at nothing to purge it.

The ancient rooms seemed to close in on him, the ceiling pressing down and the walls squeezing tight, as if the building itself shared his anger. The tall windows were mere slits in the thick stone, and the fire in the hearth flickered and hissed as if it too were angry. The dimly lit corridor, with its tapestries of valorous deeds, now seemed to mock him. Each heroic image was a haunting reminder of his failure.

The time was swiftly approaching when the Order's very purpose would be tested, and he would make sure they were ready.

He stalked the grounds, his movements sharp and predatory, his eyes filled with a dark and raging fire that matched the storm in his heart. The members of the Order, once his most trusted allies, now seemed inept and unworthy of his respect. They were failures, each and every one. Weaklings who had allowed this disaster to occur under his watchful eye.

The young initiates cowered as he passed, fearfully lowering their eyes. The seasoned warriors, once proud and strong, now seemed fragile and defeated. Even the Cleric, once a source of wisdom and guidance, was now an object of his scorn.

"Prepare yourself," he spat at the Cleric, his voice dripping with disdain. "You will go to Myrtlewood yourself."

"Me, Shepherd?" the Cleric replied, his hands shaking slightly.

"You," Father Benedict replied. "I need someone on the ground who is at least competent."

The Cleric's eyes swelled with pride at this lavish complement, but he at least had the decency to bow his head humbly.

"Disguised, of course," Shepherd continued, pleased that the Cleric hadn't been too difficult to manipulate after all. "Find out what happened, and do not return until you have answers."

The Cleric's eyes widened, but he said nothing, bowing his head further in acquiescence. Father Benedict entertained a moment of suspicion. Perhaps this was what the Cleric had wanted all along – a chance to prove himself. If so, there were ways to use such enthusiasm to the Crimson Shepherd's own advantage.

Father Benedict's judgment was swift and unyielding. There was no room for weakness, no room for failure. The world was a place of order and discipline, and those who could not uphold those virtues were worthless.

He retreated to his private study, a room filled with ancient artefacts, mystical tomes, and the lingering scent of alchemical potions. The flickering candles cast strange shadows on the walls, and the room seemed to pulse with an unseen energy.

He pored over maps and scrolls, his mind whirring with plans and strategies. The fire witch must be found, the failure of Operation Delta must be avenged, and the Order must be restored to its former glory. There was no other choice.

With a grim determination, he continued to plan, his mind a whirlwind of thoughts and strategies. He would not fail again. The fire witch would be found, the Order would be restored, and the world would once again know the true meaning of discipline, order, and honour.

# 51

## DELIA

As the path opened up to reveal the cottage, Delia noticed a rather large horned animal grazing nearby. The white goat, with a patch of black fur over its left eye, raised its head and looked at the three of them through slanted eyes before returning its attention to nibbling on a large mint bush.

"Is that a normal goat?" Delia asked, then jumped as the door of the cottage flew open.

Ingrid stood there, hands on her hips, bearing down upon them.

"You're late." She glared at them.

Agatha, Marjie, and Delia all gaped at her.

"Well, come on in. I haven't got all day."

Marjie and Agatha shared a puzzled look, while Delia couldn't help but smile.

"Come on, the tea's ready." Ingrid beckoned them in.

Marjie beamed, and Agatha looked like she'd swallowed a damp rat.

Delia simply laughed and walked in ahead of them.

Moments later, they were all seated around Ingrid's solid, old, and much-scarred kitchen table.

"You were expecting us then?" Agatha said, regaining her composure.

"It's been a long time coming," Ingrid replied, "but I was watching the signs." She looked out the window to her hawks flying in the distance. "The forest speaks to me. Tells me the things I need to know."

"Well, the forest said nothing at all to me," said Agatha. "Except for whoosh, crunch, and caw caw."

Ingrid ground her jaw. "The forest doesn't whisper to those who don't listen. Keep your ears and eyes open; nature speaks volumes. Besides, the Crone Moon is full tonight."

"I'm not really following," said Delia. "What's the moon got to do with anything?"

"Of course," said Agatha. "The last full moon before winter solstice."

"The Crone Moon is a reminder that even in darkness, there's a light to guide us. Never forget that."

Ingrid clunked an earthenware teapot in the centre of the table surrounded by four small mugs.

"I don't drink this for the flavour," Ingrid warned as she poured the tea. "But it does bring some insight."

Marjie looked as though she was bursting to ask about the ingredients but seemed to be holding herself back.

Delia, on the other hand, wasn't afraid. "What's in it?" she asked, prompting startled looks from Agatha and Marjie.

Ingrid quirked an eyebrow.

"She's new," Agatha explained. "She doesn't know it's terribly inappropriate to ask a witch for her secret recipes."

Ingrid threw back her head and guffawed. "Since when did I ever care about what was appropriate? Besides, Delia's a sensible girl. She's just checking to make sure I'm not feeding her anything she wouldn't want to consume. Isn't that right?"

Delia gave her an unimpressed look. She wasn't used to being treated like a child. "Look, I prefer to know what I'm consuming. Is that a crime?"

"Not at all, dear," said Marjie. "It makes perfect sense. Sometimes, people get very offended if you slip something into their tea without telling them what it is."

Delia nodded and then shot Marjie a suspicious glance. Marjie merely smiled back, cherubic.

Delia turned back to Ingrid expectantly.

"I won't tell you my secret," said Ingrid sternly. "Agatha is right about that. But I will warn you that this is no ordinary tea. It's a seer's brew designed to uncover our own inner mysteries."

Delia scowled. "And you expect me to drink it?"

"You ate my food, didn't you?" said Ingrid gruffly. "And what use will it be if you sit this out?"

"So you won't tell me anything at all?" Delia persisted.

A tension rose around the table as Marjie and Agatha glared at Delia. Ingrid looked livid, but then she doubled over in hoarse laughter. "You're much more plucky when you haven't just been a lost little lamb in the woods. If you must know, it's mostly mugwort, with some mullein and peppermint for a breath of fresh air, chamomile for comfort, and a pinch of rue, but that's all I'll say. Just know that it's a special brew with special effects."

Delia's eyes narrowed, then she let her shoulders slump. "Fine."

She waited to watch Marjie and Agatha's expressions as they picked up their tea and took a sip. Although each of them may have disguised a wince upon tasting, their expressions were inscrutable.

Overcome by curiosity, Delia took a small sip. It was bitter, yet not entirely undrinkable for someone used to decades of very strong coffee.

"Not bad," she commented.

Ingrid nodded firmly.

There was a moment of silence as the four women sat around the table regarding each other.

"Right then." Delia broke the silence. "I want to get to the bottom of all this." She waved her arm in the air vaguely. "Why were you expecting us, Ingrid? And what are we doing here? And what's your version of this whole story?"

"Rather a lot of questions," Ingrid mused, chewing her lower lip. She regarded Delia thoughtfully. "Fine, if you really want to know, I don't always know the why or the how of these things. I just listen to the signs. So it's a bit like walking in the dark, you might say. You never know exactly, with the rational mind, because it is simply impossible to logically comprehend these things."

"Speak for yourself," Agatha muttered.

Marjie chuckled. "It's so nice to be here," she said to Ingrid. "You've never let us in before."

"It wasn't the time," said Ingrid.

"And now is the time," Delia added. "But for what?"

Ingrid downed her tea in one gulp, then returned her hand to her hip and leaned back in her chair. "I'm hoping this brew will bring some clarity to the situation...However, I believe we all have a piece of the puzzle."

"I don't know about me," said Delia. "I'm new to all this."

"But your family isn't," said Ingrid, with such certainty that Delia was sure she knew something important. But before she could figure out how to ask about her heritage, Ingrid continued.

"There's a delicate balance holding the world together – our precious living systems – our energetic bodies – and all the different layers of things..."

Agatha regarded her suspiciously. "What is this? The age of Aquarius? I never picked you for a hippy."

Ingrid smirked. "Don't waste all your causticness on us, Agatha. Put it to good use."

Agatha wrinkled up her mouth and took another sip of tea, not bothering to wince this time.

Ingrid chuckled.

Delia took another swig of tea. It was growing on her, whatever it was in this cup. She suspected that Ingrid had added rather a lot of secret ingredients. But, as much as Delia might want to listen to her fear and get as far away as possible from these frightening older women who she now found herself ensconced among, and their odd magic, she couldn't. She at least had to figure out what was going on and how she could protect her daughter and grandkids from it. Perhaps there was some kind of magic she could learn to master – to protect them, and then somehow convince Gilly to come with her, somewhere safe, far from all this danger. Perhaps she was listening to her fear after all, but Delia had always thought it was important to protect oneself. She didn't get as far as she had in her career by being naïve.

Just then, the door creaked open. All turned to see a black cat padding in, rather regally. He jumped up and set himself on the table, eyeing them all thoughtfully.

"Cats don't belong on tables," Ingrid said slowly.

"It's just as well that I'm not actually a cat," Mephistos said primly.

"Look, you've come to visit all of us," said Marjie. "You're no familiar, and yet we don't know anything about who or what you are at all, only what you tell us."

"He hasn't told me anything useful at all," Delia grumbled. "Apart from giving me directions here when I was lost."

"You didn't seem very happy about it at the time," said Mephistos.

"Alright, if you're not a cat, what are you? And what do you know about Crones and dragons?" Delia asked, feeling rather impatient despite the fact that a part of her brain was still adjusting to the fact that she was conversing with a talking cat who seemed to be in denial about what he obviously was.

The feline entity lifted his paw and scratched his chin. "If you must know, I am a god."

"Oh yes?" said Agatha. "Or a demon, more like."

215

Mephistos shrugged his shoulders. "What's the difference?"

"And what?" said Delia. "Are you going to tell us that you're cursed to look like a cat? It's a bit Sabrina the Teenage Witch, isn't it?"

Mephistos shrugged. "Where do you think they got the idea from?"

"I thought you said you could only talk to Crones," said Ingrid. "Now you're out there, influencing the television industry?"

"I may have figured out how to cast an inspiration spell or two," said Mephistos, his eyes downcast. "I've been here a long time, with no real power, after all. It didn't work very well though, did it? I should have been the star. Not comic relief."

Delia giggled before Mephistos shot her a look of such reproach that she silenced herself.

"It's hardly relevant now, is it?" said Ingrid. "Why are you here? And what do you know?"

Mephistos narrowed his eyes at her. "I'm here because you're the only people who actually understand me properly. When I try to speak, most people just give me pats or yell at me...or feed me old fish."

Delia raised an eyebrow. "Why are you *here right now*?" she asked slowly.

Picking up the note of threat in her voice, carefully crafted from years of acting, Mephistos turned his head as if offended and sighed dramatically. "A long time ago I was cursed by a witch. I was summoned to destroy the witch, and she cursed me to this eternal damned life as a feline. And now the only way it appears that I can get back to my old life of pleasure and debauchery is to help the Crones to defeat the big-bad-threat and atone for whatever I did wrong. I've never quite been able to figure out what that was..."

"So you expect us to believe that you're on our side?" said Agatha. "When you admit yourself that you were summoned to attack witches?"

"Summoned!" said Mephistos. "It's there in the fine print. It wasn't of my own free will; it was an energetic contract. Look, I'm not what you would call good, I'll admit that. However, I'm a natural ally for you because we have the same enemy – the force that summoned me."

"You mean you want to get something out of us?" said Delia. "And the only way to do that is to help us defeat him."

"You can put it like that if you like," said Mephistos, preening.

It struck Delia as a little ironic that anyone could feel put out living a life as a cat. "You mean you're sick of all those naps in the sun?"

Mephistos yawned. "It is getting to be that time of day, isn't it?"

"How can you possibly not want to live life as a cat?" said Agatha suspiciously. "It seems ideal for a hedonist."

"It's not the worst experience," said Mephistos. "In fact, for the first hundred years or so, I did quite enjoy myself, terrorising the town. Although that was back when they feared and respected black cats as evil. I got an interesting reputation, especially because no matter how many times they tried to kill me, I'd always return. However, it gets a little repetitive after a while, and I have some rather old unfinished business to attend to in the underworld. Besides, it's important to have goals to keep moving forward, and this is the last one that I have. I cannot die until the curse is broken. Which means I cannot return home. This can grate on one's nerves after a while."

"All right. We'll take you at face value for now," said Agatha. "As witches, we must remember, a pinch of salt—"

"Or perhaps an entire salt circle." Ingrid nodded firmly. "If what you say is true, Mephistos, then you know the history better than any of us possibly could."

"Speak for yourself," Agatha grumbled.

Ingrid regarded her sternly. "Surely even a historian like yourself, Agatha, must be excited about the prospect of having a real-life witness."

"I can tell you some things," Mephistos said, "but admittedly, I was rather drunk when I was summoned. And then I woke up three days later after being cursed. It took me a long time to figure out what even happened to me and why I was stuck in this place. And it was thoughtful of the witch to leave a note. However, my cat instincts had already taken over, and I tore it to shreds before I realised what it was. Then I had to spend quite a while putting it back together and trying to decipher it. I ate about a third," he admitted.

The rest of the group listened to his tale, their scepticism evident yet curiosity piqued.

# 52

## THE CLERIC

The Cleric leaned back in his chair, a satisfied smile playing on his face. It was an unforeseen upgrade. The office was, in a word, quaint, in the way that old relatives are quaint or the way a pudding can be both understated and delightful. The Cleric stretched his legs out behind a stately old oak desk, surrounded by walls adorned with books and scrolls, the kind that looked wise merely by existing. A fireplace, hardly roaring but not without spirit, offered a pleasant warmth. It was a welcome change from the veritable dungeon of the inner chamber where the Cleric had to contend with young scribes and their tedious scratchings.

This office was not the austere, brutal space that the Crimson Shepherd would've chosen for himself. No, it was more suited to a mind that preferred to wander a bit, to engage in whimsical theories. There was room here to breathe, think, and even enjoy one's work. The Cleric revelled in it, though he would be the first to admit that he wouldn't trust Father Benedict as far as he could throw him. Not that he'd ever tried.

A peculiar instrument began to dance and flash on the desk, jingling as if it had had one too many glasses of wine. It was a communications device, and it was singing its lovely, if slightly off-tune, song to him. The Cleric's heart leapt.

The Rogue was reporting back.

"Finally!"

The Cleric buzzed with excitement, a sensation not unlike being tickled by a magical feather duster. It had been so many hours since he'd heard from the Rogue that he'd begun to entertain the notion that the best tracker in the country had perished in the fire. Not that he was supposed to be there, of course. The Cleric had made sure that the outsider contractors knew as little as possible about the Order's inner workings.

"The fire witch and her companions are still in Myrtlewood. I've located them," the Rogue's voice came through, crackling like a mischievous fire, just as his face appeared, rugged and intimidating, on the labradorite crystal slice attached to the instrument.

"I knew she'd survived that fire," said the Cleric. Though, in truth, that blasted woman had caused them so much trouble that part of him wished she was no longer of this world. He knew the Crimson Shepherd saw her as integral to the mission, at least temporarily, but perhaps he just hadn't considered all the options.

"Where?" the Cleric asked. "They must have a clever hiding place if it has taken this long to find them."

"Last I checked they were at the pub," the Rogue said flatly.

"The pub?!!" The Cleric's voice danced a jig of disbelief.

"The pub," confirmed the Rogue. "So maybe you can have your fellows pick her up and then I can leave this contract. My work here is done."

The Cleric's eyes narrowed, suspicion welling in his gut. The Rogue was sounding rather eager to leave the contract.

"No," the Cleric said firmly, tapping his desk as if underlining his own statement. "In fact, I will accompany you from now on."

"I work alone," came the protest.

"You'll find there's a clause in the contract – you didn't read the fine print, did you?" The Cleric smiled to himself. "I will be your companion and learn from you."

There was a sigh, and the Cleric could almost hear the Rogue's eyes rolling. "You'll have to up the fee."

"That will be fine," the Cleric responded, though he got the impression that there was somewhere else the Rogue would rather be. "You're still on contract until the case resolves."

The magical communications device went silent, still vibrating slightly as if it too were surprised by the turn of events. The Cleric leaned back in his chair, feeling a mixture of satisfaction, anxiety, and a small, tickling sense of adventure.

It wasn't every day one found oneself paired with the country's best tracker, on a mission to find a fire witch who'd made herself at home in a pub. A pub, of all places! He chuckled to himself. Even in the most grave and dire of circumstances, life had a way of inserting a wink and a smile.

He stared at the fireplace, the flames dancing and flickering as if taunting him with Crone secrets.

"We will find out," he vowed, his voice filled with a conviction that he hoped would be enough. "We will uncover their plot and put an end to this madness."

His hand trembled as he reached for a book on the shelf, a tome of ancient knowledge that might hold the key to unravelling the mystery.

The game had changed, the stakes raised. And the Cleric knew that he was now in a battle not just for his own life but for the very soul of The Mission.

A battle that he could not afford to lose.

With a determined smile, he began to prepare for his journey to Myrtlewood. The fire witch had been located, the game was afoot, and the Cleric was ready to dive into the thick of it.

After all, how often does one find witches at the pub? Even in a world filled with magic, some things were still delightfully absurd.

# 53

## DELIA

Delia yawned. "It must be getting late," she said, looking out into the darkening night. "I feel like I might just fall asleep right at the table."

"No, that would be the potion setting in," Ingrid said casually.

"Potion?" Delia asked.

"You might feel more comfortable lying down or at least getting into a cosy chair," Ingrid continued. "I generally prefer to lie flat on my back or my neck gets a crick."

"You're kidding," said Delia. "You fed us a potion without telling us what it would do? I'm sure that's not legal!"

She looked towards Marjie and Agatha who merely shrugged.

Ingrid chuckled. "And how much convincing would it have taken to get you to drink something if I had labelled it as a 'potion'? Besides, I told you it was a seer's draught."

Delia put her hands on her hips. "What does it do?"

Ingrid stared at her. "Like I said, it's a seer's brew. It's for the seeing. Have a little nap and tell me what you see in your dreams, and if you insist, I'll apologise later. Now quickly. Midnight is approaching and the Crone Moon is rising high. This is our best opportunity to let the magic seep in – the best timing in the entire year, in fact!"

Delia shook her head. She was already feeling droopy and drowsy. As unethical as Ingrid's actions might appear to a casual observer, the older woman didn't seem to harbour any ill intent, apart from being dangerously pragmatic.

Delia made her way back to the window seat where she had previously slept. Marjie took the chair by the fire while Ingrid and Agatha rolled blankets out onto the ground to lie on. No one else seemed perturbed that Ingrid had given them a mystery potion. And so, perhaps there was nothing to worry about. As surprising and mysterious as it might be to Delia, it did occur to her that perhaps this was a perfectly normal occurrence in Myrtlewood.

Mephistos took a few licks from one of the mugs left on the table, then curled up by the fire, too. He clearly didn't want to be left out of the action.

Delia let her eyes droop closed, relishing the warmth that drifted over from the fire, as Marjie's gentle snoring and the sound of a purring cat-slash-demon-god lulled her to sleep.

DELIA STOOD IN A FOREST, *only she felt achingly young. She looked down at her tiny hands, soft, smooth, and perfect, like a baby's. Yet, she was walking, so she couldn't have been a baby at all. Perhaps she was around five. Her hair was long, wild, and tangled, and she was clad in a plain canvas dress. She walked along a forest path she didn't recognise. The wind whipped through the trees and a crow flew overhead, then a growl echoed from the woods behind her.*

*A wolf, she knew it...a terrifying creature.*

*She began to run as fast as she could, dashing deeper into the forest. Up ahead was a cluster of rocks where she could hide. She leapt onto the rocks, but the wolf followed behind. She didn't dare turn to look back. She couldn't risk slowing down; her heart was pounding as she scaled the rocks, higher and higher into the mountain, headed towards a cave, but just as she neared it, flames burst out, knocking her backward.*

*Delia was falling...*

SHE SCREAMED AND WOKE, only to find herself back in Ingrid's house, on the window seat, at a much more comfortable age than she'd been in the dream aside from her back feeling rather stiff.

Marjie was still snoring peacefully, but Agatha was sitting bolt upright, staring at her. "What did you see?"

Ingrid was nowhere in sight, though Delia looked around for her as she recounted her dream.

Agatha huffed. "All I got were a bunch of swirly symbols that I can't understand."

"Sounds like something you'd enjoy," said Marjie, yawning as she opened her eyes.

"It was rather interesting," Agatha admitted.

"But where's Ingrid?" Marjie asked.

"Wouldn't you like to know?" Mephistos replied.

Ignoring the snarky cat, Delia turned to Marjie. "What did you dream about?"

"I was under the ocean. There were just waves and waves of feeling," Marjie replied.

"That doesn't sound very useful," said Agatha.

Delia shrugged. "Is any of this useful?"

"Well, I dreamed about chasing a squirrel in the woods. It was rather tasty," Mephistos chimed in.

Delia frowned at him. "Be careful not to get rabies."

"Excuse me?" said Mephistos.

"Never mind. Do you know where Ingrid is?" Delia asked, changing the topic. Mephistos yawned before answering, "I think she went out back."

Delia stood up, stretching her aching legs. She walked to the back of the house and peered out the window, but couldn't see anything of note. She did, however, notice a rather pleasant smell wafting from the pot above the fire.

As she pondered over her dream, Delia couldn't shake the feeling that something was stirring, a hint of tension in the air. Could Ingrid's disappearance signify something more ominous?

# 54

## THE ROGUE

Declan settled into his hidden camp nestled within the dense foliage near Myrtlewood. His long, solitary life had taught him to appreciate the comforts of nature, and his camp was an unassuming place with its small fire pit at the centre.

He reached into his bag and carefully pulled out the knuckle bones. As his fingers brushed the ancient artefacts, they glowed faintly, pulsing with a strange blue energy that danced and wove like a thin thread in the air. It was a living connection to the magic he sought, and its appearance was ethereal, almost like a phantom caress on his skin.

Using the bones, he focused on Delia Spark. The magical thread quivered and twisted, leading him to the image of the pub where he had last seen her.

She was no longer there.

The knuckle bones, still warm in his hand, quivered as their ancient magic settled.

With a sigh, he let the elemental connection guide him, the blue thread pulling him towards the edge of the forest. The energy moved, shimmered, and beckoned, winding its way through the trees, like a luminescent river.

He packed his rucksack and followed the trail, his senses tingling as the scent of moss, damp earth, and decaying leaves filled his nostrils. The forest was an ancient place, filled with whispers of hidden secrets, rustling leaves, and the distant cry of unseen creatures.

The magical thread led him deeper into the wilderness, through thick underbrush and towering oaks, their gnarled branches creating a tangled canopy that allowed only slivers of sunlight to filter through.

As he reached the edge of the enchanted forest, the trail abruptly stopped, swallowed by an unseen barrier. The scents grew more profound, infused with a mix of wildflowers and something else, something indefinable and mystical.

Declan frowned, knowing that he had reached the point where tracking was impossible.

Last time he'd tracked Delia to this very forest, he'd come up against a wall. It was a rare experience in all his years. Whoever lived here was powerful – powerful enough to have the entire living system of the forest on her side.

Tasting the magical residue of the witches' trail still hanging in the air at edge of the forest, the Rogue estimated that perhaps half an hour or more had passed since they'd been there.

Annoyance welled within him, mingled with an odd sense of relief. It was his own fault, after all. If he was being completely honest, he was sabotaging the case on purpose. And though he could admit that to himself, he could not fathom why.

Sighing again, he knew it was his duty to update the Order.

He reached for his seer's stone, its smooth surface reflecting his conflicted expression.

The Cleric's face appeared a moment later on the dark surface of the stone.

"Let me guess," said the Cleric. "No news is good news, so this thing you're about to tell me is...not good news is it?" His voice lilted in weak hope.

"No," said Declan gruffly.

227

"They're no longer at the pub, are they?"

"They've entered the enchanted forest," Declan said, the words tasting sour. "I can't follow them further. This place...it's impossible."

"I don't believe in impossible," the Cleric declared. "I'll be there in a jiffy. What shall I bring?" His eyes filled with determination. "I'm coming, and I'm bringing our best spell crackers and gadgets. We will get through the forest's defences, and then the witches will be at our mercy!"

The Rogue's eyes narrowed as he ended the communication. The Cleric's confidence was unnerving, and something about this mission was gnawing at him.

Declan paused for a moment, his thoughts swirling. The enchanted forest was a place of ancient magic, and even the whispers of the wind seemed to carry a warning.

The Cleric's confidence was a stark contrast to the uneasy feeling growing within Declan. This case was awakening something inside him, something he had long ignored. The values he thought were lost forever. But now he was sure of it. What he was experiencing included the slow awakening of a conscience he thought he had buried centuries ago.

He considered himself separate from humanity, especially as he didn't understand what he was. He used to believe he was human once, and something happened to him so that he never seemed to die. A curse, perhaps, or an aberration of magic at birth. The questions were never-ending.

His tracking powers weren't connected to his immortality. He'd traded something priceless in order to have magic, a purpose, a focus, a drive...to keep himself sane. And that also meant he couldn't leave a contract or he'd forfeit both his powers and that piece of his soul.

As much as he wanted to escape this one, he had no choice but to see it through. So far, his small sabotages hadn't done anything to erode his powers, or his soul, but it was risky. He had to keep himself in check.

The Cleric wanted to buddy up with him? Well, perhaps that was for the best. Together they would pursue Delia Spark and her companions into the unknown. But as the Rogue stared into the dark shadows of the enchanted forest, he couldn't shake the feeling that something more significant was at play, and that his own buried secrets were on the verge of being unearthed.

Looking into the forest, he wondered what was it about this case that had him slowly developing a tiny nub of a conscience? It had been centuries since he'd bothered with ethical concerns. They tended to be flavour of the month, and there were too many months in a millennium to keep up with passing fads. Over time, all the feelings, trauma, and sensations became too much. He'd locked all those things away for the sake of practicality. He couldn't get attached to anyone because they'd only die.

As he stood at the threshold of the forest, a place where time seemed to hold its breath, he wondered what it was that drew him to this case, and why he felt a growing connection to Delia Spark. She hated him and she had every right to. If he allowed himself to indulge in more emotion, he was sure he'd absolutely loathe her too. How dare she interrupt the most peaceful part of his relentless existence and have the nerve to insult him!

The question of his own existence, his curse or gift of immortality, loomed large, casting a shadow on his thoughts. He had traded a piece of his soul for purpose and power, but now, he felt the stirrings of something...else.

The forest's scents lingered, a heady mixture of life and magic, and as Declan turned to leave, he knew that he was venturing into uncharted territory, not only in his pursuit of the witches but also in the unexplored corners of his soul. The game was far from over, and his role in it was evolving in ways he had not foreseen.

# 55
## DELIA

As Delia gazed into the night, she felt a strange tingle running across her skin, followed by a wave of nausea. She barely managed to open the back door before retching and ungracefully depositing the contents of her stomach into the back garden. She stood there, leaning over the rail, feeling most disoriented and woozy.

A bleating sound interrupted her and she looked up to see another goat, only this one was black with a white patch across its face. Its horns glinted in the light of the rising full moon.

The goat regarded her suspiciously. She looked from the animal to the enormous disc of the moon – the Crone Moon, as Ingrid had called it. In that moment, as dizzy as she felt, she knew this moon, this moonlight, possessed a power deeper and wiser than she'd ever known.

She shuddered and moaned. "What did Ingrid put in that tea?"

The world began to swirl around her.

There was a cackle from the darkness and Ingrid emerged, just as Marjie and Agatha rushed outside, each succumbing to the same sickly fate as Delia had moments earlier.

"What did you poison us with?" Agatha asked, her eyes narrowed in suspicion.

A wave of fear washed over Delia.

Out here in the forest they were vulnerable, not just to imaginary wolves or rabid squirrels.

"Hold your britches, gals," Ingrid said. "Let me guess. You thought the seer's potion would induce dreams and that'd be the end of it?" She cackled. "Guess again. We're just getting started."

"Is that why the air's all shimmery?" Marjie asked, sounding surprisingly delighted as she reached out around her.

"I do believe so," Ingrid confirmed.

"So, you've drugged us with some kind of psychedelic?"

"An important part of my potion is a certain sacred mushroom," Ingrid admitted. "And yes, in order to achieve a unified wisdom, certain barriers must fall away. Just imagine that my heartfelt written apology is in the mail and stop frowning."

"Look," said Delia, "I didn't come here to partake in illicit substances. I had enough of those in the '70s."

Marjie giggled.

Although, even as Delia's outrage bloomed, fiery in her chest, she found her anger giving way to a wave of delight. She looked past Ingrid to the old elder tree, in all its majesty, and the forest beyond, where the dark green leaves seemed to shift and merge to form faces and patterns.

"I don't know about this!" Agatha complained.

"The human mind excels at shutting out the magical," said Ingrid. "Now that we've removed some of those barriers, you'll discover new layers of mystery even within your own mind."

Delia, though still outraged, was determined not to let anger give her a bad trip. She was sure Ingrid had behaved unethically and the old bat was certainly untrustworthy, but despite her frustrations, Delia felt a pleasant sense of lightness.

Marjie doubled over in hysterical laughter.

"Come over here!" Agatha called out, spinning around, her dress held out in her hands. "I feel like a child again!"

The sight of Agatha dancing in such a joyful and spirited manner, across the lawn, sent Delia into fits of giggles. Something very strange was happening. The world had turned upside down, and it was rather a lot of fun.

"Ingrid!" Agatha cried. "You're the Picasso of potion-making. No one has any idea what you're doing, so it's impossible to tell if you're any good at it!"

Ingrid grimaced. "If your spells were as good as your backhanded compliments, you'd be a high priestess by now."

Agatha turned to Marjie. "Did she just try to insult me?"

Marjie shrugged.

"Alright, enough mucking about," Ingrid said sternly. "Inside, by the fire, or you'll catch a chill. Stop your dillydallying. Don't you realise we're being pursued by a sinister order of monks?"

"Musty monks!" Marjie cried.

Delia couldn't help but laugh at the absurdity of the whole situation, but Ingrid continued to scold them, warning them of the dark and devastating power that threatened to break free if they didn't get their act together.

Still giggling, Delia, Marjie, and Agatha finally trudged back into the house, drawn to the inviting warmth of the fire.

# 56

## THE SHEPHERD

The winding stairwell at the compound of the Order of Crimson was a place of echoing silence and contemplation, adorned with carvings and lined with ancient sconces that held flickering torches. The scent of burnt wood mingled with the musty aroma of old stone, creating an ambiance of solemnity. Shadows danced on the walls, and the very air seemed to hum with magical energy. This was a place of power, of tradition, of unbreakable resolve.

Father Benedict's heart pounded in his chest as he stood at the bottom of the staircase, the anger from the earlier failure still festering within him. The sound of hurried footsteps reached his ears, and he turned to see the Cleric, laden with a plethora of bags and looking undeniably flustered.

"Where do you think you're going?" Father Benedict's voice boomed, echoing in the stairwell like a clap of thunder.

The words were harsh, filled with an authority that brooked no dissent. The Cleric stalled on the staircase, a look of terror in his eyes. His voice, when he spoke, was a pitiful quiver. "Shepherd," he stammered, "I...I..."

Father Benedict's eyes narrowed, his mind working furiously. Was the Cleric trying to escape? To run away from the responsibility that had been thrust upon him? A surge of disgust filled him, and he spoke again, his voice dripping with disdain.

"Not running away from a challenge, are you?"

Though he stood at the bottom of the staircase, he somehow managed to loom over the Cleric, his presence an inescapable force that seemed to press down upon the other man. The Cleric was several steps higher than Father Benedict's head, but physical height meant nothing in the face of such overpowering will.

"Not at all," said the Cleric, attempting to muster some semblance of dignity. "I have news. And I'm preparing, like you said. I'm going to go down there and lead."

Father Benedict's eyebrows furrowed, a sense of suspicion gnawing at him. The Cleric's enthusiasm seemed forced, his actions rushed. Something was not right, and he would get to the bottom of it.

"With your permission, of course," the Cleric added, his voice almost pleading.

"You haven't sought my permission!" Father Benedict snapped, his voice rising in fury.

"I...well, you see I was in quite a rush. It's most urgent and pressing. I had to...err."

"Out with it, man!" Father Benedict roared, his patience worn thin.

"The rogue tracker has located the witches in Myrtlewood."

"I knew it!" Father Benedict crowed, a triumphant smile spreading across his face. This was excellent news, a ray of hope in the darkness. He had been right to send the Rogue, and now they had a lead.

"You were right to prepare, but you should have sought my permission first – and informed me!" he continued, his voice stern.

"Yes...yes." The Cleric bowed his head in penitence, his voice trembling with fear. "Err, there's one more thing."

"What is it?" Father Benedict asked slowly, his eyes narrowing once again.

"They've gone back into that blasted woodland – you know, the one that makes them untraceable."

The words were like a punch to the gut, and Father Benedict's mind reeled. The woodland was a place of ancient magic, a barrier that had thwarted them before. But he would not be defeated. He would not let this setback derail them.

"Then we find a way through it," he said, his voice nonchalant, as if the task were nothing more than a minor inconvenience.

"Yes!" cried the Cleric, rather too enthusiastically. He began to mutter wildly about gadgets and spell breakers, his words tumbling over one another in a torrent of excitement.

"Enough!" Father Benedict's voice boomed, silencing the Cleric's ramblings. "I don't need to know the details. Just get to work. Be swift. And keep me updated."

"Yes, Shepherd," said the Cleric, bowing his head before scampering off, his footsteps receding up the stairwell.

Father Benedict stood in the silence, his mind a whirlwind of thoughts and emotions. The witches had been located, but they had retreated into that accursed woodland. The task before them was daunting, but he knew they could overcome it. They had to.

The stairwell seemed to close in around him, the shadows deepening, the scent of burnt wood growing stronger. It was a place of power and tradition, a reflection of the Order itself. And like the Order, it would endure, no matter the challenges they faced.

With a renewed sense of determination, Father Benedict turned and strode away, his mind already planning their next move. The Order of Crimson would not be defeated. They would find the witches, they would succeed, and they would restore their honour. The very future of the world depended on it.

# 57
## DELIA

Seated around the fire with the smell of a herby stew wafting through the air, things seemed somewhat less wobbly to Delia. Mephistos seemed to have disappeared but additional armchairs had appeared, though it was unclear where they'd come from.

They nestled in comfortably while Ingrid conjured a small table to sit between them with mysterious items that Delia observed with some curiosity. Upon the table was a black cloth and a three-legged copper pot that began to smoke with incense.

Next to it sat a large glass bowl of water, along with an enormous crystal chunk.

"Now, cronies," Ingrid said.

"Cronies? Who are you calling cronies?" Agatha asked. "Oh, you mean like crones? Very clever. I get it."

Ingrid chuckled. "Now that you're suitably empotioned, it's time to do some scrying."

"Will we read the tea leaves, dear?" Marjie asked.

Ingrid huffed. "If you must."

A cup of tea promptly brewed itself and flew through the air, barely spilling a drop, right into Marjie's hands. It was a dainty china teacup with a matching saucer, unlike any of Ingrid's earthenware pieces.

Marjie beamed as she took a sip. "Ah, Earl Grey, perfect."

"From the basket you left on my porch," Ingrid muttered.

Marjie beamed even brighter at that.

"I could do with a cup too," Agatha said.

"Or a coffee?" Delia suggested.

Ingrid shook her head, "Nonsense, refreshments come after. First we work. For the next twenty minutes or so, stare into the incense smoke, the fire, the crystal, or the water...whatever you're called to look at, and allow the elements to reveal their secrets."

Delia immediately found herself drawn to the fire, her mind stilling as she watched its dance and flicker.

The embers glowed beneath the flames like her own budding powers, ready to burst forth at any moment.

Her old life had burned to the ground.

Embers, that was all that remained.

A wave of grief washed over her, cleansing away her resistance as she let it go.

Staring into those embers, she let her mind still, as Ingrid suggested.

Delia listened to the crackle of flames and the hoots of an owl outside. She breathed in the scent of sage and thyme, and something more mysterious drifting from the incense. She found her mind drawn along a narrow and windy path.

The fire, itself, seemed to tell a story, which unfolded as she meandered along on the path towards a mountain.

She began to climb the mountain and then decided to glide up instead.

From high up in the air, she noticed glowing red cracks towards the peak.

*A volcano.*

Lava pooled in a crater, spluttering and pulsing.

Delia stared into the bright, hot, red light.

Deep within, a dark shape was revealed. A creature.

From her vantage point floating high above, Delia continued to stare.

The creature opened its eye and looked right back at her.

*A dragon!*

It was as terrifying as it was beautiful, but in that moment, Delia was sucked forward, hurtling towards the crater. The lava burned through her, but she felt no pain.

She was in a tunnel now, speeding down, down, right down into the depths of time, right back through all creation, as if somebody had hit rewind on an old VCR.

All of a sudden, she came to the precipice of nothingness. Within the darkness at the beginning of creation.

Within this void she sensed presence, a malevolence, an intelligent, chaotic, destructive force.

"What are you?" Delia whispered.

"You may call me the Abyss," it replied. "And I am your downfall."

"I don't think so," said Delia stubbornly. "I've got plenty of trouble on my own. I'm quite happy to be my own downfall, thank you very much."

"Exactly," the voice replied, sending a creepy tingling sensation through Delia's bones. "I am within you. Your downfall is the world's downfall."

The sound of a bell rang out, jolting Delia from her meditation.

She found herself back in Ingrid's house, surrounded by the fire's warmth. No longer a floating entity conversing with the Abyss, but solid and slightly hungry. The potion was clearly wearing off. All eyes turned to her.

"What?" Delia asked, noting the shocked expressions on their faces.

"You started screaming," Marjie explained. "Are you quite alright, dear?"

Delia shook her head. "Screaming? I don't remember anything like that."

"It was agony," said Marjie.

"I thought you were about to die, right then and there," Agatha added.

Delia shook herself. "How strange...Well, what did everyone else see?"

"I saw a group...a kind of convent of cloaked women," said Marjie. "They were like nuns but different. It's hard to explain. They lived in the mountains in a kind of monastery. They tended the gardens...maybe they still do, but it looked old-fashioned."

Ingrid simply shook her head.

"Well, I saw an order of monks," said Agatha. "So perhaps you were mistaken."

"Monks?" said Ingrid, quirking an eyebrow.

"I can only assume that's what they were," said Agatha. "They had red robes, and I'm sure they were all men. Possibly some old Roman sect."

Delia felt herself tremble. "I've been attacked more than once by men in red robes, remember?"

"And they led to my house burning down!" said Marjie. "So perhaps I was mistaken about the women...but I don't think so."

"And what did you see, Ingrid?" Delia asked.

"I saw you." Ingrid stared Delia directly in the eyes.

"Me?"

"You were unleashing an ancient evil!" Ingrid said crossly.

"Not on purpose," Delia protested.

"What do you mean, dear?" Marjie asked, a note of anxiety in her voice.

"Delia still hasn't told us what made her scream," Agatha pointed out.

"Look," said Delia. "All I saw was time unfolding backwards, and then I was on the verge of absolute darkness and there was some sort of malevolent force...and I had a brief conversation—"

"Brief conversation?" said Ingrid drily.

"Yes!" said Delia.

"I see."

Delia felt her rage stir at being blamed for something she had no idea about.

"I also saw dragons," Ingrid added, before Delia's anger could set the house on fire.

"Dragons?" said Delia. "One of those robed men mentioned dragons, and I've seen something like that in my dreams...but surely they're not real."

Ingrid shook her head. "I forget you're so new to this."

"Well, I've never seen a dragon," said Agatha.

"Of course, you haven't; they're ancient, mythic beings," Marjie said. "No one has seen them for thousands of years. Perhaps they're more of a metaphor..."

Ingrid stomped a foot down. "No, not a metaphor at all."

"Do you think they're connected to whatever entity I was talking to?" Delia asked.

"Probably," said Ingrid. "Everything is connected. That is part of nature."

"So what then?" said Delia. "We've got a little quest to slay some dragons?"

"And a wolf," Agatha added.

"A wolf?" Marjie asked.

"I forgot to tell you all that I was chased by a wolf in my vision, earlier," said Delia.

Ingrid looked warily from Delia to Agatha.

"Well, I forgot to say," Agatha continued, "that the cult I saw in my vision...the monks, they had some kind of beast hidden behind huge metal doors. I don't know why. But I got a sense that it was some kind of wolf or enormous dog."

Delia slumped forward, feeling overwhelmed and defeated. But Ingrid clapped her hands. "Excellent! The more we know, the less we know."

"That doesn't sound like something to celebrate," Agatha grumbled.

"Celebration sounds like a good idea, though," said Marjie, "to lift our spirits. I don't suppose that delicious smell might be dinner?"

"Of course it is," said Ingrid. She clapped her hands, and several bowls sailed across the room to be filled by a floating ladle moments later.

They sat, still nestled cosily in their chairs, with the sound of delighted slurping, enjoying dinner. The stew was different from the broth Delia had last time: richer somehow, and even more aromatic and herby, but it was exactly what she needed, almost as if the brew was seeping into her bones, and knitting back together the small fractures of her soul. "I really need to learn how to cook like you," she muttered.

Ingrid replied with a rare satisfied smile. "In your dreams," she said quietly.

Marjie chuckled.

"So what now then?" said Agatha. "Do we armour up? Go chasing dragons?"

"Surely we're not going to actually kill dragons," said Delia. "I mean, if they exist...even if they are terrible, and frightening and dangerous. Wait—they're not fire-breathing, are they?" She looked around. "Okay, so maybe they are fire-breathing, whatever they are...It's a bit like sharks. Do we really have to kill them? I mean, they're perfectly fine minding their own business as long as we don't get in their way."

"But what if they get in our way?" said Agatha. "Or come after us? Whoever these enemies are, whether they're an ancient brotherhood of monks or some kind of agrarian sisterhood, they're clearly trying to harness the power of these dragons."

"We need to be prepared," Marjie agreed.

"Which means Delia needs to work out how to use her own magic properly," Agatha added.

"Add it to my to-do list," said Delia with a sigh.

"And we all need to unlock the power of the Elemental Crones," said Ingrid.

"Ah!" said Marjie excitedly. "How do we do that then?"

"That remains a mystery to me," said Ingrid. "Legend has it that the powers are threefold and each layer requires something different to unlock it. We'll find out more once we locate the ancient grimoire."

"Right then, tally ho!" said Agatha, getting up. "Where do we start?"

"We start with rest," said Ingrid firmly.

"Rest?" Delia asked.

"Oh yes," said Ingrid. "Nothing is worth doing if one hasn't had a proper nap first."

"I like the way you think," said Marjie.

"Nonsense," Agatha protested. "There's no time to spare."

"And if we are not properly rested and nourished," said Ingrid pragmatically, "we will not be at full capacity, which is exactly what's needed here."

"Oh, very well," Agatha relented. "I don't suppose you have any sherry?"

# 58

## THE CLERIC

"**B**rother Cedric?"

The cleric was startled from his daydream as he felt the car rumble beneath him like an impatient beast stuck in a giant snail shell. It was a far cry from the magical conveyances he was accustomed to, but inconspicuousness was the call of the hour.

"Yes?" he responded, so unused to being called by name. His superiors called him 'Cleric', as did the underling scribes he usually suffered the presence of. But these companions of his, the spell breakers, well, they were peers, if not equals.

"It's just that we're approaching Myrtlewood," said Brother Berberis, his voice filled with nervous anticipation. A portly man with thinning hair, he was known for his friendly demeanour and had served the Order with devotion.

Brother Ignatius, a tall, wiry figure with an ever-serious expression, looked up from his study of an ancient tome. "You seem distant, Brother Cedric."

"Just pondering what Father Benedict and the elders might be keeping from us," the Cleric mused, momentarily wondering what secrets lay with those higher in the Order. He knew far more than the spell breakers. He was sure of that. They only knew what they needed to in order to perform their jobs, as did the larger troupe of Order soldiers and guards who were to follow on behind them on proper transportation – horseback of course. Cloaking all the horses took time, and time was of the essence, so a motorcar had been provided for expediency.

"Best not to dwell on that now," said Brother Thaddeus, the youngest of the three spell breakers. His bright eyes sparkled with excitement. "We have a task ahead."

They reached the forest, and the Cleric's heart skipped a beat. It looked ordinary, yet he knew it was far from mundane.

The Rogue awaited them, his leather hat and oilskins making him appear part of the landscape itself. His presence was both unsettling and reassuring.

After a brief exchange of nods, the spell breakers retrieved their magical implements, intricate devices, worn with age but gleaming with a power that could see beyond mere physical appearance.

"Are you sure you want to attempt this?" the Rogue asked gruffly. "It's best not to provoke wild animals, and this forest is a wild beast unto its own if ever I saw one."

"Nonsense," said the Cleric. "This is what we came here for!"

"But this forest is far from ordinary," the Rogue protested.

"It's never ordinary with magic," Berberis cautioned, pulling out a mystical magnifier, its lens etched with runes of detection.

Ignatius held a divining compass, an antique that whispered to the magical north, while Thaddeus wielded an ancient spell-breaker's mallet, its head inlaid with gems that shimmered with enchantment.

The forest was a dense and tangled place, thick with foliage and seemingly impenetrable. But as the spell breakers began to scrutinise the area, the unseen began to unfold.

Threads of magic emerged, interwoven between the branches, delicate as gossamer and strong as steel. They shimmered like moonlight, dancing in graceful patterns, casting ethereal shadows that only the trained eye could see.

Ignatius's compass spun and twirled, revealing hidden paths where the ley lines crossed and energies merged. The forest was not just alive; it was sentient, each tree a note in a symphony, each leaf a word in a poem.

Thaddeus's mallet resonated with a deep hum, a sound that was felt more than heard, aligning itself with the magical frequency of the place, acknowledging the strength and beauty of the unseen barriers.

Thaddeus raised one of the implements, waving it in the air towards the forest while the other two spell breakers recited a revealing charm.

The Cleric watched, transfixed, as the leaves began to glow with a luminescent green, a living network of energy pulsing through the veins of each leaf. His breath caught in his throat, the sight so unexpected.

Berberis gasped as he too looked through his lens. "By the ancient runes! Look at the bark, the patterns!"

As the instrument passed over the bark, the very texture seemed to shift, patterns emerging that were a fusion of geometry and poetry, a code written in nature itself. The trees were alive with magic, a hidden artistry woven into the very fabric of life.

Ignatius let out an awe-stricken whisper. "The forest...it's singing." The gentle whisper of leaves transformed into a harmonic melody that resonated with the very core of being, the magic within it becoming an audible symphony.

Thaddeus watched in awe. The Cleric followed his gaze, sure he was sharing the very same wonder at the connections between the living flora and the underlying arcane essence. Every glance brought a new revelation, a fresh sigh.

The forest was an enigma, a riddle written in leaves and water and wind. As they looked deeper, more layers revealed themselves, a complexity that was both beautiful and bewildering.

The Cleric's heart swelled with awe and trepidation as he realised the enormity of what lay before them. This was not merely a forest; it was a masterpiece of nature and magic combined, a testament to a wisdom long forgotten.

And they were about to break it apart.

A heavy silence settled over them as they reached the forest's edge, the weight of their task settling upon their shoulders.

The Rogue finally spoke, his voice low and filled with a knowledge deeper than words. "Are you ready?"

The Cleric met his gaze, knowing that what lay ahead was more than a task; it was a journey into the unknown, a path that would test them all.

"By the stars," Berberis whispered, his eyes wide with awe. "I've never seen anything like it. The magic here is not just in nature; it is nature."

"It's a crime to break such a masterpiece," Ignatius noted, his voice filled with reverence.

The Rogue merely grunted, his face inscrutable, yet his eyes seemed to share their sentiments.

"But break it, we must," the Cleric insisted. "The very future of the world is at stake."

There was a moment of silence, filled only with the soft rustle of leaves and the distant call of a bird. The spell breakers looked at each other, understanding the gravity of their task.

"It will take a long time," Berberis finally said.

The Cleric, however, rallied himself. "Then we must hurry."

The words hung in the air as they set to work. The Rogue hung back, speaking only when spoken to. The spell breakers worked with reverence, beginning the process of unravelling the magic with a sense of awe and respect.

The Cleric watched, his hands rubbing together with glee, the opportunity to see how things worked outside the compound surging through him. But he could not shake the uneasy feeling that they were meddling with something far greater than they understood.

Hours passed, yet the magic held.

The Cleric's anger began to rise. "Try harder!" he commanded.

Slowly, but surely, signs of the unravelling began to reveal themselves, like an old shirt fraying at the edges. They pressed on, the magical barrier yielding slowly, reluctantly, each thread a piece of art being undone.

As the first thread peeled away, the Cleric felt a pang of loss, but also a thrill of discovery. The world beyond the compound was indeed a place of wonder and mystery, a place where magic was not just a tool but a living entity, a partner in a dance that had no beginning and no end.

The Rogue watched silently, his presence a constant reminder of the unknown.

Finally, they reached the last layer. Brother Thaddeus looked up, exhaustion in his eyes. "It will take time."

"We don't have time," the Cleric insisted, his voice edged with urgency. "The battalion will be here soon, and they need a way through."

The Rogue's eyes met his, understanding and warning mingled in his gaze.

They began the final work, the future of the Order hanging precariously in the balance, the forest's enchantment unravelling, its secrets laid bare.

# 59
## DELIA

Delia woke, disorientated. It took her a moment to realise where she was – still in Ingrid's cabin. They'd all settled in for a nap. Agatha and Marjie still reclined in their chairs – Delia could see them from the window seat – and Ingrid had retired to bed.

Perhaps it was the hearty meal and the mead that they'd enjoyed earlier, but everyone seemed to have slept rather soundly.

In fact, Delia found herself drifting back to sleep and began meandering down a forest path in her mind. Then she was running...faster and faster.

*Dum dum dum dum dum.* A drumming sound thrummed through the room.

Delia jolted awake, her dreams of being chased down a forest path by a mysterious figure interrupted.

Ingrid clattered down the stairs.

"What's that infernal racket?" Agatha grumbled.

"My warning chimes are being activated," said Ingrid. "They're coming for us."

"Who?" asked Marjie, rubbing her eyes. "Not those bloody blokes who burned my house down?"

"Chances are high it's the same outfit," said Ingrid. "However, all I can confirm is that someone has entered this forest with ill intent, and they're looking for me."

"That's a clever piece of magic," said Agatha. "Remind me to pick your brain about it in the future."

Ingrid shot her a look that said no one would be getting anywhere near her brain.

"Or not," said Agatha, folding her arms.

"The forest will deceive them for a bit," said Ingrid.

"You talk about the forest as if it's sentient," said Delia. "Is it really?" Surely, if witches and dragons were real, a sentient forest wasn't much of a stretch.

"Of course it is!" said Ingrid. "What a question! A forest is a life system, made up of many living things that speak to each other."

"Just like the mycelium through the earth," said Delia.

"I suppose," said Ingrid.

"But will it do your bidding?" Delia asked.

Ingrid chortled. "I daresay it won't do my bidding, but I look after it, and it looks after me. That's how forests work."

"Very well," said Delia. "That sounds like it's to our advantage."

"But they'll find us eventually," said Ingrid. "Faster or slower, depending on how good their magic is."

A second rattling noise echoed through the house.

"I suspect faster," said Agatha.

"There's no time to spare," Ingrid said. "We must prepare."

"Haven't you warded this place to the nines?" Agatha asked.

"Of course I have," Ingrid replied. "But there's no point in sitting around waiting to see if they break through. We have a mission."

"We do?" said Marjie, perking up. "How thrilling!"

Ingrid shot her an unimpressed look. "It's not a party."

"What are we doing?" Delia asked.

"We need to find and activate the power of the Elemental Crones,"

Ingrid announced. "And to do that we need to retrieve an important artefact…"

"The grimoire! Of course we do," said Agatha. "What are we waiting for? And…uhh…how are we going to do that, exactly?"

"I have an idea of where it might be," said Ingrid. "I've even investigated the place, but I couldn't get through the protections alone."

"How will we even get out of here?" Delia asked. "I suspect it might be hard to go by car if there's someone in the forest…I don't suppose witches actually travel by broom?"

Uproarious laughter followed.

"Brooms are more trouble than they're worth, dear," said Marjie.

"However, it can be a bit of fun if you're in the right mood." Agatha winked.

Delia blushed, not sure whether she wanted to know what they were referring to.

"No, we travel by goat," said Ingrid, as if this was the most normal and matter-of-fact thing in the world.

"Goat?" Delia asked, her eyes wide. "You want to ride through the forest on a goat?"

"Of course. Put on your warm clothing."

"Off through the forest then?" said Marjie. "A wonderful adventure!"

"It's not supposed to be fun, remember," said Agatha, as they began to dress in warm layers of clothing.

Delia, rather baffled, put on her own coat and wrapped the scratchy but warm woollen scarf that Ingrid handed her, firmly around her neck.

After a few bustling moments, and rather rigorous pottering around, Ingrid led them out through the back door where the two goats Delia had spotted earlier now seemed to be been tethered to a small cart.

"You're serious," said Delia flatly. "I suppose it's too late for me to wish that this was some kind of practical joke?"

"Just get in," Ingrid said sternly.

They climbed into the small cart which proved to be surprisingly roomier on the inside. Agatha nodded in approval as she sat down on a worn bench at the back. "I don't suppose you have any reading material?" she said.

"Under the seat," said Ingrid, positioning herself at the front of the cart. "But careful when you turn the pages. Alright then." She snapped her fingers, and the goats stood to attention, their focus shifted from grazing to their upcoming journey, heads upright and horns held high as if waiting for further instructions.

"Hold tight," Ingrid said. "West," she instructed, and the goats took off along nearly invisible forest paths with impressive speed.

"They must be enchanted," Delia muttered as she steadied herself.

"Of course they are, dear," said Marjie as she pulled some knitting from her bag.

"Knitting at a time like this?" Delia asked, astounded.

"Well, Agatha's reading," said Marjie.

"I suppose so," said Delia, with a sigh. "Silly of me not to pack any crafts for a night time goat-cart mission."

"That's okay," said Ingrid. "You can be lookout. Keep an eye on the forest. I don't have eyes in the back of my head...at least not usually."

Delia stared out. She watched the forest rush by. Despite the speed they moved at, there was only a light breeze brushing her face and through her hair – undoubtedly another consequence of magic, which it turned out, could be quite convenient, at times. Such as when one wants a slightly roomier vehicle, to travel quickly by goat, or wants somebody else to pour the tea. Delia wondered momentarily whether there was a spell to fold a fitted sheet, but then decided that would clearly be too difficult and complex. "Best not to dabble in the dark arts," she muttered to herself, then giggled.

"What was that dear?" Marjie asked, lifting a strand of lime green wool and pulling it into another stitch.

"Nothing," said Delia. "Just entertaining myself."

Having adjusted to the surprise of their adventure, Delia felt a thrilling invigoration as they sped through her woods. Her eyes occasionally darted towards some sign of movement or flicker of light, but she could discern no noticeable threats. Besides, who could really follow them all the way out here when they were travelling so quickly?

Her mind began to race with imagined possibilities.

Perhaps the enemy, whoever they were, already had control of dragons.

She kept an eye on the skies, just in case, though Delia had no idea what she'd do in the actual event of a dragon. She made a mental note to ask the others to help her refine her powers as soon as possible. Accidentally setting things on fire was hardly going to cut it in a dragon fight.

The cart continued to hurtle through the forest, following the trails that only Ingrid and her enchanted goats seemed to see. The cool night air whispered secrets as it swirled around them, mingling with the rhythmic clatter of hooves.

Suddenly, Delia's heart leapt into her throat as she caught a glimpse of something. A shadowy movement, a drumbeat of hooves, a glint of moonlight reflecting off something metallic, and a chilling sensation down her spine.

"Ingrid!" Delia yelled, her voice cracking with alarm. "There's something following us!"

The clatter of hooves intensified, and all mirth and knitting were abandoned. Agatha's book slapped shut, and Marjie's woollen strands tangled as they turned to look.

"What is it?" Agatha demanded, squinting into the darkness.

The drumming of hooves grew louder, echoing like thunder as they reverberated through the forest. A chill ran down Delia's spine, and she gripped the edge of the cart, her fingers white with fear.

"They're on horseback!" Delia cried. "Those red-hooded hooligans!"

Her words were met with a sudden surge of energy from Ingrid, who whipped the goats into a frantic gallop. The cart lurched forward, throwing them all off balance.

"Defensive positions!" Ingrid ordered, her voice sharp with command. "They're attacking!"

Marjie and Agatha leapt to action, hands moving in swift, complex patterns as they summoned spells of protection and defence. The air sizzled with magic, and the cart was surrounded by an invisible barrier.

"Can you see them?" Marjie shouted, her eyes wide with terror.

"There!" Delia pointed as the red cloaks came into view from between the trees. There were two dozen at least, and they were fast approaching.

A gasp escaped Delia's lips as the first wave of magic hurtled towards them, a swirling vortex of energy aimed at the goat cart.

"Help!" she screamed, ducking as Marjie and Agatha's spells met the attackers' magic head-on.

Explosions rocked the air, and the cart swerved violently as Ingrid steered them through the chaos. The forest was alive with flashes of light, and the ground shook with the force of their battle.

"Fight back!" Agatha yelled, hurling a spell over her shoulder. "We can't let them catch us!"

The chase was on, a desperate race through the forest with their lives at stake. Magic clashed and sparked as they exchanged blows with the Order of Crimson, the air thick with tension and fear.

Delia's breath came in ragged gasps as she watched the onslaught, her eyes wide and unblinking. The forest was a blur, the path twisting and turning as they hurtled onward.

There was no turning back.

With a glance over her shoulder, Delia caught a glimpse of the Cowboy – Declan – his cold eyes fixed on her, his expression unreadable. Her heart pounded in her chest. He was hanging back behind the others, but he was definitely with the Order. There was no doubt about that now.

Delia's fear turned into something else, a flash of anger mixed with determination. She glared at Declan, her eyes narrowing in pure rage.

The Cowboy's hat burst into flames.

A look of shock crossed his face, and he reached up to swat at the fire, his eyes wide with surprise. His steed whinnied and reared, momentarily throwing the pursuit into disarray.

Delia burst into a cackle of laughter, joined by Marjie, Agatha, and Ingrid.

"Good one!" Ingrid said, turning her head to fire another blast of magic at their attackers.

# 60

## THE ROGUE

The Rogue reached for the brim of his hat, dowsing it in magic to put out the flames. He cursed as the smell of burning leather filled his nostrils. His horse reared in panic, and the Rogue fought to regain control, his mind a whirlwind of confusion and anger.

He looked up to see the Cleric riding beside him, his eyes blazing with righteous fury. "Fight, man, fight!" the Cleric urged, his voice filled with desperation. "We must stop them!"

"Fighting isn't in my contract," the Rogue growled, his voice dripping with disdain. "I gave that up long ago."

He pulled back on the reins, allowing the others to charge ahead, the sounds of magic being hurtled filling the air. He stayed close enough to see what was going on, his heart pounding in his chest. Under his breath, he murmured a protective charm. No one needed to die now. Not when mortal life was so fleeting and fragile. It was a loophole in his contract. He wasn't directly working against his employers, just minimising the collateral damage.

The Order of Crimson's attack became more ferocious as they hurled magical projectiles towards the goat cart. Magic crackled in the air, forming incandescent streaks that seared through the night, leaving luminescent trails behind them. The witches retaliated by weaving intricate counter spells, their fingers dancing in precise patterns, creating barriers that deflected and dispersed the magical onslaught.

The scene before him was chaotic and terrifying. Bolts of magic flew in every direction, the forest itself seeming to come alive with energy.

The old crone driving the goat cart looked familiar, but the Rogue couldn't place her. He watched, transfixed, as she stood, turned, and cried out, "Enough!"

She began to chant an ancient spell in a language long forgotten. Her voice deepened, resonating with a mystical timbre that carried through the forest.

Despite his long life, the Rogue had rarely encountered magic so ancient and powerful. He gasped as her eyes turned a milky white, and it almost looked as though she was floating above the cart. The wind howled in response, swirling leaves and branches in a mesmerising dance.

The forest itself began to react to Ingrid's call. Trees seemed to sway and lean toward the source of the magic, their bark pulsating in unison with the rhythm of the chant. Tendrils and vines emerged from the ground, slithering towards the Order's horses. They reached out, snaring and enveloping them in a tight embrace. The forest's power manifested in waves of emerald energy that rippled across the landscape, intertwining with the old woman's magnificent spell work. The fusion of nature's raw power with the crone's mastery created a mesmerising spectacle of lights, shadows, and ethereal sounds.

Darkness overtook them, and the Rogue's world went black.

He woke, not knowing how long he had been out, but the sky was growing lighter. Someone groaned next to him on the forest floor. They all lay there in piles of leaves, the Order members stirring while the horses slept peacefully, their flanks rising and falling in a gentle rhythm.

The Rogue reached for his slightly singed hat, his mind still reeling from the magnificent display of magic he had witnessed. A smile crept across his face, a mixture of admiration and awe. They had been bested by those old witches, beaten back by the very forest itself.

He looked around, his eyes taking in the scene. The Cleric was on his knees, his face pale and drawn. The Rogue knew that something had changed, something profound and irrevocable.

The forest had spoken, and they had all been humbled by its power. The battle was over, at least for now, and the Rogue felt a strange sense of peace settling over him. They had been taught a lesson, one that he would not soon forget.

The forest had protected its own, and the Rogue knew that he had been a part of something much larger than himself. He tipped his hat in silent acknowledgment, a newfound respect for the crones and their magic. It was a victory well deserved, but judging by the zealous gleam in the Cleric's eyes, he knew the fight was far from over.

# 61
## DELIA

Delia kept watch, but there were no more signs of the Order as the goat cart travelled miles west, then north, then west again, and finally northwest into wide, snowy plains. Delia wondered where they were going, but somehow she knew she wouldn't find out until they arrived.

The night sky was just beginning to lighten along the horizon as they left the cover of the forest and found themselves on a country lane. The goats continued to speed along and Delia wondered what a sight they'd be for a farmer out to milk the cows, but there was no one around to see it.

After a few minutes, Ingrid made a sharp left, directing the goat cart down a driveway that branched off the country lane towards an old farmhouse.

"Where's this, then?" Agatha inquired.

"You'll see," Ingrid responded.

"I hope we're not just showing up uninvited at some stranger's house," Marjie muttered.

Delia yawned. "Maybe there'll be no one home and we can sneak in and sleep in their beds for the night. Leave it nice and tidy in the morning."

Ingrid simply shook her head as they approached the house.

It was an old-fashioned building with stone walls and a thatched roof, the sort of place that, despite their prevalence in the countryside, seemed like it was straight out of a fairy tale.

A light came on from inside the house, and as the goat cart came to a halt, the front door opened.

A woman with long flowing white hair stepped out, holding a lantern.

"Ingrid, what are you doing here at this time of night?"

"Not strangers then," said Marjie, looking relieved.

Delia couldn't help but smile at Marjie's code of hospitality, which was evidently much stronger than her own. After all, turning up uninvited seemed like the least inappropriate thing they'd done in the past twenty-four hours.

"Who are your friends?" the woman asked Ingrid.

"Go on and introduce yourselves," said Ingrid. "We don't have all day."

The woman smiled at them peacefully. "I'm Mathilda. Ingrid's sister."

"Sister?" Agatha asked, surprised. She turned her stern gaze on Ingrid. "I never thought of you as having family."

"Everyone has family, whether you know them or want to...Some things can't be helped," Ingrid responded.

Mathilda gave her an inscrutable look. "Come inside," she said.

Ingrid whistled and the goats trotted around to the back of the house with their cart, where they would no doubt quickly unburden themselves and begin grazing again.

Delia followed Marjie and Mathilda into the house, with Agatha and Ingrid bringing up the rear.

Inside, the house was simple and clean with few adornments. It was relatively uncluttered compared to the cottages Delia had visited recently.

"What kind of trouble have you got yourself into this time?" Mathilda asked, leading them into a rather austere kitchen.

They sat around a solid oak kitchen table and accepted some bitter chamomile tea.

Delia hoped it would help her to relax, maybe even sleep. She was feeling so exhausted that her bones were practically grumbling at her, yet she was curious about this woman, Mathilda, who lived all the way out here.

She and Ingrid didn't seem especially close, and yet clearly there was a kinship bond.

"It's the Order of Crimson," Ingrid finally admitted.

"That ridiculous brotherhood," Mathilda replied. "They're after you?"

"As we suspected," said Ingrid. "I don't suppose you would mind putting us up for the night?"

Mathilda took a sip of her tea. "Of course not, sister." There was a measured silence, laden with a kind of tension that Delia didn't completely understand. Perhaps there had been an old family feud.

"What do you know about this Order of Crimson?" Delia asked, too curious to remain silent. "If I'm going to protect my family against them, I need more information."

Mathilda regarded her cautiously. "They've come after you, have they?"

"Several times," Delia replied.

"And they burned down my house," Marjie chimed in.

Mathilda shuddered. "Then it's worse than we thought. They're amassing power. They're going after the unspeakable."

Ingrid sighed. "Of course they are. We need more information, and not just about the Order. I need to go to the library."

Agatha looked rather pleased at the idea. "What kind of library are we talking about here?"

"I believe Ingrid is referring to the library in the abandoned hamlet of Gildea," Mathilda explained when Ingrid remained silent, staring down at the table. "It's believed that a sacred grimoire is hidden there, that only the Elemental Crones can access."

"Why is it abandoned?" Delia asked abruptly.

"Oh, you know. The usual. Something terrible happened there long ago," Ingrid said dismissively. "The details aren't important. What's important is that there's a library there which I believe contains an ancient book – one that will give us the information we seek."

"On the Crones," Delia asked, earning disapproving looks from Ingrid and Agatha.

"You're still going on about all that?" Mathilda queried, looking at Ingrid imploringly. "When are you going to re-join the sisterhood?"

Ingrid shook her head, "You know it's not for me."

"But you are always a member," Mathilda retorted. The statement had an ominous undertone that made Delia uneasy. She wanted to know much more, but she was both too exhausted and too frightened of Ingrid to ask.

"You may sleep here tonight," Mathilda said. "We have spare cots. It's not the most lavish of accommodations..."

"I'm sure it'll be the Ritz compared to that goat cart," said Delia.

They trudged off down the hallway. Mathilda led them into a single room with four rather plain-looking beds. Delia didn't care that the mattress was slightly too firm, or that she had only a particularly scratchy woollen blanket for warmth. She crawled into bed fully clothed and quickly drifted off to sleep.

# 62

## MATHILDA

Mathilda's mind was a whirlwind of thoughts and feelings, pulled in every direction by duty, sisterhood, family, and a certain irrational irritation that had followed her sister around like a cloud of gnats since they were children.

With a sigh, she rose from her simple cot and made her way to the ornate black mirror that hung in a private room, the connection to her superiors at the Veiled Sisterhood. She brushed a lock of hair back, hoping she looked suitably serious and mysterious. The moonlight cast an eerie glow in the room, and she looked at her reflection, her image framed by the dark carved wood of the mirror. "Why do I always look like I've been dragged through a hedge backwards?" she grumbled to herself.

She spoke the charm that activated the mirror, and it swam with swirls like smoke and clouded over. Nothing happened for a moment, but Mathilda wasn't surprised. It was very late – or very early depending on perspective. At least they couldn't scold her for sleeping in.

Mathilda waited patiently, staring into the murky mirror. "Perhaps I should try again later," she muttered.

"Try what?" Sister Breag's voice croaked.

"Oh...you are here."

The surface of the mirror shimmered, revealing the faces of the elder sisters looking decidedly grumpy.

There was Gwyneth, looking as wise as she always did, and Sister Breag, looking rattled.

"They're here – they're all here!" Mathilda practically burst out.

"Who?" Sister Breag asked. "Speak clearly, child."

Mathilda blushed. She was hardly a child. She was probably only slightly younger than Breag, but now was the time to pick her battles if ever there was one.

"The Crones."

"How do you know it is them?" Sister Gwyneth asked.

"I...I just know it's them," Mathilda replied.

"Where exactly?" Sister Breag asked. "Can we meet them?"

"Err..." Mathilda mumbled. "I sent them to bed. They arrived very late and, besides, I don't think Ingrid would agree."

"Of course she wouldn't," Sister Breag grumbled.

There was a moment's pause, and then Gwyneth said, "Well, they're with you. That's good, isn't it? It's exactly why you were sent to the outpost."

Breag frowned slightly, her brow furrowing like a very concerned garden. "Bring them in. It's time."

"No, it's too early," Gwyneth argued, her eyes narrowing with the kind of wisdom that comes from always knowing exactly when it's too early for something. "Destiny must play out."

"But Ingrid must come home!" Breag exclaimed, her voice rising in pitch. "The ancient feminine powers must be returned to the sisterhood!"

"Leave them be," said Gwyneth. "Things will happen in due course."

"Well, we can't just leave them at the outpost, can we?"

Mathilda's eyes darted between the two sisters as they bickered, her mind a whirlwind of confusion, impatience, and an inexplicable craving for biscuits.

"They won't stay here!" Mathilda finally shouted. "They're on the run from the Order. Surely there must be some plan?"

"We must consider the greater good, Mathilda," Gwyneth intoned wisely.

"Greater good? I've got four crones sleeping on cots, and they snore like a herd of elephants!"

Breag's lips twitched, but she maintained her composure. "I want to give that Ingrid a piece of my mind."

Gwyneth shook her head and elbowed Breag out of the way. "As you know, they are the key to something bigger, Mathilda. We need to guide them, not control them."

"Oh, guide them, is it?" Mathilda snapped. "Well, I guided them to their cots for the night, that's about all the guidance I've got from you."

"Ingrid's return is essential," Gwyneth said, her voice soft but firm. "But we must let the situation unfold naturally. They must unlock the ancient power first. They have their path, and we have ours."

Mathilda sighed, exasperated. "What if the Order catches them before they can unlock as much as a single door?"

But the elder sisters, now seeming to be on the same page at last, merely muttered about destiny and said nothing more useful.

Mathilda begrudgingly thanked them, ended the connection, and looked at her own reflection in the now-silent mirror. Her face looked drawn, her eyes tired.

"Blasted destiny," she muttered.

# 63

## DELIA

T he sound of a blaring horn jolted Delia awake.

"We've got to go," said Ingrid's voice.

Delia rubbed her eyes and looked up to see that the older woman was already up and dressed. Delia groaned; every ache and pain from her past six-and-a-half decades had come back all at the same time to taunt her.

"What's going on?" Agatha asked, putting on her spectacles.

"No time to explain," Ingrid answered. "They're after us. We've got to go now."

In a flurry of activity, the four women hurriedly dressed and gathered supplies, gifted or possibly pilfered from Mathilda.

They stole out into the darkness moments later.

"Where's the goat cart?" Delia asked.

"In the shed," Ingrid replied as the rumble of hooves echoed in the distance. Delia looked towards the horizon to see a group of horsemen galloping towards them.

"Quickly," said Ingrid.

"But, how on earth will we escape?" Delia questioned.

"I don't think they've seen us yet. Not properly," Ingrid assured her.

Ingrid opened the shed door. Inside, the goats eyed them suspiciously as they munched on a haystack.

"You know," said Delia, "people often complain about women being invisible. But I would quite appreciate some invisibility right now...In fact, if there was any kind of magic that I could—"

"Hurry up," said Ingrid briskly. "Get in!"

They piled into the goat cart.

"Alright, now cover your ears," Ingrid instructed.

Unsure why, Delia did as told.

The next thing she knew, Delia heard muffled words as Ingrid muttered some kind of incantation and the shed shook.

Delia gasped as the floor gave way and the cart dropped into a pit. Through billows of dust, they found themselves in an underground cavern.

Above them, the shed floor reassembled itself, forming a ceiling of the cave.

"These pathways are old," Ingrid explained. "I'm not allowed to give away the secret to accessing them. That blasted sisterhood still has me bound by oath."

"Handy though!" said Marjie cheerfully. "I must remember to set up some underground pathways of my own, although there are already plenty of those in Myrtlewood. The vampires use them to get around."

"You're kidding me," said Delia. "Vampires, too? What else is real?"

"Basically anything you can imagine," Agatha assured her.

Delia gulped.

They sped off through narrow underground tunnels with scant illumination. The goats seemed to see just fine, and the path was evidently wide enough for the cart to pass through, but Delia braced herself just the same. "What makes you so sure they didn't see us?" she asked Ingrid.

"I cloaked us as we left the house."

"So, you do have the power of invisibility?" Delia said. "But if we can hide, why are we running?"

"Cloaking magic is hard to maintain for long and uses up a lot of energy," said Marjie. "Especially when the fellows chasing us seem rather adept at breaking through our protections. But it comes in handy in a pinch, and the basics are fairly simple. I'm sure we could all do it."

"Speak for yourself," Delia replied. "All I can do is accidentally set things on fire."

"We must set up a training regime for you, dear," Marjie said with a warm smile, her face illuminated by a glowing ball she held between her hands, which Delia assumed was some sort of light magic.

"When are we ever going to find time for a training regime?" Delia asked.

"There's a more potent magic," said Ingrid. "Or legend of it. A powerful cloaking that the Elemental Crones of Myrtlewood will be able to access."

"Oh good," said Marjie. "Then the Order will leave us alone for a while. They can hopefully get on with their lives, perhaps pick up some new hobbies for themselves. What do they think they're doing, chasing a bunch of old women around the countryside? It's ridiculous!"

Delia couldn't help but laugh.

"I suggest you keep the noise down," said Ingrid. "These tunnels belong to the Sisterhood, and they don't like me being down here."

Delia desperately wanted to ask about the Sisterhood. Were they actual sisters or something like nuns? Were they the same women that Marjie had seen in her vision, and if so, why didn't Ingrid say anything? However, she intuited that now was not the time to test Ingrid's patience.

As they sped through the tunnels, many questions swirled in Delia's mind, making her feel dizzy. She was afraid she might lose her dinner, or breakfast, or whatever the last meal was that they ate.

It was hard to keep track of time. It must be early morning or was it now evening? How long had they slept? Being underground wasn't helping her circadian rhythms find any rationality to speak of. It could have been an age that passed, or it might only have been a few minutes, but eventually, a light brightened up ahead, and the goat cart slowed. Above them, shining like the sun, was a circular opening, and below it, a pool of water reflecting the blue of the sky.

"We'll leave the goats here," said Ingrid, procuring some straw for them and tethering them near the pool. Marjie assured them the water was perfectly safe to drink. Apparently she could just tell these things.

Following Ingrid's instructions, they began climbing a stone ladder built into the wall. 'Ladder' was probably too generous a term. It was more like a series of deliberately placed holes which one's hands and feet could grip onto.

Marjie and Agatha both grumbled about the climb, but Ingrid was completely silent.

Delia's problematic hip ached. She winced with every step, fearful of slipping and falling onto Marjie below.

Despite all this, the climb proved easier than it had looked and Delia suspected Ingrid was using magic to aid them, especially given Agatha's need of a cane.

Eventually, with a hand-up from Agatha, Delia reached the surface, blinking into the blinding light of the midday sun. "At least I know what time it is now," she muttered to herself.

Marjie clambered out behind her, unaided.

"So where are we, then?" Agatha asked, looking around.

They looked to be in the centre of a small village.

"This is the hamlet I was telling you about," said Ingrid.

On closer inspection, Delia noticed that the stone buildings around them had smashed or boarded-up windows. "It's abandoned...a ghost town?"

"Look over there," said Marjie, pointing to barren fields.

"Do you think there was a recent snowfall that killed everything off?" Delia asked.

"No, there'd be more green," Marjie replied. "I suspect whatever happened out there is what drove the villagers away."

"Hamlets don't have villagers," Agatha interjected.

"What do they have then?" Marjie asked. "Hamleters?"

"Hams," said Agatha drily.

Delia giggled.

"Stop dilly-dallying," Ingrid scolded. "We need to find the library."

The hamlet wasn't much to look at. Delia was slightly disappointed. She'd expected something grand – a large stately library with pillars outside, several stories high, but there was nothing like that in sight.

After poking around several of the small structures, Ingrid cried out in triumph, "Here it is! I found it!"

The four of them crowded around in front of an unassuming stone building with its front windows intact. Peering in, Delia could see rows and rows of books. "Well, that's something," she said. "At least there are still books inside."

"I can't get in," said Ingrid. "The door's locked with some kind of magic."

"Do you think that's why the windows are intact too?" Delia asked.

Marjie nodded. "This place is protected, at least more than anywhere else in this place seems to be."

Delia stood back as the three others took turns trying to unlock the door to no avail.

"Would you like to try, dear?" Marjie offered.

"I don't think so," said Delia. "If anything, I'd just set the place on fire."

"That might help us get in..." Agatha muttered.

"Actually, I do have an idea," said Delia. "What if we all try together?"

"Together?" said Ingrid.

Delia sighed, exasperated. "Look, if this was a play, we'd need to think about things differently in order to stop going around in circles. Surely there's something about the four elements that's important to this whole story arc."

"What are you talking about?" Ingrid grumbled. "This isn't one of your fantasy novels."

"I'm not a fantasy writer, I'm a director," Delia replied.

"The same principle applies," said Agatha. "And why would we follow directions from a complete novice?"

Delia glared at her. "Because this seems like a worthy direction to try! Look, I'm merely suggesting something. If you have any better ideas—"

"Fine, we'll try it," said Ingrid.

"What exactly are we trying?" Agatha asked,

Delia rolled her eyes. "I don't know, maybe everyone just put your hands on the door at the same time."

Nothing happened.

"Now what?" said Ingrid.

"Err, maybe there are some magic words?" said Delia. "Or we could just will it to open?"

Agatha huffed, but Marjie reached out with her other hand. "Alright, everyone. Let's will it to open on three. One...two...three!"

Delia sent out a silent wish for the door to open, and interestingly enough, she felt a tingle running down her arm.

Marjie reached for the doorknob and turned.

There was a slight creak and then the four of them fell forwards through the door which had now vanished.

Plumes of dust billowed out.

Delia coughed. "I wish they'd included magical cleaning when they protected this building!"

"That's harder than it sounds," said Marjie. "You really need automancy for that in the long term."

The door materialised again, behind them.

Ingrid shook her head.

"I hope we're not trapped," said Agatha.

"The more important thing to hope for," said Ingrid, "is that we can find it."

"What are we looking for exactly?" Marjie asked.

"The book!" Ingrid said. "The old grimoire, of course."

Delia waved her hand around at the stacks of books. "I think in a place like this, you're going to have to be more specific."

Agatha's eyes glistened in excitement as she observed the literary hoard. "I wonder if I could borrow a few..."

Ingrid sighed. "From my scrying, I think it's supposed to be a black book with silver lettering."

Delia looked around. Many of the books appeared to be blue and red and green, but there weren't many black books. They began poring over the shelves, pulling out volumes here and there.

"Such a collection!" said Agatha gleefully.

# 64

## THE CLERIC

The dawn was breaking, a sliver of light rising on the horizon, and the Cleric could feel a newness dawning in his life as well. The Cleric felt it in his very soul: anticipation, victory. It tingled through his veins like a promise. The horse beneath him was strong and sure-footed, carrying him and his companions, the Order of Crimson, toward their destiny.

Wind whistled in his ears, tugging at his crimson cloak, as they rode through the snowy fields. They had been bested in the forest, the stronghold of those wily crones, but out here in the open, the playing field was levelled.

The Rogue guided them, his tracking magic unerring. The Cleric tried to study him, to learn more of his mysteries, but he could gather no intel other than the general awareness that the Rogue held some mysterious small objects in his palm, which he whispered enchantments to occasionally.

The spell breakers rode ahead, their implements glowing with energy, cutting through any cloaking magic the witches threw in their way.

His mind wandered to the mission's details, murky though they were: The crones would find some kind of powerful artefact, and then the order would capture them. That was the plan.

The attack in the forest, earlier, had been a tactical manoeuvre designed by the Shepherd to spur on those unpredictable witches. Despite Father Benedict's severe arrogance, he really was a master strategist. The idea was to round them up like sheep and herd them to exactly where they were needed. The Cleric was still not privy to all the details, but he suspected the Crone power to be dangerously powerful; something the Order should certainly wield or at least take for safe-keeping. Father Benedict had been furious, yes, when they'd lost track of their targets several times, and when the fire witch had behaved in such an unpredictable way so as to thwart the Order's tight timetable. However, things were back on track. The artefact would be retrieved by the Crones, for they were the only ones who could access it, and then the Order would rightfully take control.

A flicker of doubt nagged at the Cleric's mind as he glanced towards the Rogue. He didn't trust the man, not entirely, but he respected his magic. An effective tool, but one he would discard when the time was right.

The thought of the Rogue being free, leaving all the glory to him, filled the Cleric with a satisfying warmth.

The Cleric allowed himself a small satisfied smile, one even the Crimson Shepherd would surely find no fault in.

Yes, victory was in the air. He could feel it, taste it. His heart pounded enthusiastically.

Father Benedict, in his austere ivory tower, would be proud of him finally. The Cleric was getting his hands dirty on the ground, proving himself, just as Benedict had for many years.

The Cleric would earn himself praise. The elders would take notice. Perhaps even award him a new title.

As they rode on, the snow gave way to deadened fields of crops, a grim omen perhaps, but the Cleric's heart was light.

Victory was at hand.

After several minutes they approached a village that appeared to be abandoned, windows shattered or boarded up, the life of the place snuffed out like a candle.

The Cleric's smile faded, replaced by a tightening in his gut.

This place seemed to have been struck by a curse, its crops withered, its life extinguished.

The horses slowed, hooves clopping on the hard-packed earth. Something was wrong, and the Cleric could feel it in his bones.

The Rogue turned, his face drawn, his eyes haunted. "They're here."

# 65

## DELIA

A distant rumble echoed through the library.

Delia felt a cold knot of dread in her gut.

"Hoofbeats," Agatha said. "They're on their way here."

"How do they keep finding us?" Delia asked. "Surely we've lost them enough times. But we haven't put them off the scent, not at all."

"They're using some sort of magical tracking," Marjie responded.

Delia's mind flew immediately to the Cowboy. Was that what he was – a tracker? Was he responsible for the Order always finding them? She cursed him under her breath in the ordinary non-magical way.

"Whatever it is," Marjie continued, "it's powerful, more powerful than anything Ingrid, Agatha, and I have been doing to counteract it."

"You've been using magic this whole time?" Delia asked.

"Of course, dear," Marjie replied. "It's second nature."

The sound of hooves grew louder.

"Quick, look for the book," Ingrid instructed.

Delia had already searched the rare, black volumes in the corner of the library that Agatha had assigned to her. "What if it's not here?"

"It must be. It must be!" Ingrid said, clearly losing her patience.

"Wait a minute..." Something caught Delia's eye. It wasn't a black volume, but a red one, with gold lettering on the spine that read: *The Opening*.

A tingle of intuition told her to reach for it, just as the hoofbeats grew closer and then stopped, indicating the enemy was upon them.

She pulled the spine of the volume and the shelf rumbled and swivelled through the wall, creating a doorway.

"Found it!" Delia called out. She wasn't exactly sure if she'd found what they were looking for. How could she know? *But surely anyone finding a secret chamber in a bookshelf has found something important,* she reasoned.

"Well, what are you just standing there for?" Ingrid said, staring at the new entrance. "Let's go!"

They walked through the dark doorway into a chamber that was surprisingly full of light, paved with engraved stones the colour of sand.

In the centre was a single pillar, atop of which was set *the book*.

It had to be the book, with its black cover and silver lettering. It was closed just as the door behind them now was.

The four women stood around it.

"What good is finding it if we're trapped here?" Delia asked, looking around anxiously. The stone room had no windows.

"This will give us the power," Ingrid said with a gleam in her eyes that made Delia slightly nervous.

Ingrid reached towards the book and it flew open.

Delia looked at the slanted, curly writing. The open page was clearly a spell. 'Invisibility of the Crones', the title read.

Delia couldn't help laughing.

"What's so amusing?" Ingrid asked.

"It's just like we were talking about before. Old women complain about being invisible, and now..."

"Sometimes it can be quite convenient, you'll find," Agatha said.

Marjie beamed. "Don't we all look wonderfully crony, standing around in this enchanted secret room with an ancient grimoire!"

"Who cares about looks at a time like this?" Agatha grumbled. "Focus on the spell."

Delia laughed. "You're so vain, you probably think this spell is about you."

Ingrid shot her a withering look. "This is no time for insults."

"All right," said Delia with a sigh. Clearly Ingrid didn't appreciate '70s pop references. "What are we waiting for?"

"What makes everyone so sure we should be doing this particular spell?" Agatha asked.

"This is where the book landed," Marjie said. "This is what it wants us to do."

"I'm not taking instructions from a book," Ingrid grumbled.

"What choice do we have?" Delia asked.

Ingrid shot her a grumpy look.

"Oh, fine. I'll take instructions from a book," Ingrid grumbled. "This could be very useful indeed," she added as she read over the spell.

The sound of breaking glass shattered the silence, followed by hammering and shouting.

The noises grew stronger, edging towards where they were.

"We don't have much time..." Agatha said.

Every muscle in Delia's body seemed to tighten. "And I don't know how to do magic." What if they all died here? What would Gilly and the grandkids think? Would they ever find out what happened to her poor old mad mum, or would Delia remain a missing person forever?

"We all hold hands," Ingrid instructed. "Picture your element at its most intense."

"My element?" Delia asked.

"Fire, of course, dear," said Marjie.

"You, Marjie," said Ingrid. "Picture the deepest ocean. Agatha, picture the boundless sky. Delia, picture the heart of a furnace, maybe even the sun. And I'll picture a rock."

"A rock?" said Marjie. "You think that's going to be enough?"

"Oh, alright," said Ingrid. "I'll picture the bountiful grace of the planet."

Delia nodded. "That sounds more fitting."

"Now then," Ingrid continued. "The chant is simple. The spell requires no extra paraphernalia, which I like."

"It's just as well," Agatha muttered. "Because my supplies are back at the goat cart."

They peered over the book and read the chant.


EARTH, *air, fire, and water,*
*sacred elements come to us.*
*Ignite within us,*
*Our deep and ancient power,*
*the power to be free of our enemies,*
*the power of invisibility*
*so that no one who seeks to do us harm*
*can see, hear, nor scent us.*


"WHAT DO they want to go around smelling us for?" Agatha asked, wrinkling her nose.

"The scent, you know," said Ingrid. "Like a hound, sniffing out witches. Now pay attention!"

"Are you sure we shouldn't read the fine print first?" Delia asked. "I mean, I don't want to be invisible for good."

"Don't be silly, dear. You won't be properly invisible," said Marjie. "It's just our enemies won't be able to see us. Didn't you listen to the chant?"

Delia took a deep breath as the clashing grew louder; the walls of the chamber trembled.

"There's no time for fine print," Ingrid said. "You're either in or out, and we need you to be in."

"No pressure then?" said Delia with only a mild eye roll. "Alright. Let's do this."

With Marjie's warm palm in her right and Agatha's dry little fist in her left, the crones joined hands.

There was a pulsing of energy, like light, but brighter, warmer and more thrilling, zipping around the circle between them.

"Now we read the chant," said Ingrid. "We say it three times, and then we keep going until the working is done."

"Okay then," Delia agreed.

They began to say the words scrawled in the book.

Their voices, low and only slightly croaky, sounded to Delia like monks chanting in an old temple. There was something ancient and timeless about it. She could feel it – the magic – and for a moment she felt a stab of pain, of regret.

*Where had magic been all her life?* she thought to herself.

*Where was the magic when I was a little child who thought of nothing else but it? Who dreamed of fairies and unicorns? Where was the magic when I was trudging through adolescence in a state of depression? Where was the magic in my darkest moments, in my dreary times?*

That was the reason she'd sought out the theatre, for some kind of magic, some kind of excitement steering her beyond the mundane everyday existence.

But this, this was something even more spectacular.

This was real and alive. And she knew that somehow it connected her to her lineage, though she had no idea of the specifics.

She thought of Etty, and Delia knew without a doubt that this power – this magic – was second nature to her grandmother. And yet why didn't she ever tell Delia about it? Why had she missed out on her entire life so far without the thrill and joy of knowing this was real?

The regret only pained her for a moment before she brushed it aside, focusing on the flame of the furnace, on the heart of the sun, focusing on her element of fire, allowing her anger at the injustices of the world and of her own life to burn away, as her passion for the magic grew bright.

She kept saying the words until they became mere sounds, a rhythm, losing all specific meaning, merging instead with the infinite.

A light appeared in the room between them, bright and silvery white. It began to grow – a diamond-shape – a prism. It shone as they continued to chant.

All four elements could be seen reflected in its many facets: the depth of the ocean, the clarity of wind, the passion of fire, the lushness of Earth.

"Keep going," Ingrid urged. "One more time!"

They recited the chant again, and the prism grew until it wrapped around them all, joining them together. And then, as they neared the end of the chant, it burst open.

There was only brightness, only light. Delia lost all sense of herself in a brief, blinding, beautiful moment.

And then...they were back.

"I think that worked," Marjie said with a warm tone of satisfaction.

Ingrid dusted off her hands and nodded. She reached for the book and tucked it into her satchel.

"Now what?" Delia asked.

"Now, we go," Ingrid replied.

"What?" said Delia. "We just stroll out there and hope they can't see us?"

"Don't doubt the magic," Ingrid cautioned. "Doubt tests its strength, and that's not what we need right now."

Delia gulped. "Okay then."

Delia called on every ounce of blind faith she possessed, which was not actually a whole lot – in fact it was hardly a teaspoon. She stretched for more – calling on the strength of several characters she'd played many years ago who'd had bucketloads of faith – who'd have leapt gleefully into the ocean if they'd thought it was at the request of their god. That seemed to help Delia.

"There's no handle on the door," said Agatha. "I think we're trapped here until those eedjits go away."

"Nonsense," said Ingrid. She walked towards the door and it slid open.

There was the sound of shouting and scurrying feet.

A hooded man with a big beard emerged, looking around the room as if seeing right through them.

"There's no one in here," he said. "There's a secret chamber, but it looks empty."

"What about exits?" a deeper voice called out.

"None," he replied.

"Well if there's one secret chamber, there's bound to be more," came the reply. "Keep looking!"

Delia held her breath. As the footsteps retreated, she let it out again. "They really couldn't see us," she whispered.

"And apparently, they can't hear us either," Marjie added. "Like the chant said."

"But we may want to keep quiet, just in case," said Agatha.

Delia nodded.

"Alright, coast is clear," Ingrid said.

"Not that it matters if they can't see us," Agatha muttered.

"Well, it matters if they bump into us," Marjie argued. "There was nothing in the chant about that."

"Quiet, you two," said Ingrid. "Focus. And don't touch anything."

Stealthily, they followed Ingrid out of the chamber through the now rather dishevelled library.

Books and shelves were in disarray, and Agatha would have probably been shedding tears if she was capable of it. Delia noticed her grab a few volumes and stuff them into her bag when Ingrid wasn't looking.

There were no more red-hooded figures on their path out of the library, aside for a few guarding the exit.

Delia held her breath as she followed Ingrid straight out between them.

The guards seemed to look straight through them.
Invisibility was clearly brilliant.
Then her eyes landed on *him*. The Cowboy. Declan.
And he was staring right at her.

# 66

## THE ROGUE

The taste of dryness lingered in Declan's mouth, a physical response to the arid surroundings, and his fingers itched towards the dagger at his side, a constant companion, a silent promise.

He stood back as the Order breached the library, the musty darkness within swallowing them whole. What were they really looking for? What secrets lay buried within those rotting shelves? The questions gnawed at him, feeding his curiosity, his desire to know more, yet he knew his place. He was the outsider, the observer, bound by unseen chains to watch but never to participate.

As the minutes ticked by, the abandoned hamlet seemed to hold its breath, the weight of history pressing down, the very air thick with anticipation. The Rogue's instincts tingled, a warning, a whisper of danger that lurked unseen.

He had led them here as his contract bound him. Even so, seeds of doubt had been planted, and they were beginning to take root.

Upon arrival, the Order's spell breakers had gone to work on the heavy fortifications, ancient enchantments woven into the building. At first they'd advised the Cleric that it was impossible to break in, but he'd assured them the witches had already broken through the strongest protections, weakening what was previously an impenetrable fortress of magic.

It took several minutes, but it turned out the Cleric was right. As the Order broke through the barriers and stormed the building, a blast of powerful magic pulsed out from the humble building, and Declan felt it in his very bones.

On the instructions of the Cleric, the Order attempted a coordinated assault. Declan, however, lingered outside. This was not his war.

As the members of the Order moved through the library, confused shouts echoed outwards. There was no sign of the crones, no trace of their presence. The scramble turned into chaos as soldiers dashed through the hallways, overturning books and searching hidden crevices.

In the midst of the disorder, Declan's eyes landed on them: the four crones, strolling out as if they were on a crowded London street, looking only slightly suspicious.

It was a thrilling sight.

Clearly no one else could see them through the heavy magic surrounding them, swirling like gas in the air.

His eyes fell on Delia. His nemesis. The fault line in all of this. The thorn in his side.

A surge of rage that rushed through him. Yet, something else tugged at the edge of his anger. Admiration. Respect.

A decision presented itself: he could alert the Order, have them capture the crones, and call off his contract.

He would finally be free of this nightmare. But something held him back. Could it be morality?

No.

That was an ancient memory for him. Curiosity. That's what it was.

If the crones were captured, the outcome would be too obvious. They'd be tortured and manipulated, maybe even stripped of their powers. But to let them go free? Well, that led to all kinds of more interesting possibilities. This intrigued him. It breathed life into the centuries-old weariness that weighed him down.

What was another few months or years of torture in an endless existence? Yet, this contract had worn him down to the point where his soul begged for release.

In that moment, as he stared her down, the choice tore at him.

Freedom or intrigue?

# 67

## DELIA

**D**elia froze, staring into the dark eyes of the hunter who had continued to hound her.

It was all over. He could see through the magic.

Whatever kind of magical being he was, he didn't seem to be affected by the magic of invisibility, no matter how potent it was.

He would alert the Order any second now, and the guards would seize them.

Delia's mind rushed with thoughts of Gilly and the children. What would they think of her mysterious disappearance? How could she have been so foolish to get mixed up in all this magical nonsense? And what of her life? Her legacy? Would she be forever remembered as the nutty old bat who set her husband's mistress's bra on fire in the theatre? Sixty-three years was far too short a life.

"Hurry it up!" Agatha hissed at her. "My bag is rather heavy."

Delia glanced around, but none of the Order members had noticed them, and none of her friends had noticed Declan's gaze, but she was sure as daylight that he could see them, or at least, see her.

But he hadn't said anything.

He was the tracker. Surely it was his job to raise an alarm. Surely…

She took in a quick inhale of breath and stepped forward.

The Cowboy remained exactly as he was, but she was sure that as he shifted his gaze, he winked at her.

By the time they had made their way through the muttering and somewhat frustrated troop of the Order of Crimson and back to the well, Delia was positively bursting with glee.

They scaled down the inside of the well with some magical assistance from Agatha and stood there looking at each other for a moment.

Delia let out an excited, "Eeee!"

She spun around with her arms out, almost bumping into the walls. "I can't believe it, that was amazing! I've never felt so alive."

Marjie chuckled.

"Alright, you thrill-seeker," said Ingrid. "Back in the cart."

They piled back into the cart and made their way slowly but surely, and rather cheerfully, back through the tunnel.

The journey seemed quicker than Delia had expected and she wondered what magic her new friends were working silently while she simply watched the countryside fly by. Perhaps it included an anti-aching charm because sitting in a goat cart as often as she had recently surely should have taken its toll on her hips, but Delia wasn't complaining. Before she knew it, they were pulling up outside the pub in Myrtlewood.

"Are you sure it's safe?" Delia asked the others as Sherry waved to them from the window. "They can see us."

"These aren't our enemies," Marjie reminded her. "It's only the people who mean to do us harm who can't see us."

"Sure it hasn't worn off?" Delia asked.

"It won't wear off, not just through time alone," Ingrid said. "It would take a great magical force to undo that working. It's powerful magic."

"That's brilliant," Delia exclaimed. "So, we've unlocked the Crone power?"

"Oh no, dear," Marjie said. "That was just one spell. And I'm glad it worked and that we were able to retrieve the grimoire. It means we probably *are* who we think we are."

"Probably?" Delia said, feeling a touch of disappointment. "Are you joking? There's still doubt?"

"Nothing will be certain," said Ingrid, "until we've unlocked the magic of the Myrtlewood Crones. This book will show us how to do that."

"Shouldn't we stick together then?" Marjie asked. "Why are you dropping us off at the pub?"

Ingrid shook her head. "I work alone."

Marjie deflated, clearly disappointed. Delia gave her a pat on the shoulder.

Agatha grimaced. "I work alone too, but if we really are the Crones, we need to work together, at least part of the time."

"Very well," Ingrid acquiesced. "How about you come over for tea next Tuesday?"

Marjie beamed. "That would be brilliant."

# 68

## MARJIE

**M**arjie's knitting needles clicked together, a comforting sound that melded with the soft creaking of the goat cart and the murmur of Agatha and Ingrid's conversation.

She wound the soft green wool around yet again. It was a scarf for Athena. It would match her eyes. Marjie had recently completed one for Rosemary. She glanced across at Delia, noticing her hair was long and wild again with that intriguing fiery streak. Perhaps she would be next to receive some knitting.

Delia caught her gaze and grinned, a spark in her eyes that wasn't just from the excitement of their recent adventure. Her budding fiery power was something to behold, and Marjie felt a sense of pride in how they had all grown together.

As Marjie's hands continued in their rhythm, she cast her eyes towards the mysterious Ingrid. The woman had been an enigma when they first met and had fought off all Marjie's generous attempts to get to know her, despite all the gifts of baked treats, but now, Marjie felt a connection and understanding. Ingrid was no longer a stranger but an ally, driving the cart with a steady hand and a knowing, confident expression.

Even Agatha's bickering tone was less grating now.

The four of them had found a balance, a connection that went deeper than mere acquaintance. They had faced danger together, and they had triumphed.

The foundations of a strong friendship were there, and Marjie knew that it would only grow with time. But all that would come later. Now, the fatigue of their journey weighed heavily on her, and her eyelids drooped.

With a start, she snapped awake, realising that she had nodded off. She returned to her knitting, the needles clicking again, a soothing reminder of the normality they were returning to.

She thought of Rosemary and Athena, back in Myrtlewood, preparing to embark on their own dangerous journey as the winter solstice drew near. Marjie wished them well, knowing that they too would find growth in their adventures. She would be there for them when she could, but they had to forge their own paths too.

The landscape rolled by, the trees and fields a blur as the cart made its way toward Myrtlewood.

Delia laughed at Agatha's grumbling, and Marjie smiled, content in the knowledge that they had captured the grimoire and returned, tired and victorious.

With a satisfied sigh, Marjie's thoughts turned inward once more. They had done it, and they had done it together. Her knitting needles clicked together, echoing her contentment. Now, after all the excitement, she was good and ready for a nice cup of tea and a lie down.

# 69

## DELIA

Ingrid had gone home, of course, but Delia, Agatha, and Marjie settled in for a nice meal at the pub. They sat in a corner booth with big bowls of stew and a medley of meads between them, and a few glasses of sherry, which were exclusively for Agatha.

The food was delicious and hearty, as usual.

Sherry brought over three helpings of sticky date pudding on the house. "That's right. There was something I wanted to ask you about," she said to Delia.

"Oh, yes? What is it?" Delia asked, wondering if rumours about her had already started to circulate around town.

"Are you looking for a place to rent?" Sherry asked.

Delia looked from Marjie's beaming smile to Agatha's rather subtle grin. "I might be," she replied. "Do you know of anything?"

"My aunt recently moved in with her boyfriend in the south of Spain," said Sherry. "And her house is free. Three bedrooms, close to town. Not too far from Thorn Manor, actually."

She turned to Marjie, who nodded enthusiastically and then grinned at Delia again.

"I might be interested," said Delia.

"Excellent," said Sherry. "I'll let her know. Maybe you can view the place tomorrow."

For a moment, Delia felt a pang of longing for her old life. Perhaps it wasn't the thought of actually living in a small town that made her yearn for the city, but she felt a distinct sense of loss.

"What is it, dear?" said Marjie, clearly noticing her expression.

"Maybe I should go back to London. It's been nice, and altogether magical being here. But I had a life, you know. I had a career and it feels like I've just given up on it."

"Oh, no, dear. You can't possibly do that. It'd be far too dangerous," Marjie responded.

"You really think so?" Delia asked, to which Agatha nodded.

"Yes," said Agatha. "In London, you're definitely Delia Spark, or whatever your old name was. They'll be able to find you far more easily there. And if they do find you, they'll more easily be able to lift the magic and find the rest of us. Myrtlewood is more protected, you see."

"That didn't stop them from getting in here before," Delia pointed out, waving her arm around the pub.

"Not that time," Marjie admitted. "But you might notice an absence of burgundy hoods now. Myrtlewood is protected."

"How?" Delia asked.

"The magic we unleashed is powerful and connected with the magical foundations of Myrtlewood. Let's just say the invisibility powers spell we performed goes far beyond just us. I didn't realise it at the time, but I've been tuning into the magic and I do believe it's cloaked the whole township and the area around us, adding to the protections already in place. Myrtlewood has always been hard to find unless it wants to be found, you know."

"You know, when I came here, I could have sworn every road was a dead end," Delia confessed.

"But you made it here," Agatha replied with a wry smile.

"Besides, we have Myrtlewood Players here," Marjie chimed in. "If you want a job, I hear they're looking for a new director since Ferg is trying to step down from most of his other roles now that he's the mayor."

"How many jobs can one person have?"

"You should ask him," Marjie suggested. "I believe he was up to twenty-one at one point, though he's whittled it down to five or six now."

Delia shrugged. "Small town players? It's not exactly my forté."

"Look, just give it a few weeks," said Agatha. "If the threat settles down and we unlock our true powers, maybe you can return to London."

"I suppose I could do with a few more weeks of holiday," Delia conceded. "Especially after what we just went through."

"Not entirely a holiday," Agatha corrected. "The winter solstice is coming up – that's when Crone power is at its strongest. We're going to need you for that."

"Why does it feel like I'm always being roped into things?" Delia grumbled.

"Now you're sounding like a crone!" Marjie said encouragingly.

Delia smiled. Despite the fact that her life seemed to have shrunken to the size of the small town, her circle of friends had multiplied threefold.

"It still bothers me that we don't understand the motives of this ridiculous Order of Crimson," Marjie admitted.

Delia sighed. "Maybe one day they'll do us the honour of explaining themselves. What do they really want? Whatever it is, they seem very sure about it, and they're zealous enough to think they're in the right."

"That's what makes them so dangerous," said Agatha. "Secrecy and fundamentalism are a recipe for disaster."

"A lot like your cooking then," Marjie quipped.

Delia chuckled. She checked her phone to find several missed calls from Kitty and felt dreadful about it, but she wasn't in the right mood. There was also a message from Gillian reminding her of something...

"That's right. I've got an appointment with the lawyer sometime in the next few days to sort out my divorce."

"Sounds cheerful," Agatha commented.

"Which lawyer, dear?" Marjie asked.

Delia checked her phone. "Someone called Perseus Burk."

Agatha spat out her sherry.

"Oh yes, he's very good," Marjie commented, while Agatha shook her head, mumbling something about 'bloodsuckers'.

Delia wasn't sure whether it was an insult to lawyers in general, or this one in particular. Either way, she didn't mind as long as he knew exactly what he was doing and could get her a fair share of the settlement.

She looked around the pub, at the eccentric residents of Myrtlewood enjoying their evening.

"You know, this place is very strange and unusual," Delia commented. "It's just as well I am too. I feel as if I fit in rather well, actually."

"Of course you do, dear," said Marjie. "And you might well find, even though you miss your old life, that Myrtlewood seems like home."

# EPILOGUE: THE SHEPHERD

F ather Benedict's feet struck the cold, unyielding stone of his
austere chamber, each step resonating with the turmoil of
emotions roiling within him as he paced back and forth. His usually
humble dinner, a thin broth, sat abandoned on the plain wooden table,
its steam fading into the chill of the room.

Bad news had arrived, news that gnawed at the very core of his
being. The latest operation had failed, just as the others had. The crones
had bested the Order, retrieving the powerful artefact and simply
vanishing without a trace. The Cleric had assured him that even the
Rogue's unparalleled tracking magic had failed to find even the ghost of
a trail.

Anger swept through him, followed by waves of grief and, to his
shame, occasional satisfaction that the Cleric had not earned himself
glory from one small mission. His own selfless sacrifice in the field,
years of clandestine service that had earned him the title of Crimson
Shepherd, would not be overshadowed by a simpering oaf seeking
victory in a single day.

He looked out the window at the compound, meticulously laid out
and shrouded in the silver light of the moon. The Order's compound

stood as a fortress, its walls lined with ancient runes and wards, embracing the magical energies that had protected it for centuries. The crimson banner of the Order fluttered atop the towers, defiant against the wind. Beyond the walls, gardens nurtured with mystical herbs lay dormant, a place of meditation and reflection for the members. In the distance, the training grounds, a testament to discipline and rigour, lay silent but ready for the morrow's exertions.

But now was not the time to wallow in anger, grief, or petty satisfaction. The last few operations had failed, yes, but they were mere attempts, learning experiences. After all, what was the use of failure if not as grist for the mill? There was a higher purpose – a higher power – guiding him, and it nudged him to look at the bigger picture.

Each apparent failure was simply a stepping stone to his eventual triumph. His scheming had many layers, deliberately and intricately designed with such strategy that each operation, no matter how botched, simply peeled the onion of his master strategy, ready to be chopped into soup. His eyes wandered back to the broth, a physical reminder of the sustenance he drew from both victory and defeat.

It was time.

A small smile curled his lips, an uncommon expression for a man who rarely indulged in emotion. The world might see a setback, but he saw a pivot, a change in direction that would ultimately lead to the triumph he sought.

The Order would rise, and he would lead them, his place as the Shepherd assured, his purpose unshakeable. His mind already began to unfold the intricate plan, a dance of power and intrigue that would once again set the Order on the path of glory.

He turned away from the window, leaving behind the abandoned broth, his determination renewed, his path clear. The world was waiting, and he would answer its call. The Crimson Shepherd had work to do, and failure was merely a lesson learned.

Yes, it was time for Operation Theta.

With a gleam in his eyes, Father Benedict's mind turned to the Order's secret weapon.

DEEP within the heart of the compound, a low growl shook the very foundations of the ancient stone walls. The powers of the beast were growing, humming a dissonant tune that echoed in the labyrinthine corridors, causing monks to stop in their tracks in dread before hurrying on their way.

Locked in its chamber, the beast's red eyes gleamed malevolently in the darkness. Change was coming, and the scent of freedom in the air brought with it a hunger. The beast growled again, louder this time. Soon it would be time to feast.

*A PERSONAL MESSAGE from Iris*

Hello my lovelies! Thank you so much for joining me and the Myrtlewood Crones. If you enjoyed this book, please leave a rating or review to help other people find it!

If you're ready to read more, you can order the second Myrtlewood Crones book, Crone of Solstice Flames.

If this is your first time reading my books, you might also want to check out the original Myrtlewood Mysteries series, starting with Accidental Magic.

If you're looking for more books set in the same world, you might want to take a look at my Dreamrealm Mysteries series too.

I absolutely love writing these books and sharing them with you. Feel free to join my reader list and follow me on social media to keep up to date with my witchy adventures.

Many blessings,

Iris xx

P.S. You can also subscribe to my Patreon account for extra Myrtlewood stories and new chapters of my books before they're published, as well as real magical content like meditations and spells, and access to my Myrtlewood Discord community. Subscribing supports my writing and other creative work!

For more information, see: www.patreon.com/IrisBeaglehole

# ABOUT THE AUTHOR

Iris Beaglehole is many peculiar things, a writer, researcher, analyst, druid, witch, parent, and would-be astrologer. She loves tea, cats, herbs, and writing quirky characters.

f facebook.com/IrisBeaglehole
X x:com/IrisBeaglehole
O instagram.com/irisbeaglehole

Made in United States
North Haven, CT
17 October 2024

59038533R00182